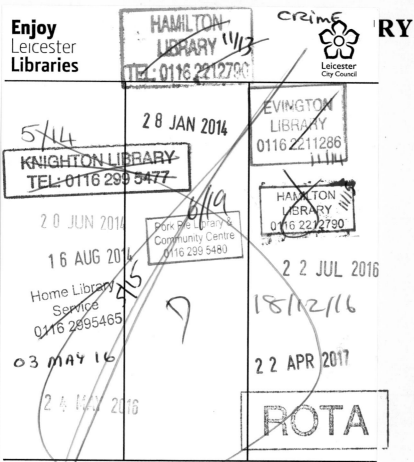

THE
WHISPERING GALLERY

MARK SANDERSON

ISIS
LARGE PRINT
Oxford

First published in Great Britain 2011
by
HarperCollins Publishers

Published in Large Print 2012 by ISIS Publishing Ltd.,
7 Centremead, Osney Mead, Oxford OX2 0ES
by arrangement with
HarperCollins Publishers

British Library Cataloguing in Publication Data
Sanderson, Mark.
   The whispering gallery.
   1. Serial murder investigation - - England - -
   London - - Fiction.
   2. Journalists - - Fiction.
   3. Nineteen thirties - - Fiction.
   4. Detective and mystery stories.
   5. Large type books.
   I. Title
   823.9'2–dc23

ISBN 978–0–7531–9036–4 (hb)
ISBN 978–0–7531–9037–1 (pb)

Printed and bound in Great Britain by
T. J. International Ltd., Padstow, Cornwall

To Miriam, without whom . . .

Let us be grateful to the mirror for revealing to us our appearance only.

Erewhon, Samuel Butler

Foreword

It made no difference whether or not she opened her eyes. She was smothered in complete darkness. It was impossible to distinguish night from day.

How long had she been here? And where was here? It had to be somewhere underground. Her voice-box had cracked from screaming for the help that refused to come. She longed for the relief that unconsciousness lent her.

The chain attached to the tight spiked collar round her neck — What had he called it? A throat-catcher? — clanked as she tried once again to pull it off the bare brick wall. She was so thirsty she had resorted to licking the damp stone. The tip of her parched tongue was already torn. The collar prevented her getting any closer to the precious moisture.

She had broken all her nails — her lovely, long nails that she manicured daily — scratching in the search for a way out.

Hunger gnawed her insides. She was empty now: the stench of her piss and shit filled her nostrils. She could not stop shivering. The only thing in her favour was that it was July: had it been winter she would have already frozen to death.

She blushed at her nakedness and immediately reproached herself. What did it matter when she was about to die? And she had no doubt that she would soon be dead. He had told her as much on his last visit as he shortened the chain. Tears sprang to her eyes once more. She tried to catch them with her tongue. They felt shockingly hot on her cold, filthy skin.

The silence was shattered by the clang of a metal door. She shrank back into a corner and began to shake uncontrollably. A candle-flame pin-pricked the darkness. He was coming again. So far he had not touched her but he had made it quite plain what he eventually intended to do.

She screwed her eyes shut, terrified at what she might see. He would blindfold her and, to begin with, say nothing at all as he watched her for what seemed like hours. She could feel his eyes creeping over her flesh, lingering between her legs. It was only then that the whispering would begin.

PART ONE

Wardrobe Place

CHAPTER
ONE

Saturday, 3rd July 1937, 2.30p.m.
He was going to take the plunge. It had been almost eight months now and he loved her more than any other girl in the world.

Even though the remorseless sun came slanting through the clear glass, it was cool in the vast interior of St Paul's. Johnny, impatient as ever, strolled down the nave, dodged gawping tourists, and took a seat beneath the magnificent dome which, thanks to the exhibition in St Dunstan's Chapel, he had already learned was actually three in one: the outer dome of fluted lead and stone that could be seen from all over London; a brick spire that held up the lantern at the very top of the cathedral; and, sixty feet below the outer one, an internal dome decorated with scenes from the life of St Paul in grisaille and gold. Biblical history had never been one of his strong suits — or interests — at school, but Johnny recognised the shipwreck on Malta, the conversion of the gaoler and the Ephesians burning books — just like the Nazis today. Nothing changed.

What little remained of his faith had been buried along with his mother after her early, excruciating, death from cancer. However, he was not in St Paul's to pray but to propose marriage to Stella, the green-eyed, glossy-haired temptress he had met in The Cock, her father's pub in Smithfield, back in December. They had been seeing more and more of each other since Christmas — and Johnny had been falling deeper and deeper in love. Although she still sometimes helped out behind the bar, Stella was now a fully qualified secretary who worked at C. Hoare & Co., a private bank in Fleet Street — which just happened to be a minute's walk away from the *Daily News* where Johnny was a crime reporter.

Johnny checked that his mother's engagement ring was still safely tucked in the inside pocket of his jacket — his father had died in the battle of Passchendaele when Johnny was three — and looked up to the Whispering Gallery where he intended to make his proposal. The acoustics were such that words whispered behind a hand travelled round the wall of the dome and into any ear pressed against the stone. There were only four people up there at present. One of them, a beanpole of a man, gaunt and unshaven, stood directly above the keystone of an arch decorated with a cherub behind a pair of crossed swords. He leaned over the ornate railings and watched those milling around a hundred feet below.

Johnny got to his feet. He was beginning to feel really nervous now. Stella wasn't due for at least another ten minutes and she always made a point of being eight minutes late: "It makes you all the happier to see me." She didn't seem to understand that this was impossible.

"She can only say no," said Matt, his oldest friend, in characteristically blunt fashion when Johnny had told him of his plans over several pints of Truman's the night before. "But she'd be a fool if she did."

Blunt, perhaps, but unswervingly loyal. Passing his sergeant's exams had given Matt more than promotion in the ranks of the City of London Police; it had boosted his self-confidence — not that Johnny thought he needed any help in that department. Self-doubt was his own speciality.

He ambled through the quire — why the earlier spelling of choir was insisted upon was anybody's guess — gazed at the dazzling blue and gold mosaics above him, passed the organ that would be bellowing out Old Hundredth the following morning, and turned right to face the windows where the unruly sun came streaming in. The funerary effigy of John Donne, the metaphysical poet who became Dean of St Paul's in 1621, was now on his left. It was supernaturally realistic: every whisker of his beard, every crease of his shroud, stood out.

Johnny preferred prose to verse but he could still recall a few of the lines that Old Moggy had made them study, beating the rhythm with his wooden leg — supposedly made of mahogany, hence the teacher's nickname. This, for example, from "The Anagram":

Love built on beauty, soon as beauty, dies.

Stella would always be beautiful to him: even when she was sixty. Every time her almond eyes met his own his heart flipped. It seemed to liquefy and flood his body with euphoria. At such moments he felt he could do anything — and there was certainly nothing he wouldn't do for her. The attraction wasn't just physical — although he existed in a state of constant desire for her. He had never before made love to the same woman over such an extended period of time. His past was littered with a succession of brief but intense flings with actresses and dancers who had hoped he could help their careers by persuading colleagues to mention them in print. It still amazed him that sex with Stella got better and better, that the novelty did not wear off. She was his new-found land that he would never tire of exploring.

And yet he was equally happy simply doing nothing. It was enough just to be in her company. When they were together he felt complete. They made a handsome couple. They were the same height — five foot six; Johnny was accustomed to being looked down on — and shared other characteristics besides their startlingly green eyes: both were quick witted, with a fiery temper and a deep sense of fair play. However, Stella would not hesitate to knock him off his high horse when he was raging against social injustice.

It was not that she was in favour of inequality: she just couldn't stand intellectual soppiness. Johnny had a tendency to get dewy-eyed about the plight of the underdog. Then again, he had seen a lot more than she had: more reality, more poverty and more death. Her protective father, a lumbering bear of a man who had no difficulty handling awkward customers, had done his best to shield her from the worst aspects of life in the capital. His possessiveness had ensured that they had yet to spend a whole night together. Johnny was not looking forward to asking him for permission to marry his daughter — if she said "yes".

He hoped she wouldn't make too much of a fuss about the 259 steps up to the gallery: a notice warned those wishing to ascend towards heaven that there were no stopping-off points on the way. It wasn't as if he had chosen the Stone Gallery (378 steps) or even the Golden Gallery (530 steps).

On their second date they had climbed to the top of the Monument, the tallest isolated stone column in the world. Designed by Christopher Wren to commemorate the Great Fire of London, which had started in Pudding Lane 202 feet away, it was consequently 202 feet high and contained 311 steps. When they had finally reached the iron cage at the top — built to prevent suicides — Johnny, checking no one was looking, had kissed her full, red lips and murmured, heart still pounding from the ascent: "You take my breath away." Their laughter had hung between them in the frosty air.

He had felt on top of the world and wanted Stella to feel the same way. Together they had seen the City in a whole new light — a light enhanced and reflected by the flaming golden urn above them.

Johnny had made a point of going to places where neither of them had been before. The relationship was new territory for them both. Finally, in Postman's Park, with its wall of plaques dedicated to local heroes, including Daniel Pemberton — *foreman LSWR, surprised by a* train when gauging the line, hurled his mate out of the track, saving his life at the cost of his own, Jan 17 1903 — Stella, fed up with all the talk of death, had said: "Next time, let's go to the pictures like a normal couple." The fact that she had referred to them as a "couple" had gone a long way towards mollifying him.

A love of the movies was another interest they shared. The death of Jean Harlow the month before had shocked them both. Hollywood's first "sex goddess" was only twenty-six: four years younger than they were. Johnny had been mesmerised by her breasts the first time he had seen them burst out of the silver screen. He preferred her as a femme fatale in gangster flicks such as *Beast of the City* and *Public Enemy* rather than as a dizzy blonde in comedies like *Hold Your Man* and *Wife versus Secretary*. However, his reporter's instincts were still intrigued by the echoes of Harlow's personal life in *Reckless*.

The suicide of her on-screen husband Franchot Tone in the film recalled the death of Harlow's second real-life husband Paul Bern, who was said to have shot himself in 1932. His apparent suicide note had a claim to being one of the worst ever:

Dearest dear. Unfortunately this is the only way to make good the frightful wrong I have done you and to wipe out my abject humiliation.

Paul.

You understand that last night was only a comedy.

10

What was more humiliating than being reduced to blowing out your brains? Yet the suicide rate had been climbing on both sides of the Atlantic throughout the decade. On the face of it Bern appeared to have had a lot to live for: he was both rich and respected. Even so the director had chosen to roll the end credits of his life story. Or had he? The men from MGM had been on the scene long before the cops or the coroner. What had the young Harlow seen in the much older, and reputedly impotent, man? She might have shot him herself in frustration. Johnny smelled a cover-up. One day he would write a book about it.

He had arranged to meet Stella in the middle of the sunburst on the floor beneath the centre of the dome. It was a visual representation of heaven on earth, a sign that Wren's Masonic masterpiece was designed to unite the two. If Stella agreed to be his wife, the two of them would become one, and he would be in paradise. He stood 365 feet — one for each day of the year — beneath the golden cross that topped the dome. It didn't seem a second since he and Stella had been laughing on top of the Monument — so much had happened since then. He glanced around yet again, hoping to spot her making her way towards him. No: as usual she was making him wait the full eight minutes.

CHAPTER
TWO

A woman screamed. A sickening crack echoed off the Portland stone. Tourists scattered across the black-and-white chequered marble. Johnny turned and, instinctively going against the flow of fleeing sightseers, moved closer to the centre of the action.

The jumper had fluked a soft landing but was surely dead. Black blood seeped from his head. Johnny knelt down and, using his fore and middle fingers, felt for a pulse behind the man's ear. To his amazement, he detected a faint beat. He rolled him off the unfortunate clergyman he had landed on. It was too late: the corpulent priest resembled a beetle crushed by a callous schoolboy. He lay face down, his limbs and neck splayed at crazy angles. There was a hole in the sole of his left shoe.

Johnny, feeling nauseous, took a deep breath and exhaled slowly. If he had stood his ground for just a few seconds more it could have been him lying broken on the floor. Perhaps there was a god after all.

The suicide opened his eyes. The escaping blood had created a sticky halo round his head. His lips moved. Johnny bent down to hear what the beanpole was trying to say.

12

"I'm sorry. I . . ." His eyelids fluttered.

"What's your name?" asked Johnny, already thinking of the piece he was going to write. He felt in vain for a pulse. The wretch was wearing a black suit of good quality. It was as if he had dressed up for the occasion. Johnny went through the man's pockets. That was odd — they were completely empty. There was no wallet or loose change, no keys, not even a handkerchief.

"Can you believe it? He's robbing the poor guy!" An American, flushed with indignation, pointed a pudgy finger at Johnny. The rubberneckers, reassured that it had not started raining men, had slowly gathered round to get a closer look. The circle tightened round him.

"Don't be ridiculous. I'm trying to find out who he is. Why don't you make yourself useful and go and find someone in authority?"

"There's no need." A middle-aged man in a dog collar gently cut through the crowd. Beady eyes took in the scene. They showed no sign of shock or grief. Countless funerals — in Britain and in France during the Great War — had inured him to death. "Please stand back." He was plainly accustomed to being obeyed.

"Is he one of yours?" Johnny nodded at the flattened priest.

"And you are . . . ?"

"John Steadman, *Daily News*."

"Ah." The gimlet eyes bore into him. "Mr Yapp was a member of our chapter. I presume he's beyond our help?"

"Indeed. My deepest condolences."

The clergyman searched for but could not detect a note of insincerity. "I'm Father Gillespie, Deacon of St Paul's."

"How d'you do." They shook hands. Johnny reached into his pocket and flipped open the notebook with its miniature pencil held in a tiny leather loop. It went everywhere with him. "What were Mr Yapp's Christian names?"

"Graham and Basil. He was proud to share his initials with Great Britain."

"Thank you. I don't suppose you know who the other man is? It seems he jumped from the Whispering Gallery."

"He wouldn't be the first to have done so." The deacon sighed and lowered his voice. "And doubtless won't be the last." The eavesdroppers craned their necks. "Ladies and gentlemen, please stand back. This is a house of God, not a freak show."

"The police will have to be informed."

"The call is being made as we speak."

Johnny was impressed. "That was quick." It wouldn't take long for the Snow Hill mob to get here. He handed Father Gillespie a business card. "May I telephone you later?"

"Of course. But what's the hurry? You're an eyewitness. The police will want to talk to you."

"Actually, I'm not. I didn't see the man jump. For all I know, he could have been pushed. However, by all means tell the cops I was here. They know where to find me."

14

The ring of spectators that was growing by the minute reluctantly parted to let him through. Forgetting, once again, where they were, they broke into an excited chatter. A look of exasperation flitted across Gillespie's face. Would he have to close the cathedral?

Johnny, using shorthand, scribbled down a few details while they were still fresh in his memory — the exact location of the bodies, the appearance of the two corpses, their time of death — before hurrying down the north aisle and out of the door by All Souls Chapel.

It was like standing in front of a blast furnace. He squinted in the sunshine, blinded for a moment, then hurried down the steps which in the dazzling light appeared to be nothing more than a series of black-and-white parallel lines. It was so hot even the pigeons had sought the shade.

Should he wait for Stella or run with the story? He only hesitated for a moment. She was not expecting him to propose so would not be particularly disappointed. Besides, it would serve her right for being late yet again. She would guess what had happened when she saw the bloody aftermath where they were supposed to have rendezvoused.

As he made his way down Ludgate Hill, overtaking red-faced shoppers, he slipped off his jacket and slung it over his arm. He took off his hat and loosened his tie. It made little difference. Sweat trickled down his spine, made his shirt stick to the small of his back. He licked his top lip. He was glad the office was only five minutes away. He could see it in the distance, shimmering in the haze.

The newsroom was a sauna even though all the third-floor windows were flung wide open. The roar of traffic competed with the constant trilling of telephones and the machine-gun tat-a-tat of typewriters. Fans whirred uselessly on every desk. Any unanchored piece of paper would be sent waltzing to the floor. The sweet smell of ink from the presses on the ground floor and dozens of lit cigarettes failed to mask the odour of unwashed armpits.

Johnny checked his pigeonhole for any post, memos or telephone messages. There were several slips from the Hello Girls on the ground floor and two envelopes. Before he could open either of them, Gustav Patsel, the news editor, came waddling up to him.

"It is your day off, no? What are you doing here?"

Rumours that Patsel was going to jump ship — go to another newspaper, or goose-step back to his Fatherland — had so far proved annoyingly untrue. He made no secret of the fact that he disapproved of Johnny's recent promotion from junior to fully fledged reporter, but hadn't had the guts to say anything to the editor, Victor Stone. Like most bullies he had a yellow belly. Johnny's previous position remained unfilled. The management, trying to slow the soaring overheads, had ordered a temporary freeze on recruitment.

"Pencil" — as Patsel was mockingly known — considered Johnny disrespectful. He could never tell when he was being serious or insubordinately facetious.

However, Steadman was too good a journalist to sack. His exposé of corruption within the City of London Police the previous Christmas was still talked about. Patsel couldn't afford to lose any more staff from the crime desk — Bill Fox had retired in March — and furthermore he didn't want Johnny working for the competition.

"I've got a story and I guarantee you no one else has got it — yet. A man's just committed suicide in St Paul's."

"So what? Cowards kill themselves every day."

"Only someone who doesn't understand depression and despair would say that," said Johnny, bristling. He held up his hand to stop the inevitable torrent of spluttering denial. "There's more: he took someone with him. When he jumped from the Whispering Gallery he landed on a priest."

"Ha!" The single syllable expressed both laughter and relief. Patsel's eyes glittered behind the round, wire-rimmed glasses. "So much for the power of the Saviour. Has he been identified?"

"I know who the priest was, but the jumper didn't have anything on him except his clothes. No money, no note, no photograph."

"How do you know this?"

"I was there. I went through his pockets."

Patsel was impressed — but he wasn't about to show it.

"What?" Johnny could tell his boss was itching to say something.

"It is not important. Okay. Give me three hundred words — and try to get a name for the suicide."

Johnny nodded. He had an hour and a half to develop the lead into a proper story. The copy deadline for the final edition was 5p.m. There was a sports extra on a Saturday so that most of the match results could be included. He flopped down into Bill's old chair and tipped back as far as he could go, just as his mentor had. Fox had taught him a great deal — in and out of the office. Although Johnny had no intention of following in the footsteps of the venal but essentially good-hearted hack, he had taken his desk when he left. It was by a window — not that it offered much of a view beyond the rain-streaked sooty tiles and rusting drainpipes in the light well at the core of the building.

"Stood you up, did she?" Louis Dimeo, the paper's sports reporter, had slipped into the vacant seat at the desk opposite, which used to be Johnny's. A grin lit up his dark, Italian features. Johnny was handsome enough but Louis, who spent most of his spare time kicking a ball or kissing girls, was in a different league — as he never stopped reminding him.

"Who?"

"Seeing more than one woman, are we? Surely you haven't taken a leaf out of my book? Stella, of course." They sometimes had a drink together after work — always with other colleagues, never alone — but Louis was too concerned about his physique to sink more than a couple of pints.

"An exclusive fell into my lap. Well, almost." His telephone started ringing. "Haven't you got anything better to do?"

"It's all under control. The stringers will soon be calling the copytakers."

"Why aren't you at a match?"

"I drew the short straw. Answer the bloody thing!" He sloped off back to his own desk.

"Steadman speaking."

"You must know by now that leaving the scene of a crime is against the law."

"So is suicide, but there's not much you can do about it, is there?" He smiled. It was always good to hear from Matt.

"What did she say?"

"I haven't asked her. She hadn't turned up by the time I left. She was late, as usual."

"Constable Watkiss tells me you spoke to Father Gillespie. As you're no doubt aware, the man who jumped had no identification on him. We'll be releasing an artist's impression of him on Monday — if his wife hasn't reported him missing by then."

"How d'you know he was married? He wasn't wearing a ring."

"We don't. I'm just hazarding a guess. His appearance doesn't match that of anyone on our missing-persons list."

"Is it okay for me to describe him in my piece? It might prompt someone to come forward." Johnny held his breath.

"Yes — but I didn't say that you could. Understood?"

"Of course. Thank you. Have you informed Yapp's next of kin yet?"

"We're trying to find out who that is. He was unmarried. Your piece might prove doubly useful."

"I aim to please. Fancy a drink later?"

"Aren't you going to see Stella?"

"Why can't I see both of you?"

"I thought you had something to ask her."

"I still want to do it in St Paul's. I'm not going to let what happened stop me." Some might have chosen to see the accident as an ill omen — but not him. He refused to believe in such nonsense.

"Very well. I'll be on duty till eight p.m. If I'm not in the Rolling Barrel, I'll be in the Viaduct." Matt hung up before he could say anything else.

Instead of replacing the receiver, Johnny dialled the number of The Cock. He knew it off by heart.

"Hello, Mrs Bennion. It's Johnny. Is Stella there?"

"I've told you before: call me Dolly. I thought she was seeing you today."

"We were due to meet this afternoon but I had to come in to the office. I assumed she'd be back home by now. Perhaps she's gone shopping."

"Wouldn't surprise me." She lowered her voice. "Did you see Stella last night?"

"No. I haven't seen her since Thursday. Why?"

"She told us that she was going to visit a friend in Brighton and since she didn't have to go to work the next day she would spend the night there. Her father took some persuading. He thought you were behind it!"

"Alas, no." Should he have said that? "So you haven't heard from her since yesterday?"

"Not a dicky bird."

"Well, don't worry. I'm sure she'll turn up any minute now."

"I hope so." She did not sound convinced. Johnny had said the wrong thing: telling people not to worry just served to raise their concern. It was like the dentist, drill in hand, telling you to relax: the very word made you tense up in anticipation of pain.

"I know so. Give my regards to Mr Bennion."

"I will. He's having his afternoon nap before the doors open again." Johnny cursed himself silently. He had probably just woken up his prospective father-in-law, who already suspected him of whisking off his daughter for a prolonged bout of seaside sex. Now *that* was inauspicious.

He replaced the receiver and stuck his face in front of the desk-fan. The back of it, which contained the tiny motor, was too hot to touch. The place would probably be cooler if all the fans were turned off.

He should have waited for Stella. What if she hadn't gone to St Paul's? Perhaps she had not meant to be late. Something — something bad — could have happened. He crushed the thought. Maybe the beach and the sea breezes had proved too much of a temptation and she had decided to spend the entire weekend away from the stifling City. He wouldn't blame her if she had.

Stella had never mentioned a pal who lived in Brighton. He'd assumed he'd been introduced to all her friends by now: she'd certainly been introduced to all of his. He enjoyed showing her off, being told that he'd done well for himself, batting away such envious remarks as "Lost her white stick, has she?" Then again, if he had chosen well, so had she. Stella held his heart in her hands. She knew she could count on him.

He checked that the plain gold band was still safely buttoned up in his jacket. It should have been on her finger by now. He sighed in disappointment — but there was no use dwelling on what might have been. He got out his notebook. He had work to do.

It took him less than half an hour. Father Gillespie was unable to furnish him with any further information except the fact that Graham Yapp had been forty-eight. As he bashed out the report, Johnny recalled the other dead man's expression as he had looked down from the gallery. Even from where he was sitting Johnny could tell it had been one of anticipation rather than fear, of anger rather than regret. And yet his last words had been *I'm sorry*: an apology for breaking the God-botherer's neck? A believer was unlikely to have chosen such a place to kill himself.

He handed in his copy to the subs and returned just in time to catch the tea lady. His mother had always said a hot drink was more cooling than a cold one — but only because it encouraged perspiration. He sipped the stewed brew and stared into space. The story was a minor scoop but it had made him a hostage to fortune. If the jumper turned out to have been pushed he would look like an incompetent fool.

He read his messages — there was nothing that couldn't wait till Monday morning — then turned his attention to the mail.

22

The two envelopes were the same size but there the similarity ended. The first one was cream-coloured and unsealed. The thick weave of the paper felt pleasurably expensive. It contained a postcard of Saint Anastasia. The martyr, golden-haloed, was draped in red robes. She held a book in one hand and a sprig of palm in the other. A look of ecstasy spread across her pale face. There was a single sentence, carefully inscribed in a swooping hand, on the back:

Beauty is not in the face; beauty is a light in the heart.

There was no signature. He was always getting letters from cranks. To begin with he had kept them in a file along with the threats of grievous bodily harm — or worse — from people who disagreed with what he had written or objected to having their criminal activities exposed in print. Nowadays he just threw them straight in what the public schoolboys, who were everywhere in the City, called the wagger-pagger-bagger. However, he liked the image of the serene saint so he simply put it to one side.

The second envelope, a cheap white one that could have been bought in any stationer's, was sealed. Wary of paper cuts, he used a ruler to slit it open. An invitation requested his presence at the re-opening of the much-missed Cave of the Golden Calf in Dark House Lane, EC4 on Friday, 9th July from 10p.m. onwards. A woman, one arm in the air, danced on the left side of the card. Johnny studied the Vorticist design: the way a straight black line and a few jagged triangles conjured up an image of swirling movement, of sheer abandon, was remarkable.

Much-missed? He had never heard of the place. Still, it was intriguing. What was the Cave? A new restaurant? Theatre? Nightclub? There was no telephone number or address to RSVP to, so he would have to turn up to find out. Perhaps Stella would like to go.

CHAPTER
THREE

He hung around for as long as he could, willing the telephone to ring. It didn't.

Patsel, throwing his considerable weight about as usual, provided a distraction. Bertram Blenkinsopp, a long-serving news correspondent, had written a piece about widespread fears that the groups of Hitler Youth currently on cycling tours of Britain were actually on reconnaissance missions. The smiling teenagers — who looked, at least in the photographs, very smart in their navy blue uniforms of shorts and loose, open-neck tunics — were said to be "spyclists" sent to note down the exact locations of such strategic sites as steelworks and gasworks. Why else would they have visited Sheffield and Glasgow?

However, Patsel, putting the interests of the Fatherland above those of his adopted country, spiked the article — "Where's the proof?" — and accused Blenkinsopp of producing anti-Fascist propaganda. A stand-up row ensued. The whole newsroom kept their heads down and pretended not to be listening as the irate reporter lambasted his so-called superior:

"You're not fit to be a journalist. You wouldn't know a good story if it came up and kicked your fat arse."

Such exchanges were not uncommon — Patsel had given up complaining to the high-ups; their inaction was widely interpreted as a suggestion that the German should quit before he was interned — but they had become more frequent as the heatwave lengthened and tempers shortened.

The oppressive temperatures only added to the sense of a gathering storm. The "war to end all wars" had been nothing of the sort. It was becoming increasingly obvious each week that diplomacy — or, as Blenkinsopp put it, lily-livered appeasement — had failed and that Britain would soon be at war again.

The argument stopped as suddenly as it had started. Blenkinsopp knew there was nothing he could do: the Hun's word was final. He stormed off to the pub leaving Patsel pontificating to thin air. Johnny, catching Dimeo's eye, had to bite the inside of his cheek to stop himself grinning. Blenkinsopp had the right idea: it was time for a beer.

Johnny joined the exodus of office-workers as they poured out into the less than fresh air. The north side of Fleet Street remained in the sun: its dusty flagstones radiated heat. A stench that had recently become all too familiar hung over its drains. Johnny, ignoring the horns of impatient drivers, crossed over into the shade. He still had a couple of hours to kill before he was due to meet Matt.

He lit a cigarette and strolled down to Ludgate Circus, jostled by those keen to get back to their families, gardens or allotments. It was not an evening to go to the pictures. Cinema managers were already complaining about the drop in audiences. On the other hand, the lidos were packed out. People were fighting — literally — to get in.

In Farringdon Street the booksellers were closing up for the day, a few bibliophiles browsing among the barrows until the very moment the potential bargains disappeared beneath ancient tarpaulins. He cut through Bear Alley and came out opposite the Old Bailey.

A crowd of men, beer in hand, sleeves rolled up, blocked the pavement in West Smithfield. It was illegal to drink out of doors but in such weather indulgent coppers would turn a blind eye — in return for a double Scotch. Squeals and shouts came from children playing barefoot in the recreation ground. A couple of them were trying to squirt the others by redirecting the jet of the drinking fountain. There was a palpable sense of relief that the working week was finally over.

The swing doors of The Cock were wedged open. Stella's father was behind the bar. Johnny perched on a stool and waited for him to finish serving one of his regulars, a retired poulterer who didn't know what else to do but drink himself to death.

"So she really isn't with you then?"

Johnny noted the choice of words — *isn't* not *wasn't* — and shook his head. "Still no word?"

"Not a blooming thing. This isn't like her." Bennion ran his hand through greying hair that was becoming sparser by the day. "What'll you have?"

"Pint of bitter, please." Johnny put the money on the bar. He had always made a point of paying for his drinks. It had made little difference though: Stella's father had never liked him. Johnny didn't take it personally: no man would ever be good enough for his Stella.

"We brought her up to be better than this." He put the glass down on the mat in front of Johnny then helped himself to a whisky. He ignored the pile of pennies.

"Has she ever forgotten to call before?" Johnny opened a pack of Woodbines and, out of politeness, offered one to Bennion. To his surprise, he took one.

"Thanks. It'll make a change from roll-ups."

Johnny did not understand the attraction of rolling your own: flattening out the paper, sprinkling the line of tobacco that always reminded him of a centipede, licking the edge of the paper and rolling it up — usually with nicotine-stained fingers. It was such a fiddly, time-consuming business. Why go to all that trouble when someone else had already done so? To save money, he supposed: in the long run, roll-ups were much cheaper. Dolly preferred ready-made cigarettes as well: Sweet Aftons. They were, according to the ads, good for the throat.

"She won't have forgotten. There are only two reasons why she hasn't rung: either she's unable to or she doesn't want to. Dolly's been asking around but not heard anything encouraging. A lot of her friends don't have a telephone."

"Perhaps she's just staying on the beach for as long as she can," said Johnny. He never sunbathed: his pale skin soon burned.

"Are you still in touch with Sergeant Turner?" Bennion, who generally made a point of looking everyone in the eye, gazed over Johnny's shoulder. So that was it: he wanted something. That explained his embarrassment.

"I'm seeing him later," said Johnny, and drained his glass.

"Another?"

"Please." The publican, having served a couple of customers, returned with a fresh pint. The pile of pennies remained untouched.

"Could you ask him to make a few enquiries?"

"I'm as anxious as you are to see Stella again," said Johnny. "She's only been gone for a day though. It's too early to report her missing. Besides, she could turn up at any second."

"And what if she doesn't?"

"I'll do everything I can to find her — and that includes enlisting the help of Matt and his men. If she's not back by Monday morning I'll raise the alarm myself." The possibility that some ill had befallen her filled him with panic. He drowned it with beer.

He was half-cut after his third pint. The heat increased the power of the alcohol. There was still no sign of Stella. The pavement beneath his feet felt spongy. He sauntered down Hosier Lane, along King Street and into Snow Hill where John Bunyan's earthly pilgrimage was said to have come to an end.

It was cooler now: the incoming tide had brought a freshening breeze which felt delightful against his hot skin. The cloudless sky was a brilliant blue dome that stretched serenely over the exhausted capital. A kestrel hovered overhead. Johnny stopped and enjoyed one of those rare, uncanny moments when, despite its millions of inhabitants, thousands of vehicles and ceaseless activity, there was complete silence in the city. Seconds later it was shattered by the sound of smashing glass and an ironic cheer.

The Rolling Barrel was only a few doors down from Snow Hill police station, so it was the first place that thirsty coppers made for when they came off duty. It was gloomy and smoky inside the pub. All the tables were taken so Johnny went to the bar. The clock behind the bar showed it was five past eight.

"What are you doing here, Steadman?" Philip Dwyer, one of Matt's colleagues, glared at him. "Haven't you done enough damage?"

The sergeant's eyes were glazed and his speech was slurred. Surely he couldn't have got in such a state in five minutes?

Dwyer leaned forward. A blast of beery breath hit Johnny in the face. "Be a good chap and fuck off."

As a journalist, Johnny was accustomed to being unpopular. However, his unmasking of corruption at Snow Hill in December had hit a nerve both within the force and without. The ensuing scandal had made Johnny's name — but at considerable cost to himself and Matt. His investigations had also led to the deaths of four other men. They would always lie heavily on his conscience. Rumours about what had happened to him and Matt continued to circulate — out of Matt's earshot. No one wanted to get on the wrong side of the big, blond boxer.

Johnny was in no mood to be pushed around by a drunken desk sergeant, especially when he could see that Matt wasn't in the boozer. There was no point in buying a drink just to annoy Dwyer: in the state he was in he might throw a punch, Johnny would throw one back and then end up being arrested. Johnny strolled out and soon he found Matt propping up the bar in the Viaduct Tavern, round the corner in Giltspur Street.

"Dwyer just told me to fuck off."

"Glad to see you did as you were told for once."

"It's good to see you too."

Johnny meant it. He immediately felt at ease in Matt's company. He always did. It was as if a chemical reaction took place, their personalities somehow combining to produce a sense of well-being. No one else had this effect on Johnny. Matt was a winner of the lottery of life: he was tall, very good-looking and popular. He literally saw the world in a different way to other, shorter, people. As much as Stella made Johnny happy and alleviated his habitual loneliness, she didn't make him feel safe, secure and stronger in himself the way Matt did. It was, he supposed, his role to make her feel that way. At the moment, though, Stella was making him nervous and fearful. Nervous about what she would say when he eventually popped the question and fearful about her disappearance. He needed some Dutch courage.

"Same again?"

"I'll have one for the road, thanks. I promised Lizzie that I'd be home by ten — and given the mood she's in these days there'll be hell to pay if I'm not."

Once upon a time Johnny would have experienced a stab of jealousy at such a remark. He had fallen for Lizzie as soon as he set eyes on her and had been heartbroken when she had — quite understandably, in his opinion — chosen Matt as her husband instead of him. Lizzie had worked hard to convince Johnny that his love for her was just an adolescent crush. Now they were, in the time-honoured phrase, "just good friends". Nevertheless, a part of Johnny remained unconvinced. He was happy for Matt — he and Lizzie had an enviable marriage — yet in his eyes she would always be "the one that got away".

"How is Lizzie?" They moved over to a table that had just been vacated by a pair of postmen. Johnny set down the glasses on its ring-stained veneer.

"She's finding the heat unbearable — although it's not quite as suffocating in Bexley."

Johnny had been afraid that he would see less of his friend when he moved from Islington to one of the new housing developments that were sprawling out across the virgin countryside round the capital. However, because police officers were not permitted to live more than thirty minutes from their station, the move had produced the opposite effect. Matt had to sleep in the officers' dormitory at Snow Hill more often than in the past.

Lizzie, who had cajoled Matt into the move, now complained that he was hardly ever at home. She had been forced to give up her job in Gamage's, the "People's Popular Emporium", when she became noticeably pregnant. Apparently customers did not wish to be served by mothers-to-be — even in the maternity department. Six months on, she was stuck in the new three-bedroom house, miles away from all her friends and with only the baby inside her for company.

"When's the big day?" said Johnny.

"A couple more weeks — but we've been warned that first babies are often overdue."

"Who can blame them?" Johnny took another swig of his bitter. "What a time to enter the world."

"At least I won't have to enlist: being a copper is a restricted occupation. Pity, really. I fancy killing a few Nazis. What will you do if and when the balloon goes up?"

"I haven't given it much thought. My flat feet will keep me out of the army. Perhaps I'll get a job with the Ministry of Information, or I could be a stretcher-bearer."

"Let's hope it won't come to that. Chamberlain might yet save the day."

"Sure — and I'm going to win the Nobel Prize for Literature."

"You'll have to write a novel first."

"As a matter of fact I've started."

"Pull the other one. You've been talking about writing a book for years."

"It's true. I've only written the first few chapters, but I'm enjoying the process so far. It makes a change from having to report the facts. It's so liberating to be able to make things up. It's like taking off a straitjacket."

"Have you got a title?"

"*Friends and Lovers*. But I'll probably change it."

"What's it about?"

"You and me, amongst other things. Most first novels are autobiographical."

Matt put down his pint. His blue eyes stared into Johnny's. "I trust you'll be discreet."

"Of course. You've got nothing to worry about, Matt — even if it ever does get published."

"I hope so. Does Stella know you're writing about her?"

"She knows I'm writing a novel. Actually, she's the reason I haven't been making much progress."

Matt laughed. "Real-life lovers are more fun than made-up ones."

"In most cases, certainly. However, it seems Stella's gone missing. Her parents haven't seen her since yesterday morning and I still don't know whether or not she turned up at St Paul's this afternoon."

"Perhaps she's punishing you for putting the job first."

"The thought had crossed my mind. But it doesn't explain why she's taking out her frustration on her parents. She told them she was staying in Brighton last night. If she'd decided to stay another day, she should have let them know."

"She probably guessed you were going to propose. That'd be enough to make any woman run a mile."

"Thanks for the vote of confidence." Johnny lit a cigarette but didn't offer Matt one. He was trying to give them up. Lizzie didn't like him smoking in their new home. "Any news about the nameless suicide?"

"Nothing. A post-mortem will be held on Monday."

"Perhaps the *Daily News* will come to your aid."

"I saw your piece. It was good of you to play down the horror of the situation. Imagine learning of your husband's death in a newspaper."

"I did — hence my reticence. However, the bloody halo round the dead man's head was too good an image not to use. Some will no doubt find it sacrilegious and/or inappropriate. There's never any shortage of readers willing to go out of their way to be offended."

Matt checked his watch. Should he tell Johnny now? No, there was no point worrying him unnecessarily. The postcard might prove to be nothing more than an empty threat. Johnny had enough on his plate as it was. He got to his feet. They still ached at the end of the day, even though he no longer had to pound the pavements the way he had before his promotion.

"I must be off. Why don't you come down to Bexley on Wednesday? I've got the day off and could do with some help in the garden. I say 'garden' — at the moment it's just a square of dry, brown earth. Lizzie would love to see you."

"It will be a pleasure — kind of. As long as there's plenty of beer."

He watched Matt make his way out of the pub, the crowd parting like the Red Sea. No one, sober or not, wanted to pick a fight with the handsome giant. Johnny felt very fortunate to have such a friend.

Stella lay in the darkness, alone and afraid in the strange surroundings. She had a raging thirst. The pain came in waves, ebbing and flowing as she tried to find a more comfortable position. She had been an utter fool to trust the man. To make matters worse he was the only person who knew where she was. She was still scared by his blithe assurance that her ordeal would soon be over.

The bleeding had stopped — eventually. She had to get out of here. But how could she, when each move made her cry out in agony? She was paying for her impulsiveness now.

A sudden draught told her that somewhere a door had been opened and closed. Stealthy footsteps came down the stairs.

"Ah, still not in dreamland?" His whisper was menacing rather than soothing. "Here, this will help." He took her arm. The needle sank into her flesh. Moments later she was unconscious.

CHAPTER
FOUR

Sunday, 4th July, 4p.m.
He left the bedroom window open, lay naked under one sheet, but still found it difficult to sleep. The heat seeped down from the cooling roof-slates. Stella haunted his dreams, one moment laughing at his foolish fears, the next lying dead in a back alley. She had no right to treat him like this. The ring was back in his mother's jewellery box.

It was the first Sunday they had not been together in months. Johnny had spent the morning reading the papers: Amelia Earhart was still missing somewhere over the Pacific. The sports pages were dominated by the Wimbledon singles finals. The American Donald Budge had beaten the kraut Gottfried von Cramm — which was something — and Dorothy Round had saved Britain's pride by defeating a Pole called Jadwiga Jedrzejowska.

However, Johnny wasn't particularly interested: tennis was a game for posh people.

He was too restless to sit indoors and work on his novel so, after a stale potted-meat sandwich, he walked up to Islington Green, which was so crowded there wasn't a blade of grass to be seen. Even the steps of the war memorial were crowded with families. Dress codes had been abandoned. It may have been the Sabbath, but rolled-up shirt-sleeves and knotted handkerchiefs were everywhere. The sellers of wafers, cornets and Snofrutes were making a fortune.

He strolled beneath the wilting plane trees on Upper Street and, just as he knew he would, found himself going down St John Street to Smithfield.

The Cock was closed. His knocking went unanswered. If Stella had returned there would surely have been someone home. He had been looking forward to a surreptitious beer but had to make do with the drinking fountain across the way.

Johnny hated being at a loose end. Work, as Thomas Carlyle observed, was a great cure for boredom and misery. The "great black dome" of St Paul's, seen bulging behind Newgate Prison in *Great Expectations*, beckoned.

Charles Dickens was, as far as Johnny was concerned, the greatest writer that had ever lived. He had read his complete works twice, fascinated by how much and how little his native city had changed. Only three of his characters had ventured into the cathedral: Master Humphrey; David Copperfield, when giving Peggotty a guided tour of the capital; and John Browdie who sets his watch by its clock in *Nicholas Nickleby*. However, the image that struck Johnny most deeply was that of Jo, the young street-sweeper in *Bleak House*, who stares in wonder at the cross on its summit as he gobbles his hard-earned food on Blackfriars Bridge.

He was glad to find there was no service currently in progress. Not a speck of blood besmirched the polished marble where the two men — one by desire, one by ill-luck — had gone to meet their maker. The Whispering Gallery was closed — so even if Stella had been with him he could not have proposed to her.

"We meet again." Father Gillespie regarded him over a pair of half-moon glasses. "I saw your item in the *News*. The bit about the halo was most amusing." Was he being sarcastic? The deacon sat down beside him. "Any developments?"

"I haven't been back to the office since it appeared. I'll find out tomorrow morning." Johnny didn't want everyone knowing he had nothing better to do on a Sunday.

"I prayed for them both," said the priest. "Especially the man who jumped — he won't be buried in hallowed ground. Mr Yapp, on the other hand, will be. The one consolation is that he probably didn't know what — or rather who — hit him."

"And they say God looks after his own."

Gillespie frowned. "Such cynicism in one so young. What are you doing here, if you're a non-believer?"

"Just revisiting the scene of the crime. I take it you deem suicide to be a criminal act?"

"Indeed. God has plans for us all. He believes in you even if you don't believe in Him."

"I'm glad someone does. I was going to ask my girlfriend to marry me yesterday, but she's gone missing."

"Ah. Many girls run after an ill-starred suitor pops the question."

"Are you married?"

"No — but . . ." He held up a forefinger to silence him. "That doesn't mean I don't know what I'm talking about." He looked around for a moment, as if making up his mind about something. "Here you are —" He produced a key and a piece of paper from beneath his surplice. "These were found in the collection box last night. I telephoned the police, but they didn't seem that interested."

The key was a brass Chubb, the teeth of which, when turned upward, resembled the turrets of a castle. It was probably a door-key. The piece of paper was more interesting. It was old and creased, as if it had been carried in a wallet for years. There were four words written on it in a childish scrawl: *I love you daddy.*

Johnny was unexpectedly moved. Had he ever said those words to his father?

"This is not the sort of thing you'd throw away casually."

"I agree." The deacon nodded. "Which is why I kept it. You'd be amazed at what we find in the collection box: sweet wrappers, cigarette ends, prayers and curses . . ."

"How often is it emptied?"

"Every evening when the cathedral closes. We can't be too careful nowadays. It's been broken into twice recently. We live in desperate times."

"Did they get away with much?"

"A couple of pounds. Donations have dwindled and yet the list of vital repairs gets longer each year. Secular needs, alas, have supplanted spiritual ones."

"Whose responsibility is it to empty the box?"

"The sacristan's. He brings the money to me and, having counted it, I lock it in a cash-box kept in my office."

"So these items must have been put in the box yesterday. Why?"

"I was hoping you would find that out, since the police clearly consider the matter unworthy of their attention. Of course there may be no connection between the two items. However, I suspect they could have some bearing on what happened yesterday."

Johnny was not convinced.

"If you're about to kill yourself, surely you'd keep something of such sentimental value on your person. *I love you daddy* . . . The first thing to ascertain is whether or not the jumper was a father."

"Well," said Father Gillespie. "That should be easy, once you know his identity. I expect the key may prove more of a problem. I've heard of the key to the mystery, but not the mystery of the key!" He laughed at his own joke, then quickly composed himself. "I must prepare for evensong."

"Thank you," said Johnny. "I'll keep you informed."

"I'd appreciate it. I hope the lucky young lady says yes. God bless."

He hated sunlight. He was a creature of the night, a lover of winter, a denizen of darkness where he could breathe and behave more freely. He was as old as the century, very rich — his dead father had been a banker and his late mother a cheese-parer — and, if viewed from the right, an extremely handsome man. However, those who caught the left side of his face would either stare, quickly avert their gaze or scream.

His townhouse in St John's Square, Clerkenwell, was a shrine to modernism and, in particular, Art Deco. Chrome and glass sparkled throughout the spacious, sparely furnished rooms. Mirrors, however, were conspicuously absent.

An only child, he had long looked forward to disposing of his father's art collection which consisted mainly of works by Lawrence Alma-Tadema. The pictures were too tawdry, too decadent; the women were too languorous, draped in too many clothes. He preferred nudes by Gustav Klimt and Egon Schiele, and would spend many daylight hours studying the intricacies of the female form and its precious, perfect skin. At night he prowled the streets of the capital, relishing the liberty that the shadows granted him.

He had no need to work — and the thought of having to mix with colleagues terrified him — so he spent his lonely days reading and planning long trips abroad: Paris, Rome, Venice and, his favourite destination, Berlin.

His money isolated him from the common herd and silenced the exclamations of flunkeys. His extensive range of hats and scarves, plus the use of cosmetics, enabled him to pass unnoticed for at least some of the time. Heat, though, made his make-up trickle on to his upturned collars.

Top-class prostitutes were regular visitors at his London home — until, while being taken only from behind, they made the mistake of glancing back at their generous, eccentric client. Goose-feather pillows could stifle screams of horror as well as ecstasy.

He lay naked on the vast bed, waiting for the heat of the afternoon to subside. His pale, muscular body was surprisingly unmarked. He stroked his flat stomach slowly and admired the curves of his long, straight legs. Legs that had carried him out of trouble on countless occasions. He exercised every day with a pair of Indian clubs, swinging them until his body gleamed with sweat. His hand moved to his groin.

No, not again. He had to save himself for tonight. She wouldn't last much longer. He smiled in anticipation. The Dom Pérignon was already on ice. The thought of her tears, as he drank the champagne from a silver tankard, was exquisite.

Ignoring his erection, he got up to run a bath.

CHAPTER
FIVE

Monday, 5th July, 7.45 a.m.
The start of a new working week usually filled Johnny
with optimism and excitement. Who knew what it held
in store? This particular Monday, though, he was filled
with foreboding. He had slept only fitfully, tormented
by dreams of entrapment and deceit. His claustrophobia
had worsened since December.

Stella was still missing. Acting out of character was
a sure sign that something was wrong. Her worried
parents had not heard from her. The silence was
torturing him. He would call the bank on the stroke of
eight o'clock.

The sound of someone whistling made him look up.
Reg, one of the boys from the post-room, was heading
through the maze of desks towards him.

"Mornin', squire." Reg plonked a large parcel down
in front of him. "Ain't you going to open it?"

"Give me a chance!" Johnny stubbed out his
cigarette.

The long, narrow box was wrapped in brown paper
and secured with string. There was something familiar
about the handwriting on the label. Reg produced a
pocket knife from his trousers and handed it to him. It

was unpleasantly warm. "Haven't you got anything better to do?"

"You're the one who goes on about the virtues of an enquiring mind."

"I don't 'go on' about anything. If Patsel catches you lurking, you'll get a clip round the ear."

"I can move a lot quicker than that Nazi."

Johnny cut through the string, tore off the paper and blushed. The cellophane in the lid of the box showed it was full of red roses.

Reg whistled in mock-admiration. "Who's a lucky boy then?" He didn't even try to hide his giggling.

"Shut your face," hissed Johnny. No one gave a man flowers. Whoever had sent them was trying to humiliate him. The stems were freshly cut, the buds half-open. Johnny counted twelve — the lover's cliché. Their glowing colour reminded him of Stella's lips.

"Who sent them?"

"That's what I'm about to find out, I hope." Johnny opened the cream envelope. Saint Basilissa — another unheard of martyr — beamed out from the postcard. The image was identical to that of St Anastasia except that the robes were blue. The back, unsigned, simply stated:

By plucking her petals, you do not gather the beauty of the flower.

Another bleeding quotation. Reg, who was now perched on the corner of his desk, sniffed. Johnny, taking the hint, did the same. The heady scent of the roses overlay something less alluring yet equally sweet. He looked at the boy, who had stopped grinning.

"Bit heavy for just a dozen roses." Johnny picked up the box. He was right. There was a brain behind the bravado.

Wary of thorns, Johnny cautiously parted the thick, green foliage. Reg, unable to restrain himself, peered over his shoulder. They both recoiled when they saw what it was.

"Is it real?" Reg, curiosity conquering his instinctive revulsion, leaned forward to take a closer look. Johnny could smell the brilliantine on the lad's hair.

"I think so — but there's nothing to be afraid of. It can hardly grab you round the neck."

They stared at the human arm that had been severed at the elbow. Even if the broken nails had not been painted red, the slenderness of the fingers and the lack of hair on the forearm suggested it had once belonged to a woman. Its smooth, soft skin was now blotchy, the flesh pulpy like that of an overripe peach.

"Need a hand?" Louis Dimeo stared at the limb. "Bit whiffy, isn't it?"

"What d'you expect in this heat?" Johnny pushed the vile object away from him.

The sports reporter shrugged. He didn't seem at all revolted. "Of course, it doesn't necessarily mean that she's dead. The arm could have been amputated. As far as I can see, there's not a speck of blood."

"She? I hope you're not implying this is Stella's arm." The sickening thought had crossed his mind. He refused to dwell on the possibility of such an atrocity —

46

but the arm had belonged to someone, someone who he hoped had been dead already.

"Certainly not. She . . ."

"Go on."

Dimeo, aware that he had better tread carefully, swallowed. "I didn't mean anything, Johnny, honest. I was just wondering why it was sent to you."

"It's a good question." Johnny, trying not to shudder, replaced the lid on the box and waved away his colleagues, who were threatening to gather like flies on shit. Clearly, news of the parcel was spreading rapidly. The hacks returned to their desks muttering in disappointment.

"It's more than likely just an armless prank," said Dimeo. Johnny sighed in exasperation. The newsroom thrived on gallows humour, but for some reason this seemed personal.

"Don't you have anything better to do?"

With a final wink for Reg's benefit, Dimeo strolled away.

"I don't suppose you saw who delivered this?"

Reg shook his head. "It was left outside the back entrance. Charlie found it when he arrived at seven."

The delivery manager was a punctilious timekeeper and expected his minions to follow suit. They worked twelve-hour shifts that began at 7.30 a.m., with only a thirty-minute break for lunch.

"Okay. Tell Charlie the police will probably want to speak to him. Go on, sling your hook."

The telephone rang.

"The jumper's name is Frederick William Callingham. Doctor Callingham, actually. He was a General Practioner."

"Matt! I was just about to call you."

"Well, I've saved you the trouble. His wife Cynthia contacted us last night. A neighbour saw your piece and, knowing her husband was missing, took it round to show her yesterday. She's going to officially identify the body this morning."

The week had hardly started yet already Matt sounded exhausted. He was certainly not in the mood for chitchat.

"Where's the body now?"

"At the mortuary in Moor Lane."

"Can I interview Mrs Callingham?"

"I would, of course, normally say that it is not the role of the City of London Police to aid and abet gentlemen of the press, but in this case the lady in question has expressed a wish to talk to the man who was with 'her Fred' when he died."

"Excellent. What time should I turn up?"

"She should be available from ten fifteen. Don't forget what she'll have just been through."

"As if." It wasn't like Matt to tell him how to do his job. Johnny prided himself on his sensitive treatment of interviewees — assuming they deserved it.

"Was there anything else?" Matt put his hand over the mouthpiece and spoke to someone. Johnny, waiting for his friend to finish, couldn't hear what was said.

"Don't you want to know why I was about to call you?"

"Stop pussyfooting around, Johnny. Just spit it out!"

"There's a woman's arm on my desk. It was delivered in a box with a dozen red roses this morning."

"Why the devil didn't you tell me right away?"

"I could hardly get a word in."

"Pull the other one. You were waiting till I'd spilled all the beans." Matt placed his hand over the receiver again while he spoke to whoever it was. This time Johnny heard him tell them to bloody well wait a minute. "I take it you're not spinning me a yarn."

"When have I ever lied to you?" There had been a few occasions.

"Very well. I'll send someone to collect it and take your statement."

"I won't be here, though: I'll be at Moor Lane."

"A possible murder is more important than a grieving widow's sob-story. Stay put until you've spoken to the detective." Without waiting for a response, Matt hung up.

Johnny was fed up with being told what to do: he didn't work for Matt. Then again, the last time he had ignored Matt's orders he had nearly got both of them killed. He was about to make the same mistake.

It was five past eight. He gave the switchboard the number for Hoare & Co. The answering telephonist, having ascertained his name, asked him to wait.

"Mr Steadman?"

"Yes."

"This is Margaret Budibent. May I enquire the nature of your business with Miss Bennion?"

Johnny could picture her: a stout woman in her mid-fifties. He could see the half-moon glasses perched on the end of her powdered nose. Her affected way of speaking did not quite disguise her working-class vowels.

"No, you may not."

"Oh." She wasn't accustomed to being challenged. "She's not here. She's sick. Well, that's what the man said."

"What man?"

"The man who called. He wouldn't give a name."

"What exactly did he say?"

Miss Budibent had another try at asserting her authority. "What business is it of yours?"

"I'm her fiancé" — well, he would be if all went according to plan — "and neither I nor her parents, with whom she lives, have seen her since Friday morning. For all we know, Stella could have been abducted."

"That is indeed somewhat alarming." Margaret Budibent could not have sounded less concerned if she tried. "Miss Bennion was not in the office on Friday — she took the day off at the last minute. And most inconvenient it was too. But she said she would be back at work today. Then this stranger called, just five minutes ago."

"What did he say?"

"Simply that he was calling on behalf of Stella, who was 'indisposed' — that's the word he used. Before I could ask him anything else, he hung up. Some people are so ill mannered."

50

"What did he sound like? Did he have an accent?"

"I can't say as I noticed. Let me think." Johnny could hear her wheezing as she silently replayed the conversation in her head. "He had a local accent."

"Cockney?"

"No, better than that. I mean he sounded as if he was from the Home Counties. Then again, there was something stilted about his speech. That's it: he sounded as if he were reading a script rather than just talking."

Johnny gave her his extension number at the *Daily News*, then, having extracted a promise that she would call if she heard anything more, thanked her and hung up. Why hadn't Stella called the bank herself? Had the stranger called The Cock as well?

"Mrs Bennion? It's Johnny."

"Hello, dear. You must be so relieved."

"About what?"

"Ain't no one called you?"

"No, not in connection with Stella."

"That ain't right. What's she playing at?"

"I wish I knew. Where is she?"

"Still in Brighton. She's decided to stay on for an extra day. According to her friend, she's having a whale of a time."

"Friend?"

"The person who called." Dolly sounded as if she'd realised she had said too much.

"Was it a man or a woman?"

Dolly hesitated. Johnny let the silence build.

"A man. At least I think it was a man . . ."

"Did he give a name?"

"No. I was so pleased to get some news, I didn't ask. This heat's making me even dafter than usual. We'll most likely get all the details when she comes home tomorrow."

"Tomorrow? So you don't want me to speak to the police?"

"There's no need. Ah, the brewery's arrived. I'll say one thing for this summer — it ain't half giving folk a thirst. Bye, Johnny. I'll get Stella to call you as soon as she gets back."

He sat at his desk, nonplussed, staring into space. His initial relief and gratitude that Stella was all right gradually gave way to disquiet and irritation. Why hadn't this mystery man called him? Stella must know he'd be going out of his mind. Why hadn't she called her parents and the bank herself? And why weren't her parents more concerned about the stranger who was apparently keeping their daughter company? No doubt they would interrogate her when she eventually returned home. In the meantime, though, it was unlike Stella to be so thoughtless. Something wasn't right. What was she hiding?

A large pot-belly blocked his view.

"What's this about a rotten bit of woman?" Patsel mopped his brow. There were already two dark circles under the arms of his starched shirt.

"Help yourself." Johnny nodded at the box that was still on his desk. His boss didn't need a second invitation. He lifted the lid with all the glee of a child opening a present on Christmas Day. What he found seemed to fill him with both disgust and delight.

"Have you any inkling of who this once belonged to?"

"I'm not a clairvoyant. What d'you want me to do? Read her palm?"

"Ha ha! You are joking, yes?"

"Sort of. Why would I — how could I — know who this woman was?"

"I'm sure you know lots of painted ladies." Patsel's lips curled as he surveyed the bloated fingers. Johnny's colourful sexual history had long since earned him the nickname "Stage Door".

"Nail polish isn't a sign of moral degeneracy — at least, it isn't in this country."

"Why send flowers to you?" Patsel picked up the card and read out the quotation. "Rabindrath Tagore."

"How on earth d'you know that?" Johnny was seriously impressed. He would never have guessed that Patsel read Indian poetry.

"It is on a tea-towel in my wife's kitchen."

"I see." Johnny was relieved that the German's philistine reputation remained intact. He had no wish to start respecting him. "I'm as mystified by this as you are. However, I believe the same person also sent me this." He retrieved the postcard of Saint Anastasia from the drawer in front of him.

"*Beauty is not in the face*," recited Patsel in a singsong voice. "*Beauty is a light in the heart*." He gave a snort that befitted his porcine features. "Pure schmaltz. Still, let us hope you receive soon another gift."

"Well, I don't," said Johnny. "Why on earth would you want someone else to be mutilated?"

"This is a godsend, no? A great story has been handed you on a plate — or rather in a box. You need to track down the rest of the body and identify it."

"The police are on their way. They want a statement from me. Meanwhile, my item on the jumper at St Paul's has produced a widow. I'm going to see her later this morning."

"*Sehr gut*. Well done, Mr Steadman. Keep me informed." The German's eyes continued their inspection of the newsroom. "Mr Dimeo! Feet off the desk, please!"

Johnny wrapped up the box, stowed it under his desk, then — glad to put some distance between himself and the unwanted gift — went over to where all the newspapers of the day were displayed on giant book-rests. He always kept an eye on what his rivals were up to: Simkins, for example, in the *Chronicle*, was exposing, with characteristic relish, a Tory MP's penchant for nudist holidays. The article would no doubt induce another fit of apoplexy in his long-suffering father, the Honourable Member for Orpington (Conservative). Good.

As he flicked through the pages, ink smearing his fingers, his mind returned to the gruesome delivery. There was one person who did have easy access to body parts: Percy Hughes. The unprepossessing young man, one of Johnny's secret informants, was an

54

assistant in the mortuary of St Bartholomew's Hospital. Johnny still suffered an occasional nightmare in which he was trapped in one of the morgue's refrigerators while Hughes played with the corpse of his mother.

It was half past eight already — and there was still no sign of the police. If he left the office now he could call on Hughes before he went to Moor Lane police station. It was tempting. The arm would stay put, but Mrs Callingham wouldn't. He didn't want to miss her — somebody else might get to her first.

Instinct told him there was more to the story than a freak accident. Besides, from the crime desk's point of view two dead men took precedence over a single unidentified body part. Matt would be more than displeased, but what did he expect him to do? Sit here twiddling his thumbs? He had waited half an hour — well, almost. Johnny grabbed his jacket.

The lift door opened to reveal a towering police constable and an equally tall man in a dark suit. Johnny had not set eyes on either of them before.

"The newsroom is to your right gentleman," said the lift-boy. Johnny, avoiding their gaze, stood aside to let the two men pass. He didn't breathe out until the concertina door was closed again. The boy just stared at him.

"What are you waiting for? Get me out of here."

"Been naughty, have we? Don't you like bluebottles or red roses?"

"Mind your own business."

"You do know they're here to see you?"

"Indeed. I'll catch up with them later. Don't worry, I'll see that you don't get into trouble."

The youth, who would be quite good-looking once his acne had cleared up, sniffed.

"Ta very much — but don't go out on a limb for me."

CHAPTER
SIX

Johnny, pushing his luck, stuck his head round the door of the switchboard room. It was stifling. A dozen young women, plugging and unplugging cables, intoned "*Daily News*, good morning", "One moment, please" and "Connecting you now."

"I'll be out of the office for a couple of hours, girls." He was answered by a chorus of wolf-whistles and cat-calls.

"Hello, Johnny!" Lois, a suicide blonde old enough to be his mother, winked at him. "When are you taking me out for that drink you're always promising me?"

"The next time I get jilted."

"And what, may I ask, d'you think you're doing?"

Johnny jumped. He could feel hot breath on the back of his neck. He turned round. The basilisk eyes of Doreen Roos locked on to his. "Mr Steadman, I might have known it was you. You know very well that reporters are not allowed in here."

"As you can see, I haven't actually crossed the threshold."

The supervisor tut-tutted in irritation. "Why can't you phone down, like everyone else?"

"I was in a hurry."

"Well, don't let me stop you." She stood aside to let him pass.

"Bye, Johnny!"

"Bye, girls. I'll bring back some lollies."

"Oh no, you won't," said Mrs Roos. Food was strictly forbidden in the exchange.

Johnny slung his jacket over his shoulder and, with a nod of sympathy to the doorman sweating in his long coat and peaked cap, went out into the swirling heat and noise of Fleet Street. No one wanted to walk in such oppressive weather. It took him five minutes to find a cab. The breeze coming through the open windows as it trundled up Ludgate Hill — St Paul's straight ahead — provided scant relief.

He got out of the taxi across the road from The Cock and entered the courtyard of the hospital by St Bartholomew-the-Less. A father fondly watched his child playing in the fountain at the centre. Such scenes moved Johnny. Would a father's love have made him turn out differently?

It was cool in the basement. A tunnel connected the main block to the mortuary at the back. Before it was built, the dead would have been wheeled across the courtyard with only a sheet to protect them from prying eyes.

As he approached the double-doors of the morgue the pungent smell of disinfectant grew stronger. Johnny peeped through one of the round windows and saw the back of the duty pathologist, bending over the naked body of an old man. Hughes, his assistant, looked up and blanched. He said something to his superior, pulled a curtain round the dissecting table, and, with a scowl, came out to join Johnny.

"What's the matter? You look like you've seen a ghost."

"I was hoping I'd seen the last of you." Hughes tossed his lank, greasy hair away from his face and wiped his bloody hands on his apron. "What you want?"

"Don't be like that. Haven't you missed me just a teensy-weensy bit?"

"No."

"I bet you missed my money, though." Johnny nodded towards the pathologist. "Does he know about your little sideline?"

Hughes ignored the question.

"I haven't got all day."

"Be like that then. I just came by to thank you for your little gift." Johnny studied the lugubrious thug carefully.

"Dunno what yer talkin" about."

"So you're not short of a woman's arm? Nothing's gone missing recently?"

"Dunno what you mean."

"Someone sent me the forearm of a woman this morning."

Hughes curled his lip — in amusement rather than distaste. "Well, it weren't me."

"Sure about that?"

"Sure as eggs is eggs."

"OK. I believe you."

"Why would anyone do such a thing? It's sick."

Johnny suspected the attendant was no stranger to midnight perversions. "Indeed. That's what I'm trying to find out."

"Hughes — get back here this minute!" The pathologist rapped on the door and glared through the porthole. Whatever he held in the palm of his hand dripped on to the black-and-white tiled floor.

"I assume I can count on your discretion," said Johnny. "I don't want anyone else stealing my thunder."

"Your secret's safe with me. And if I hear anything about missing body parts, I'll give you a bell."

"Thank you. I'll be more than generous."

The butcher's boy slipped through the doors and disappeared behind the green curtain that hid the outspread, opened corpse.

Johnny blinked as he re-emerged into the sunshine. A dust devil made him sneeze. He'd never get away with taking another cab — the top brass were enforcing one of their periodic clamp-downs on expenses — so he would have to walk.

As he emerged from the shade of the gate-house into West Smithfield he saw an instantly recognisable figure in the distance. He immediately turned on his heels and dived into St Bartholomew-the-Less. Had he been seen?

60

The church was empty: no one — not even an anxious parent, bereaved lover or just a lost soul — was seeking succour from above at this moment. He entered a pew, knelt on a battered hassock and lowered his head as if in prayer. The phrase *whited sepulchre* came to mind.

Johnny licked the sweat off his upper lip and waited. It was so quiet he imagined he could hear his heart beating. Dust motes danced in the slanting sunbeams. A plaque on the wall stated that Inigo Jones had been christened here in 1573. A few seconds later Matt's heavy footsteps echoed off the vaulted ceiling of the covered gateway.

The police had clearly got their act together — assuming Matt was here to enquire about any missing pieces of a human jigsaw. And why else would he be here, in person? He had sounded so busy on the telephone. The fact that both uniformed and plain-clothed officers were already involved suggested they were taking the case seriously. Perhaps it would have been wiser to have stayed in the office. His guilt at disobeying his friend was now mixed with relief that he had not bumped into him — literally. It would not have been a pleasant encounter.

Johnny got to his feet and re-entered the real world. At the end of Little Britain he crossed Aldersgate Street and cut through Falcon Square where John Jasper stayed in *The Mystery of Edwin Drood*. The public house that gave its name to the square was still shut up. Johnny licked his dry lips: a swift half would have just hit the spot.

Addle Street eventually gave way to Aldermanbury. The police station, home to A Division, came into view on the corner of Fore Street and Moor Lane.

When he saw who was standing on the steps outside he broke into a run.

CHAPTER
SEVEN

"Pipped at the post once again, dear boy. Never mind. It's always a pleasure to see you." Henry Simkins, sleek and cool in a linen suit, looked the new arrival up and down with amusement.

Johnny was aware how hot and dishevelled he must be. As he caught his breath he inspected the smart, well-to-do lady waiting beside his rival. In spite of the heat she was dressed all in black. Her red-rimmed eyes suggested she had been crying.

"Mrs Callingham. How d'you do? I'm John Steadman." He touched his hat and held out his hand. Ignoring it, she turned to Simkins in confusion.

"Ha, ha, ha, Simkins! Don't try and deceive this poor woman," said Simkins. "She's been through quite enough as it is." His eyes shone with mischief as he watched Johnny's already red face get redder.

"Mrs Callingham, this unscrupulous toff is in fact Henry Simkins from the *Chronicle*."

Simkins laughed and shook his bare head. His chestnut curls gleamed in the sunlight. They were so long they almost touched his narrow shoulders.

"If you don't admit who you are this minute I'll knock the damn truth out of you." Johnny clenched his fists. He turned to the widow they were fighting over. She must have been about forty years of age. Her almost oriental eyes exuded misery. "This man is an impostor. He wasn't with your husband when he died. Has he shown you any identification?"

"Leave her alone, Simkins," said Simkins. "You're adding to her distress." He put an arm round her shoulders and tried to shepherd her away. "I must say, Simkins, I find your joke in somewhat poor taste."

Johnny showed the woman his press card. She studied his photograph.

"It certainly looks like you." Simkins laughed.

"Where's yours?"

"I have no need for such fripperies," sighed Simkins. "Anyone can fake them. Shame on you, Simkins, for trying to dupe this grieving widow."

Johnny remembered the slip of paper that Father Gillespie had passed on to him. It was worth a go. He retrieved it from the back of his notebook.

"If I wasn't with your husband, how did I get this?" He thrust it towards her. Simkins read out the proclamation — *I love you daddy* — and tried to snatch it, but Johnny was too quick for him. "Oh no you don't, you bastard."

Mrs Callingham gasped at the coarse epithet.

"I beg your pardon, ma'am. D'you recognise it?"

"Yes, yes I do." Tears sprang into her eyes once more. "Freddie kept it in his wallet. Daniel gave it to him when he was four — he's fifteen now."

Simkins knew the game was up. Before either of them could shower him with recriminations — or worse — he made off towards London Wall.

"See you Friday evening, Steadman. You'll have a ball, I promise!"

As if he could trust any promise Simkins made. Johnny assumed he must have been invited to the Cave of the Golden Calf as well.

"So you really are Mr Steadman?" She returned the lace handkerchief she was clutching to her handbag. They finally shook hands. "Why was that gentleman pretending to be you?"

"He was intending to hijack your story. Simkins has the morals of a snake. He must have inherited them from his father, who's a Tory member of parliament."

"And he chooses to write for the yellow press?" She blushed, realising what she had said. "Excuse me. I meant no offence."

"None taken." Johnny was used to being held in low esteem — at least in certain quarters.

"How did he know I wanted to see you?"

"I'm afraid I'm not the only one with connections at Snow Hill. Money loosens most tongues and he's not averse to using his own to do it. After all, he's not short of a bob or two."

They were impeding the constant stream of foot traffic that flowed in and out of the police station.

"We can't talk properly here. Fancy a cup of tea?"

They walked down to Moorfields and found a café opposite Moorgate Street station. The sound of slamming doors and whistles reached their table through the open windows. Once the harassed waitress had taken their order — Johnny, having skipped breakfast, was starving — Mrs Callingham launched into what was clearly a pre-prepared speech.

"I can't thank you enough, Mr Steadman, for being there on Saturday. I know you tried your best to help Freddie. If it weren't for you I'd probably still be tearing my hair out at home." Her immaculate coiffure gave no sign of being disturbed.

"Call me Johnny." He waited for her to reveal her own Christian name. She remained silent. He produced his notebook. "Cynthia is your first name, isn't it?"

"Is it relevant?"

"I can't keep referring to you as Mrs Callingham in the interview."

"There isn't going to be an interview. I merely wanted to express my deep gratitude and find out if Freddie had said anything apart from 'I'm sorry'."

"No, he didn't. Any idea what he was apologising for?"

"I presume it was for injuring the other man. I do hope he didn't know that he'd gone and killed him."

"Why don't you want me to write anything further?"

"I've got Daniel to think of. He's just lost his father. The last thing he needs is a pack of newshounds chasing after him. We require privacy now, not publicity." A minute ago she'd been grateful for the attention he had created.

"How is your son?"

She looked at him as if it were a stupid question.

"Awfully upset. What did you expect? Daniel's a very private child, though. He doesn't talk about his feelings.

66

It's even an effort to get him to tell me what's going on at school."

"Which school is that?"

"St Paul's."

Johnny's antennae quivered. "Bit of a coincidence, isn't it?"

"Not really. The school is in Hammersmith."

"It used to be next-door to the cathedral."

"That was years ago."

"OK. Have you any idea why your husband was in St Paul's?"

"None at all." She waited until the waitress had unceremoniously deposited two cups of tea and a bacon sandwich in front of them. Johnny tucked in straightaway. It gave him time to think. He swallowed the mouthful he was chewing and went on the attack.

"Why did he kill himself?"

"He didn't!" Her eyes welled up. "He wouldn't! He'd never do such a thing. He was a religious man. He was a devoted father. Freddie was not the type to deliberately leave us in the lurch."

"You haven't found a note then?" He couldn't see a doctor, no matter how desperate, scribbling *Dearest dear* . . .

"No." She pressed her thin lips together firmly. Suicide was a crime — just attempting it could land you in prison. Was she so anxious to avoid the social stigma that she preferred to think her husband may have been murdered?

"So you're suggesting he was pushed?"

It was theoretically possible. Although he hadn't seen anyone do it, someone could have hidden at the top of the stairs and shot out at an opportune moment to shove Callingham in the back. Surely though — with all those necks craned upwards to admire the dome — someone would have spotted them?

"Not at all. Most likely it was a terrible accident. He must have tripped and fallen over the railings." That was a precise choice of word. Most people would have said "banister" or "balustrade". Had she been there at the time? Perhaps she had already visited the crime scene.

"Then why was there nothing — and I mean absolutely nothing — in his pockets?"

"There was this —" She held up her infant son's loving message. Johnny, concluding that he no longer had any use for it, had let the widow keep the childhood relic.

"It was found in the collection box. Why would he voluntarily give away such a cherished memento, unless he knew he was going to die?"

"I don't know. Perhaps someone else put it there."

"Who? Did anyone hold a grudge against your husband?"

"He was a doctor. Doctors don't have enemies."

"Oh, I don't know. Any of his patients die recently? The bereaved, in their grief, are prone to suspect foul play or gross incompetence."

"My husband was a very good doctor and a very popular man. I'll thank you not to cast aspersions on his character." She made as if to get up from the table.

"Please wait, Mrs Callingham. I'm sorry. Writing about crime day in and day out tends to make you think the worst of people. You and I are on the same side. We both want to know exactly what happened on Saturday, but we never will unless we continue to talk." He fished for the key that Gillespie had given him. "Have you ever seen this before?"

Somewhat mollified, she held out her hand for the key. She examined it with interest.

"No, I haven't. It wouldn't fit any of the locks in our house. Where did you find it?"

"It was in the same collection box."

She looked up. "That's as maybe, but I can assure you it did not belong to Freddie."

"Perhaps your son might recognise it."

"Why would he?" She sighed. "If you wish, I'll ask him this evening."

"I'd prefer to ask him myself."

"That's out of the question."

"Why? It would be in your presence."

"I don't want you coming anywhere near our home."

Johnny chose not to be insulted. "Where do you live?" Seeing her hesitate, he added: "I can easily find out. Your husband will be listed in the Medical Register."

"Number 21 Ranelagh Avenue, SW6."

Johnny knew his GPO codes. The Callinghams lived in Barnes.

"Was your husband's practice there?"

"Indeed. Two rooms and a lavatory on the ground floor. The separate entrance made it ideal."

"Will you stay, or are you planning to move?"

"It's far too early to say. Daniel's unsettled enough as it is."

"Did your husband have life assurance?"

"Is impertinence another concomitant of the job?" The narrow eyes glared at him. "You think I pushed Freddie over the edge?"

"You wouldn't be the first wife who valued money more than their spouse's life — but no, I don't suspect you of murder. Are you the sole beneficiary?"

"Daniel will receive his share when he's twenty-one — not that it's any business of yours."

Johnny tried again. "I really would like to meet him."

"Impossible, I'm afraid. Term ends this week, then he's off to France for a fortnight on a cultural exchange organised by the school."

"He still wants to go?"

"Why wouldn't he? It will do him good."

"Do you have any other children?"

"No." She turned away from him and stared out of the window. A coal wagon rattled past. No matter how high the temperature people still needed hot water. He waited for her to say what was on her mind. "We did have a daughter, but she died sixteen years ago. Scarlet fever. Freddie did everything he could but the infection just kept on spreading."

"I'm sorry." His sister's premature death would have made Daniel, their only son, even more precious. No wonder his mother was so protective of him. "Was your husband particularly religious before your daughter died?"

70

"He didn't turn to God afterwards, if that's what you mean. We've always gone to church once a week."

"Which one?"

"St Mary's in Church Street. It's only a short walk away."

"I'm still puzzled why a religious man would choose to kill himself in a house of God."

"I told you: he didn't!"

"Just humour me for a moment. What were his views on suicide?"

"Freddie was a man of science rather than superstition. He saw a lot of suffering in his work and did his best to relieve it. He said there was nothing noble about suffering. It was quite meaningless. He disapproved of those who seemed to take pleasure in wallowing in Christ's agony on the cross. He found it sadistic and distasteful." Johnny couldn't have agreed more. "He was a good man and he did his best to help others. He valued life too much to take his own: suicide went against everything he stood for."

"Who did he see when he needed a doctor himself?"

"What business is it of yours?"

"Perhaps he had discovered that he was terminally ill and wanted to spare you the pain of watching him die inch by inch. Believe me, there's nothing worse. It is agonising for both parties. My mother succumbed to bone cancer — eventually . . ." A lump came into his throat. Lack of sleep was making him emotional. The older he became the more his memory ambushed him.

"You have my condolences — and my assurance that Freddie was fit as a fiddle."

"He didn't appear so on Saturday. He was gaunt, thin as a rake and, at a guess, in mental turmoil. When was the last time you saw him?"

"It was around eleven, I think. He said he was going to visit a patient in Mortlake."

"Did he give a name?"

"No."

"What time did he say he'd be back?"

"He didn't." Her cup of tea remained untouched. "I can't believe I'll never see him again. The thought of being alone for the rest of my life is terrifying. Are you married?"

"Not yet. As a matter of fact, I was going to go down on bended knee on Saturday."

"You're like my Freddie: always putting work first."

"I didn't have much choice. Please don't take this as further impertinence, but you're an attractive lady. I'm sure, in time, you'll meet someone else."

"I don't want anyone else! I want Freddie back." She burst into tears. Johnny remained silent. Sometimes words were useless.

When she had calmed down again the widow got to her feet, her anger still simmering. "Thank you for being there for my husband. Please leave us alone to grieve. I'm not familiar with the *Daily News* but I have no wish to provide entertainment for its readers. Freddie took *The Times*. Goodbye."

She walked out of the café leaving Johnny to pay. He didn't mind though. Her parting shot was worth more than sixpence.

72

If her husband was a reader of *The Times* she would no doubt announce his funeral arrangements in the classified advertisements on the front page. He would go to the funeral and, one way or another, whether she liked it or not, make the acquaintance of young Daniel Callingham.

CHAPTER
EIGHT

When he got back to the office, much in need of a cold bath, the box of roses had gone. A terse note in his pigeonhole ordered him to attend Snow Hill police station forthwith. There was also a message from Matt: *Call me*. Johnny knew what was coming.

"Hello, Matt."

"Which part of 'Wait for the detective' didn't you understand?"

"I couldn't sit around all day until he deigned to turn up. You know I had to meet Mrs Callingham. And it's just as well I went when I did, because Henry Simkins, the slippery bastard, was already at Moor Lane pretending to be me!"

"I don't care. You deliberately disobeyed a police officer. I've a good mind to arrest you for obstructing a murder investigation."

"Oh fuck off! How d'you know it's murder anyway? Percy Hughes tells me the arm is unlikely to have come from Bart's. Hello?"

Matt had hung up. The muscles in Johnny's neck and shoulders — which had been acting up since he got up — tightened once again.

"How did you get on?" Peter Quarles, the deputy news editor, pencil behind his ear as usual, stopped by Johnny's desk. He spent most of his time smoothing down the feathers ruffled by Patsel. Ten years older than Johnny, he was ten times more popular than their superior. He was the proud father of identical twin boys, now aged six, who looked just like their father: open-faced, button-nosed and with enviably neat ears.

"Callingham's widow says she doesn't want any more publicity — but she's adamant he didn't kill himself, so there's a story here somewhere. She wouldn't let me speak to her son although she confirmed that the note saying *I love you daddy* was written by him. I'm going to make sure I'm at the funeral though, and I'll try and corner him then."

"OK. In the meantime see what you can find out about the other bloke who died."

"Graham Yapp."

"That's him. It'll be one way of keeping the story alive. However, your main priority is this morning's unwanted gift. The detective who turned up was most put out you weren't here. He gave poor Reg a hard time."

"What was the chap's name?"

"Detective Constable George Penterell. I got the impression he hasn't been in the job long and is keen to make his mark. You better not keep him waiting any longer."

"Should I show him this?" He got out the postcard of St Anastasia which had arrived on Saturday. "It must have been sent by the same person."

"You better had," said Quarles. "You don't want to be charged with withholding evidence. *Beauty is not in the face; beauty is a light in the heart.* In my humble opinion that's both true and untrue. There's got to be an initial spark of attraction, hasn't there? Something to make the pupils dilate. Speaking of which: how's Stella?"

"I wish I knew. She spent the weekend in Brighton, apparently. With a bit of luck I'll see her tonight — assuming I'm not banged up at Snow Hill."

Johnny arrived at the police station fully appreciating the meaning of the phrase "muck sweat". He felt — and smelt — filthy. Usually he was glad of the opportunities his job afforded him to get out and about — after two hours at a desk he was more than restless — but the dog days had left him dog-tired. He was sick of being at everyone's beck and call, resentful of having to traipse all the way to Snow Hill in the heat. By the time he got there he was out of breath and out of sorts.

"Mr Steadman? Glad to make your acquaintance — again." They shook hands. "You look like you could do with a glass of water. This way." DC Penterell towered over him, a smile of amusement playing on his thin lips. Large brown eyes with long lashes looked down on him benevolently. He was a giraffe in a new double-breasted suit.

Somewhat relieved at the unexpectedly polite welcome, Johnny wiped his brow and followed the detective through the swing doors with their bull's-eye windows and down a corridor painted dark grey below the dado and light grey above it. Penterell showed him into one of six grim interview rooms. Like the others, it contained a battered table, four sturdy chairs and absolutely nothing else.

"Have a seat. I won't be a moment. Take your jacket off, if you wish."

Johnny did not need asking twice. He would have liked to take his shoes off as well, but that would have been going too far. His feet were singing.

Fortunately, Penterell had left the door open. He hated being in windowless rooms. Clangs and yells drifted up from the cells below. The single bulb in its enamelled tin shade above him was dazzling.

"I thought you might prefer tea." The young man was carrying two cups and saucers and a glass of water on a tray. Not a drop had spilled. What next? An invitation to lunch? There was a brown cardboard folder under his right arm.

Johnny emptied the glass in one go. "Thank you."

"What was so important this morning that you couldn't wait for me?" The large brown eyes hardened. Johnny felt the chair press into his clammy back.

"Another story. I was at St Paul's when the chap fell to his death on Saturday."

"Fell?"

"Fell or jumped. You tell me."

"It's not my case. I'm only interested in the owner of the arm that landed on your desk this morning."

"Anybody reported one missing?"

"We wouldn't be sitting here if they had."

"Am I your only lead then?"

"More or less . . . Which is why it would have been useful to speak to you earlier."

"A couple of hours hasn't made any difference. The lack of blood suggests the arm — I'm assuming it was real — must have come from a dead person."

"Your assumption is correct. Now all we've got to do is find the rest of her."

"It is a woman's then?"

Penterell smiled again. "How many men d'you know paint their nails?"

"The killer could have painted them afterwards."

"It wouldn't have flaked off if he had."

"True. Although I don't think it's a coincidence the nail polish exactly matches the colour of the roses." It would not have been a particularly difficult task. There were dozens of varieties of rose. "Why did you say 'he'?"

"The chances of a woman doing such a thing are remote, to say the least."

"Why? Just as many husbands are murdered by their wives as vice versa."

"The victim was a woman."

"Perhaps she had been seeing someone else's husband."

"Are you?"

"I beg your pardon?"

"Sorry. That came out wrong. Are you currently seeing a married woman?"

"No. I never have — well, not once I found out they were married. Why d'you ask?"

"There must be a reason why the arm was sent to you."

"I get rubbish from all kinds of lunatic. It's usually just a pathetic plea for attention."

"Rubbish?"

"You know what I mean." Johnny reached into the inside pocket of his jacket that hung on the back of the chair. "I received this on Saturday."

Penterell's eyes lit up. "It must have been sent by the same person."

"Indeed. The killer, if that is what he or she is, must be a religious nut. I've never heard of St Anastasia or St Basilissa. Have you?"

"No. Perhaps he's going to work his way through the alphabet: A, B, C . . . You should have produced this straightaway. It corroborates the suggestion that you're specifically being targeted."

"I doubt they'll find any decent prints apart from mine — and yours."

In his eagerness to see the postcard, the detective had forgotten standard procedure. He flushed and dropped the evidence on to the table.

"I don't suppose you still have the envelope?"

"No — but it was the same as the one that arrived today. What are you going to do?"

"It's not up to me — not that I'd tell you, even if it were. Inspector Woodling is in charge of the investigation." He carefully picked up the postcard by a corner and placed it in the folder, which appeared to contain a single piece of paper.

"Well, I'll let you know if anything else turns up."

"Thank you." Penterell's drily ironic tone was not lost on Johnny. "And I'll let you know if you have to make an official statement. In the meantime, I wouldn't be too worried if I were you."

"Worried? Why should I be worried?" Johnny hadn't been worried — but he was now.

"If someone's trying to gain publicity, they're not going to chop off your arms — they need you to be able to use a typewriter."

"That's good to know." Johnny grabbed his jacket and made for the door. Before he could turn the knob, Penterell placed a large hand on top of his. Unlike Johnny's, it was cool and dry.

"You won't say anything about the postcard will you?"

"No. Why should I? I'd already mucked up any incriminating fingerprints." Penterell looked relieved.

"Thanks. I'd hate your friend to get the wrong impression of me."

"Friend?"

"Sergeant Turner."

So that was why he'd initially been so ingratiating. Although they had never deliberately kept their friendship secret, Matt and Johnny hadn't shouted it from the rooftops either. Even so, it seemed their connection was common knowledge at Snow Hill. Perhaps that's why Matt had been so angry. He loathed being put in a compromising position.

The detective constable led Johnny back to the reception. For once he was glad not to see Matt. It was probably wise to give him time to calm down.

The meat market had long since ceased trading for the day. Nevertheless, the streets of Smithfield were thick with hatless office-workers on their lunch breaks seeking somewhere to bask in the sun. Johnny didn't feel like sitting at a desk either. He wasn't hungry but he could do with a drink. The Cock was only round the corner . . .

Stella's father was behind the bar. When he saw Johnny he broke off chatting to the half-pissed poulterer and wiped his hands on his apron. Before her husband could say a word, Dolly flung her arms round Johnny.

"I'm so relieved, dear. I can't wait to see her. I'll make sure she calls you as soon as she comes in." She held on to him for so long that he had no choice but to breathe in her sweaty aroma that no amount of cheap perfume could disguise. An image of Lizzie, behind the cosmetics counter at Gamage's, popped into his head. There was a note of panic in Dolly's voice. The toxic combination of prolonged heat and high anxiety had clearly taken its toll.

"I'm not just here for the beer," said Johnny. "I'd like to make a telephone call, if I may. Of course, I'll pay for both."

"There's no need," said Bennion. "They're on the house. What can I get you?"

"A pint of Double Diamond, please." He was hoping to ask Dolly about the man she had spoken to that morning, but she had scuttled out of the bar while his back was turned. Everyone seemed to be behaving oddly today.

"I'm glad you didn't have to bother your mate," said Bennion.

"Do the Snow Hill lot come in much nowadays?"

"Only when they want to sell some lottery tickets."

"I thought that racket had been stamped out."

No one ever won a prize. It was a way for coppers to pick the pockets of the public they were supposed to be protecting from crime.

"It's started again."

Nothing changed.

Johnny drank his beer a little too fast. He was feeling light-headed by the time he slipped behind the bar and into the hallway of the pub where the telephone stood on a rickety three-legged table.

The Hello Girls had a couple of messages for him, neither of which needed an immediate response, so he asked to be put through to PDQ. Quarles's middle name was Donald, so his nickname — which coincidentally stood for "pretty damn quick" — was inescapable.

"They let you go!" His superior sounded almost disappointed.

"Indeed. They're of the opinion that I'm being targeted by a potential killer."

"Good to know the *News* itself is not in danger."

Such concern for his welfare was touching.

"It still could be. Goodness knows what I've done personally to deserve such attention. Do you want me to write a sensational piece to stir things up?"

"You mean, chance your arm?"

It was amazing how murder was a laughing matter to some.

"Ouch. Perhaps it would be better to await any further developments. We don't want to tip off the competition."

"I'll raise it at the three o'clock conference. Where are you?"

"Smithfield. I thought I'd go and interview Yapp's housemates. If we know what sort of life he led, it might cast light on his death."

"Good idea. Be back by four though, in case you have to file today."

Johnny left a couple of shiny threepenny bits on the table. Two months after their introduction the novelty of the new coins still hadn't worn off. He shouted goodbye to Dolly, thanked Bennion for the beer, then headed out into the unrelenting sun.

Stella, lying on her bed upstairs, looked up at her mother. Dolly did not return her smile. She closed the door behind her.

CHAPTER
NINE

Whenever possible Johnny remained in the shade. At the end of Old Bailey he cut straight across Ludgate Hill and entered Pilgrim Street. It was downhill all the way: the ground only stopped sloping when it reached the Thames. In Broadway a middle-aged couple sprawled on the pavement passing a bottle of gut-rot between them. A pungent whiff of cheese — and other things — hung above them. Only homeless people wore overcoats in this weather.

"Your good health, sir!" said the man, his tone of hail-fellow-well-met immediately putting Johnny on his guard. "Could you possibly spare sixpence so my dear wife and I might eat today?" The woman in question smiled to reveal an incomplete set of green teeth. Two pairs of yellow bloodshot eyes stared up at him.

Without breaking his stride Johnny flicked the coin towards the couple. Christ! He would rather kill himself than be reduced to such a servile state. What kept them going? The fact that they were, in spite of everything, still together? It was impossible to imagine himself and Stella in such reduced circumstances — and yet everyone was at the mercy of the economy. Stella had her family, but Johnny was alone in the world — which was one of the reasons she meant so much to him. The more he thought about her recent behaviour the more insecure he felt. She was not given to caprice. There was always a reason for her actions. Why had she suddenly made herself scarce?

"A thousand thank-yous, sir! God bless." The beggar's words rang hollow. The good Lord had not shown him much benevolence. Johnny kept on walking and soon turned left into Carter Lane.

Wardrobe Place, where Graham Yapp had lived, was on the right, opposite a school for infants. Although all its high windows were wide open not a sound came from any of the classrooms.

A covered passageway led into the deserted courtyard; another one straight ahead led out to Knightrider Street. The space in the middle was rectangular rather than square. Five Georgian terraced houses, only the top floors raked by the sun, faced five more across the narrow divide. The heavy air pressed down on Johnny's head and shoulders. It was like entering a cockpit.

According to Father Gillespie, the Church Commissioners owned all the property in the yard. Yapp had lodged at Number Five. Johnny grasped the knocker — inappropriately shaped like a turban — and rapped on the freshly painted door. God was obviously a good landlord.

The knocks echoed off the surrounding blocks. Nothing happened. Johnny took out the mysterious key and tried it in the lock. It did not turn. However, before he could remove it, the door was opened with such force that Johnny was dragged forward. He almost fell over the step.

"What the devil d'you think you're playing at?" An old man in a collarless shirt, braces dangling, snarled at Johnny. His full head of snow-white hair was haywire. "You woke me up."

"Who are you?"

"What's it to you?" The geriatric bantam put his hands on his hips.

"I'm John Steadman from the *Daily News*." The door would have slammed shut if he hadn't had his foot on the threshold. He winced in pain. "Father Gillespie sent me."

That wasn't quite true — the priest had merely given him the address — but it had the desired effect. The door swung open again.

"Should've said so right off."

"You didn't exactly give me much chance."

A smirk replaced the snarl. "Haggie's the name. I looked after Father Yapp, God rest his soul. Now what can I do for you?"

"You can let me in, for starters."

The housekeeper stood back. Johnny entered a bare hallway. A smell of baking — Dundee cake? — filled the air. He could almost see his face in the green linoleum beneath his throbbing foot.

A Victorian painting of Jesus in the Garden of Gethsemane hung on the wall. It was always hot in Palestine: why would anyone go around with all that hair? The mere thought of a beard was enough to make him feel itchy. Only a man with something to hide would cultivate so many whiskers.

"Did Father Yapp live here alone?"

"Not likely — he was only a subchanter. He shared the house with three others."

"Are they based at St Paul's as well?"

"No. One of them works in the Dean's office, but the other two are attached to different churches in the City. I look after them all."

"Do you live in?"

"No thank you very much. I still like to go home to the missus — even after forty-three years."

"Are residents allowed female guests?"

"This ain't a knocking shop!"

"That's not what I asked."

The janitor gave a snort of derision. "What d'you think? Course not. Don't mean they have to be celibate, though. We're not bloody Romans here."

"When was the last time you saw Father Yapp?"

"Saturday morning. I cook breakfast and dinner for the boys every day except Sunday. They have lunch wherever they happen to be."

"It must be very hard work."

"For them or for me?"

"For you." Johnny met Haggle's eyes. "It must be exhausting if you need a siesta."

The old man was the first to look away. He shuffled his feet.

"The heat gets to me, that's all. It's not every day. How about a cuppa?"

Johnny followed him along the hall and down the steep stairs to a basement kitchen. The low ceiling didn't bother him.

"How long have you worked here?"

"Sixteen years." The housekeeper filled the kettle and set it on what looked like a new gas stove. "It was my first job after leaving the army. Damn lucky to get it, I was. There's always a demand for religion — especially in hard times — and men of the cloth don't walk out on strike."

"It can't pay much."

"Enough to keep the tallyman from the door. Like a slice?"

Johnny, all too aware that he had skipped lunch, was eyeing the fruitcake on the dresser hungrily. "Please." He pulled out a chair and sat down at the well-scrubbed table. "What sort of man was Mr Yapp?"

"He had a heart of gold. Do anything for anybody, he would." Haggie set a generous piece of cake before him proudly.

"Thank you. Did he have many friends?"

"Everybody liked Graham."

"Anybody in particular? I know he wasn't married."

"Not that I know of. He didn't discuss such matters with me. You'd have to ask the others. The Church was his life — I don't know as he had much of a one outside it."

"What did he do at St Paul's? I haven't a clue what a subchanter does."

"Graham was an assistant to the precentor."

"I'm still in the dark."

88

"Go to church much, do you?"

"Not at all." Saturday had been the first time he'd set foot inside a house of God since he'd followed a possible informant into St Bartholomew-the-Great in December.

"The precentor is responsible for the liturgy and all the music. He runs the choir as well."

"Important man, then."

"Very. Which is why he needs an assistant. I take it you're a non-believer?"

"I believe in some things, but the Holy Ghost isn't one of them. The idea of an all-seeing, omniscient old man who sits on a golden throne in heaven surrounded by trumpet-tooting angels and fluffy clouds is ridiculous. If he existed he'd have to be a sadistic bastard to allow so many of his children to suffer such agony, misery and deprivation. It sounds highfalutin, but I suppose what I believe in is truth and justice — or the fight for them, at least — and . . ." A tone of defiance crept into his voice. "I do believe in love."

"God is love." It was said sincerely. Johnny smiled.

"I'll stick with the more earthbound version, thanks. Religion is just a means of control, a con trick that promises jam tomorrow only if you put up with dry bread today." He took a bite of the cake which, packed with raisins, was rich and moist. "Mmmm. Delicious. You certainly know how to bake."

"The army teaches you a lot." He got up, poured boiling water into an enormous brown teapot and returned to the table.

"Does the name Frederick Callingham mean anything to you?"

"Not offhand. Why?"

"He's the man who broke Mr Yapp's neck. He was a doctor."

"I thought pill-pushers were supposed to save life, not take it."

"It could have been a freak accident. From what you've told me, no one appeared to bear a grudge against him. Perhaps he was just in the wrong place at the wrong time."

"You can say that again."

"D'you recognise this?"

The housekeeper studied the key. "I don't think it'll open anything here." He took out a large key-ring from one of the dresser's drawers. "We've only got one Chubb lock and that's in the back-door. See . . ." He showed Johnny one of the keys on the ring. "They don't match."

"Can we try it, all the same?"

"If you must — but you're wasting your time." His knees cracked as he got to his feet. "Follow me." He led Johnny down the dark passage to a door at the rear of the building. "Go on then, see if it fits."

It didn't. Johnny was disappointed.

"What's on the other side?" Haggie, anticipating the question, had the correct key at the ready.

"Nosy blighter, aren't you?"

"Have to be, in my job."

Johnny expected to see a postage stamp-sized yard containing nothing but a washing line. However, although a couple of table-cloths hung limply in the humid air, they were stretched across a common paved area, not more than eight feet wide, to which all the houses backing on to St Andrew's Hill had access. The angry horn of a tug-boat drifted up from the Thames.

"Is there any other way into here?"

"A passage leads to the church round the corner."

Johnny, pushing the laundry on other lines aside, headed to where the housekeeper had pointed. A dog-legged path between high brick walls ran all the way to St Andrew's. The plain, rectangular church, designed by Wren, had attracted some attention the previous year after one of its three bells from Avenbury — which had only been installed in 1933 — had tolled all by itself when a rector of the Wiltshire parish had died. Johnny didn't believe in ghosts. He jumped as a single peal marked the half-hour.

The housekeeper stood waiting impatiently for him. "The tea will be stewed now."

"I'm sorry. It's half-past three. I've got to be off."

"Suit yourself."

"When will the other residents be back?"

"Not till this evening. Dinner's at six." He locked the door behind him and led Johnny up the stairs to the hall. Before the housekeeper reached the front door it opened. A sturdy young man, blond hair plastered to his forehead, sweat beading his upper lip, burst in.

"Ah, Haggie. I . . ." He stopped when he saw Johnny. "Sorry, I didn't mean to interrupt."

"You didn't. I was just leaving."

"This is John Steadman. He's a reporter from the *News*," said Haggie.

"How do you do. I'm George Fewtrell." He wiped his palm on his cassock before shaking hands. "Excuse me, but I must get on." He headed for the stairs.

"I'm investigating the death of Father Yapp," said Johnny. "What can you tell me about him?" The cleric turned to face him.

"Nothing that you probably don't already know. It's a tragedy. Graham will be sorely missed." He resumed the climb.

"Well, if you think of anything, no matter how insignificant it might seem, I'll be back again this evening."

"I'll look forward to it."

Johnny doubted that very much. He thanked Haggie for the fruitcake. The dogsbody nodded a farewell and closed the door.

Johnny looked up at the flat-fronted house. No one could be seen at the open windows but he was sure he was being watched.

Why had the word *reporter* made the colour drain from Fewtrell's face?

CHAPTER
TEN

Three hours later Johnny returned to Wardrobe Place. A muffled din from the nearby printing works revealed that the early editions of the next day's newspapers had already gone to press.

PDQ had told him to hang fire on the story of the gruesome bouquet. A body of a young female, with or without a missing limb, had still not been reported. Johnny's sole contribution to the evening edition was a paragraph identifying the man who had plunged to his death in St Paul's on Saturday. Simkins, who had written a similar item in the *Chronicle*, would be pleased at his apparent failure to land a scoop.

A thorough search of his desk failed to unearth any more postcards of obscure saints or anything else that might have been sent by the lunatic with beauty on the brain. However, beneath the mess of discarded typescripts, cuttings and invitations — to press conferences, parties, tree-plantings, unveilings and openings — he did find a sub-layer of paper-clips, treasury tags, rubber bands, pencil-shavings, crumbs and fluff. He had emptied the drawers when he inherited Bill's desk. It was astonishing, and a little disgusting, how much detritus had accumulated in three months. This was not the sort of muck-raking he enjoyed.

The only connection he could see between Frederick Callingham and Graham Yapp was St Paul's — and it was more than tenuous. So far Yapp was defined by his job: he was what he did. Johnny realised the same could be said of him: but there was more to him than crime-reporting, even if it did consume most of his life. As well as being a newspaperman he was an only child, a friend and lover — though he was trying not to think about Stella at the moment. Yapp had to have been more than just a shuffler of sheet music.

Johnny grasped the brass turban and knocked on the door.

The man in the broad-brimmed sunhat and dark glasses picked up a copy of the *News* on the way to the cinema. He never ventured far in daylight. The Globe was only a three-minute walk away from St John's Square on the corner of Skinner Street opposite the public library.

Before he entered the picture house, the man dodged into Northampton Buildings across the road and, sitting at the top of the coal-cellar steps — his back to any unlikely passers-by — hurriedly leafed through the paper. When he did not find what he was looking for he cursed and went through the rag again with more care. No, his gift had been ignored. He flung the newspaper down the steps.

The Globe, formerly the People's Picture Palace, was an archetypal fleapit which actually made him glad its tip-up seats, instead of being upholstered, were made of slatted wood. The barn-like auditorium was similarly devoid of embellishment. A female attendant in a tatty excuse for a uniform walked down the aisle spraying a concoction of water and scent that simply added to the soupy atmosphere.

The manager, in a desperate — or ironic — bid to boost his dwindling box office returns, had selected *Heat Wave* as the main feature. The man had no desire to see Albert Burdon and Anna Lee warble their way through the dismal comedy. It was the audience, a dozen lost souls, that interested him. The flickering light cast the upturned faces in silver. One of them made his heartbeat quicken.

Stella, still lying on her bed, sighed and turned over. She wiped her face with a damp flannel. The flimsy, floral-patterned curtains swayed in a soft breeze that brought with it a faint hint of river-stink. According to her oval Waterbury wristwatch — a present from Johnny — it was already after seven yet hardly any cooler.

The roar of well-oiled conversation two floors below suggested they had a full house tonight. She was much better physically now — the stabbing pain had been replaced by a dull ache — but mentally she felt wretched.

She seethed with self-recrimination. Her much-prized independence — not to say her life — had been in jeopardy.

There was a tap on the door. Her mother, not waiting for a reply, came in.

"You've got a visitor." Stella sat up, swinging her bare legs over the edge of the bed. She was panic-stricken.

"Please tell me it's not Johnny. He's the last person I need to see."

"He should be the first, though, shouldn't he?" Dolly's anger had given way to bitter disappointment. "You said it was different this time. You said he was Mr Right."

"Well, I was wrong." She ran her fingers through her tousled hair. She must look an utter fright. "Who is it?"

"See for yourself. I've shown him into the parlour." She turned on her heels and clomped wearily back to the bar.

Stella spent ten minutes painting her face — Johnny called it gilding the lily — before putting on a pink-and-white candy-striped dress that showed off her slender figure. The frock belled out as she twirled in front of the mirror. It was all about appearances.

As she glided down the stairs, finally deigning to welcome her gentleman caller, she found herself wishing that everything could be repaired so easily.

Haggie, the sleeves of his collarless shirt rolled up, nodded towards one of the doors on the left. An aroma of braising steak and boiled cabbage made Johnny's stomach rumble. A bacon sandwich and a slice of cake was not enough for a working man — but it was more than many people had in a day.

"I'll leave the introductions to you," said the housekeeper. "Don't worry, you're expected. As soon as I've done the dishes, I'm off." He skedaddled back to the scullery.

Two men, both in clerical garb, were drinking coffee at a circular dining table. They exuded an air of postprandial satisfaction. It was all right for some. They were housed by the Church of England, fed and watered by the Church of England and even clothed by the Church of England — albeit in frocks. Furthermore, instead of paying for all this they received salaries as well. No wonder the collection plate was always being passed round.

The sinecurists did not get up when he entered.

"Evening, gents. Sorry to disturb you. I'm John Steadman from the *Daily News*."

The priests — with their identical short back and sides, freshly shaven cheeks and shining eyes — might have been real siblings rather than mere Christian brothers. They were no older than he was, but their smug, half-mocking attitude made them seem prematurely middle-aged. They had got their feet under the table — literally — and had no intention of moving. Johnny felt like punching them. Would they hit back or turn the other cheek?

The one that was smoking put down his coffee cup.

"I'm Jabez Corser and this is Adam Wauchope." He waved his hand vaguely in the direction of his colleague. "No need for titles here. We're not at work now. Do sit down. Would you care for some coffee? I believe there's some left. Haggie can always make a fresh pot."

"No thanks." Johnny sat down between the two men. Wauchope, eyes half-closed, had his hands folded over an incipient bay window. If it was an attempt to convey disinterest, it wasn't working. "Where's your house-mate?"

"Fewtrell? He couldn't wait, I'm afraid. Parochial business." Corser sighed as if to imply the Lord was a harsh taskmaster. "I believe you met him this afternoon."

"Yes, but he didn't have time for a chat. Apparently."

"Why are you so interested in Georgie?" Wauchope refilled his own cup. "Aren't we good enough for you?"

Johnny ignored the question. "Does he work at St Paul's?"

"Hardly. That's my privilege. Georgie's attached to St Vedast-alias-Foster."

"That's in Foster Lane, I presume?"

The church and its Baroque steeple stood in the shadow of the cathedral.

"Spot on. Not just a pretty face, are you?"

"So why d'you think poor old Yapp was murdered?" said Corser. "You wouldn't be here if you thought his death a tragic accident."

"An act of God," added Wauchope. "He has such mysterious ways." The flippant remark betrayed a certain lack of faith. Perhaps he was just trying to rile Johnny.

"Can you think of anyone who might have held a grudge against him?" Johnny took out his notebook.

"Absolutely not. Graham wouldn't hurt a fly, let alone a fellow human being," said Wauchope. "He was meek and mild all the way through — just like a mug of Horlicks."

Johnny bit his tongue. What did this pair know about "night starvation"? The malted drink was said to stave off the non-existent phenomenon. Then again, they knew all about marketing something that did not exist.

"Was he a popular man?"

"Not exactly popular," said Corser. "But not unpopular either. He kept himself to himself."

"His life was like his death," said Wauchope. "It scarcely left a ripple."

"Was he close to anyone in particular?"

"You mean a lady friend?" asked Corser. "If you'd met him, you'd know what a ridiculous question that is."

"Why's it ridiculous?"

"He wasn't exactly a catch," said Wauchope. "He was interested in spiritual matters, not his personal appearance."

Johnny recalled the hole in Yapp's shoe.

"Only superficial people don't judge by appearances," said Corser.

"I say, Jabez, that's very good. Too good for you. Who said that?"

"Oscar Wilde," said Johnny.

"Ten out of ten," said Corser. He didn't bother to mask his surprise. "Where did you go to school?"

"Nowhere." Johnny was used to such queries. They were put-downs, attempts to reinforce the pecking order. "Essex Road School for Boys."

"Ah," said Wauchope. "I suppose you wouldn't be a journalist if you'd gone to Winchester or Rugby."

"There are plenty of public school boys in Fleet Street."

"He's right," said Corser. "D'you know Henry Simkins?"

"Only too well," said Johnny.

"He was at Westminster College the same time as me. His father's an MP."

"I know. Any idea who's Yapp's next of kin?"

"There isn't one," said Wauchope. "Father Gillespie told me this afternoon. He was hoping to make the funeral arrangements, but the police are refusing to release the body."

"So you're not alone in suspecting foul play," said Corser.

Johnny was pleased: it meant that the cops were still investigating Callingham's demise. His wife would have to wait to place her death notice in *The Times*.

"Does the name Frederick Callingham ring a bell?" The two priests looked at each other.

"No," said Corser.

"No," said Wauchope. "Who is he?"

"He was the man who killed Yapp."

"Ah," said Wauchope. "Gillespie said it was a suicide."

"Congregations are falling across the City," said Corser with a poker-face.

"I would have thought the threat of another world war would be good for the prayer business," said Johnny.

"You can pray anywhere," replied Corser.

"Where do you work?"

"St Lawrence Jewry in Gresham Street."

"Do either of you recognise this?" Johnny produced the key.

"No," said Corser.

"No," said Wauchope. "Where did you find it?"

"I didn't find it," said Johnny. "It turned up in the collection box at the cathedral on Saturday. Take a closer look."

"There's no need." Corser held up a key-ring. "All present and correct."

"Well, if there's nothing else . . ." said Wauchope. He got to his feet and strolled over to the window.

Corser, while Johnny's attention was diverted, leaned over and grabbed his notebook. Unable to decipher the lines and squiggles, he threw it back across the table.

"That's another reason why shorthand is so useful," said Johnny.

The basement door closed. Wauchope's back stiffened. Was Haggie on his way home to his wife? No, Johnny could hear him still clattering away downstairs. He rushed to the window.

George Fewtrell was hurrying towards St Andrew's.

Johnny grabbed his notebook — "I thought you lot were not supposed to bear false witness" — and dashed down the stairs to the basement. The housekeeper came out of the kitchen.

"You should have told me he was here!" Johnny didn't wait for an answer.

The tablecloths had been taken in but a few items of laundry still hung in the muggy air. Johnny shoved them aside and ran down the passage that led to the church. He tore round the corner of the dog-leg totally unprepared for the waiting fist and the cold brass knuckleduster.

PART TWO

Dark House Lane

CHAPTER
ELEVEN

Tuesday, 6th July, 12.05 a.m.

The bells of St Andrew by the Wardrobe brought him round. As they tolled midnight they were joined by the bells of other Wren churches, the doleful carillon growing in number and volume, slowly spreading through the breathless air, heralding another day of stress and heat-stroke, swelling until the bells seemed to be ringing inside his throbbing head. He made no attempt to get up. The clappers fell silent and unconsciousness reclaimed him.

It was only when something started licking his face — a strong tongue rasping his cheeks, hot death-breath filling his nostrils — that Johnny opened his eyes. What he saw was enough to make him sit up and yell — in pain and surprise. His legs kicked out ineffectually as he scrabbled back against the wall. With a backward glance — the bottomless black in the amber eyes betraying no fear — the fox slunk off in search of easier prey.

Someone had given him a right going-over. His head felt as if it had been stamped on. His nose was bleeding — the blood must have been what attracted Reynard — and, judging from his difficulty in breathing, at least a couple of ribs were cracked. His clothes — but not the ground — were damp. Sweat? He sniffed his fingers gingerly. Unfortunately not. The bastard or bastards had pissed on him. Foxes didn't eat asparagus.

Wincing and cursing, he dragged himself upright and leaned against the wall. He swore even more when he realised his wallet and notebook had gone. The key was still in his pocket though. Why hadn't it been taken? Perhaps his assault had nothing to do with the Callingham case or George Fewtrell. The police had said he was a target. Nevertheless, what had he done to deserve this? To urinate on someone was to show them utter contempt. Anger stung him into action. He had to get out of these clothes.

Wardrobe Place was round the corner but he wasn't going to let Corser or Wauchope see him like this. Besides, he wouldn't accept charity from a pair of liars. Actually, when he thought about it, they hadn't lied: they had only misled him. Corser's reply to the question of Fewtrell's whereabouts — "He couldn't wait, I'm afraid" — was worthy of a Jesuit. It wasn't the same as saying: "He's already left." Similarly, "parochial business" could hide a multitude of sins. He needed to grill the priests again. An unchristian image of St Lawrence on the gridiron came to mind. For now though he would let the sleeping dog-collars lie.

What about The Cock? Smithfield was a lot closer than Islington. He would no doubt be calling on the Bennions later in the day. There was no point in disturbing them now. He could just see Stella's father staring at him in dismay, thinking how could he possibly look after his daughter when he couldn't even look after himself. No, the sensible thing was to go across the road from the pub and use the emergency department at Bart's. The *News* would pay.

He saw stars when he started walking, even though his eyes were on the ground. The dizziness and nausea came in waves. He hugged himself but his ribs stabbed him viciously each time he stumbled. It was impossible to take more than the shallowest of breaths.

St Andrew's Hill seemed far steeper than he remembered. As he crossed Carter Lane and entered Creed Lane, which would take him up to St Paul's, he heard the welcome sound of a cab approaching. Raising his arm caused more pain, but the thought of his wounds being dressed by a sexy, sympathetic nurse gave him strength. The lane was badly lit, and the driver didn't appear to have spotted him, so he stepped off the pavement and, wincing once again, waved at the taxi. The cab was on the point of swerving out of the way when its brakes were slammed on.

"What you playing at? Trying to get yerself killed?" The unshaven cabbie glowered at him. Even in this weather he was wearing a flat cap. "My ticker nearly burst out me chest."

"I'm already half-dead. I've been attacked." Johnny breathed in and out rapidly. Surely he wasn't going to faint? "I really need to get to Bart's."

The driver's eyes narrowed. He sniffed suspiciously then let out the clutch and pulled away, not caring that Johnny was leaning into the open window. "Fucking tramp!"

Johnny, whose nose was now blocked with bloody mucus, had momentarily forgotten how vile he smelt. He trudged on, up Ave Maria Lane, down Warwick Lane — where he was forced to rest on a bench outside Cutlers' Hall, and would have nodded off if it hadn't been for his splitting skull — until, at last, he turned the corner into Giltspur Street.

He rang the bell. Nothing happened. It could have been a matter of life and death. These people were paid to be on call twenty-four hours a day. He rang again. It can't have been much after twelve thirty. The human body didn't clock on and off. He kept his finger on the doorbell until, a whole minute later, a buxom, middle-aged woman in a matron's uniform, a look of thunder on her face, drew back the bolt and, arms folded, looked down her pointed nose at him. Her nostrils flared as the unmistakable tang reached them.

"I'm not a tramp," said Johnny, aware that if he didn't sit down soon he would fall down. His battered mouth made it difficult to speak clearly. "Someone's assaulted me. I'm a reporter on the *Daily News*."

"That explains it then." She made no attempt to help him. "What it doesn't quite explain though is the bad smell . . ."

"My attacker added insult to injury." What was she waiting for? She must be accustomed to such bodily odours. "Where's the doorman?"

"He's sick." Before Johnny could make a sarcastic reply, his knees buckled. He was mercifully out cold when he hit the ground.

★ ★ ★

St John's Square was lit by four flickering gaslights that would soon be replaced by modern ones connected to the mains. The thought did not fill the man wreathed in a silk scarf with pleasure. Old London was being destroyed by the march of progress. Every week its nooks and crannies were flattened by the wrecking ball; rookeries were still being demolished by the meddlesome Peabody Trust. There were times when he liked nothing better than to slum it.

This evening, for example, he had stooped lower than expected. She had turned out to be more than a little rough — and, as the bite marks on his cock would testify, full of fighting spirit — until he had produced the tongue-tearer. When he had finally taken leave of her, a few short minutes ago, she had been only too willing to try and lick the last dew-drop off his tip as it glistened in the candlelight — but, of course, she couldn't. He'd wiped it on her raven locks instead. The thought of her chained up, the bloom on her naked flesh slowly fading, put a spring in his step.

Once more he congratulated his parents on their choice of location. The house was perfectly situated for all his needs. Mount Pleasant, for instance, was just two minutes away. Mount Pleasant. Mons Veneris. Mont Blanc. They were the three points in the triangle that now made up his life.

He was looking forward to a long, luxurious soak, letting the smell of blood and sex leach away. However, before he could relax, he had to do one more thing. Steadman had to be given a gentle reminder.

If the hack was not taking him seriously yet, he soon would be.

Johnny's first thought was that he must be the victim of a practical joke. He was wearing someone's pyjamas — they couldn't be his because he didn't own a single pair; he slept in the nude in summer and wore one of his father's night-shirts in winter — but it wasn't this that made him laugh: it was the turban wrapped round his head. He started to giggle then stopped as his battered ribs reminded him what had happened. He turned his bandaged head on the mound of pillows and realised he couldn't open his left eye. He was in a dimly lit side-ward off the emergency department from which new arrivals requiring further treatment could be transferred to other parts of the hospital when the day shift began. There was only one other patient: a shrunken old lady who was snoring gently.

"They gave you something for the pain," said the young nurse. She smiled down at him as she checked his pulse. The gap between her two front teeth was charming — it set off the neatness of the others to perfection. Her watch was pinned on to a freshly starched apron that covered an ample bosom. This was more like it. The brownest eyes he had ever seen — the colour of fresh toffee — watched him take in the view. She smiled again.

"There's a sight for sore eyes — sore everything, really."

"That's what I said when we cleaned you up."

Johnny felt himself blushing. He realised he wasn't wearing any pyjama bottoms. Why? To prevent him making a quick getaway?

"Your face matches your hair, now." She smoothed down the grey blanket on his bed. "I've never been out with a ginger-nut. I usually prefer the looks of conventional leading men."

"Stan Laurel, James Cagney and Spencer Tracy have red hair."

"Not exactly dreamboats, are they? Besides, how d'you know?"

"I know lots of things. I'm a reporter."

"So matron said. You going to report me?"

"Only if you want me to. You better give me your details."

"It's strictly against the rules." She glanced over her shoulder to check the coast was clear. "I'm Millie," she murmured, her lips tickling his ear. "I'll tell you more when we meet. Perhaps you'll be able to come out to play next week. I'll be on days then. We have a drink in The Cock most evenings."

Johnny's heart leapt — in guilt and shock. Stella would have scratched his eyes out. He must have brain damage. Millie, oblivious to his pricked conscience, stopped whispering and adopted a more professional pose.

"In the meantime you should rest. You've got three cracked ribs, mild concussion and lots of cuts and bruises. I do hope the boys in blue get the blighters who did this to you. The doctor will probably discharge you in the morning. Rounds start at ten."

"What time is it now?"

"Ten past four."

Johnny was surprised. He had been unconscious for hours.

"I've got to get out of here. I need to go home and change. I start work at eight."

"And how are you going to do that?" She glanced at his legs beneath the blanket.

"You're going to help me, Millie."

"Am I now? What's it worth?"

"Dinner?" He now had no intention of ever seeing her again — but he'd have suggested a kiss if it did the trick.

"Is everything all right, Nurse Popert?" Neither of them had seen the battle-axe glide up behind them.

"Yes, Sister. Mr Steadman was asking to leave." Millie widened her big brown eyes to warn him to tread carefully.

"Out of the question. You can't be discharged until a doctor has examined you again, Mr Steadman. You've been subjected to a severe beating. There could be complications. You need to rest."

"What's to stop me discharging myself?" He threw back the covers, got out of bed and, ignoring the lightheadedness, began to unbutton the pyjama top. Millie swallowed a giggle.

"Get back into bed at once, you ridiculous man." For a moment Johnny thought she was going to smack his bottom. "You're not fit to be out in public — in more ways than one."

112

"You can't keep me here against my will. I'm not under arrest."

"You will be if you attempt to leave the hospital without paying the bill."

"But my wallet was stolen. You can send the invoice to the *Daily News*."

"Is there someone who can guarantee such an arrangement at this ungodly hour?"

"No, of course not. It's not as if you don't know where to find me, though."

"We've only your word that you are who you say you are. And even if we did believe you, and agreed that your employers would pay for your treatment, do you actually propose to leave here stark-naked?"

"I thought you could lend me some clothes."

"As I've already told you, Mr Steadman, what you need is rest."

Johnny looked to Millie for support, but she refused to meet his gaze. It was no good: he was trapped.

"Can I at least make a telephone call?"

"To whom?"

"The police." He had to give the cow credit: nothing fazed her. She simply raised her eyebrows and waited for an explanation. "My best friend's a sergeant at Snow Hill."

CHAPTER
TWELVE

Johnny would have called Stella had she been at home. He'd given her a key in May, not that she'd ever had cause to use it. He usually came to meet her. Fortunately Matt had a key too — there were times, usually after too many toasts to yet another boxing victory in the police league, when it was either too late to return to Bexley or he was in no fit state to sleep at the station-house. Appearances had to be maintained: his authority would be undermined if his subordinates saw him the worse for wear. He had been drinking more since December.

Johnny always did his best to be there for Matt — during and after the match — but, inevitably, a breaking story would sometimes take precedence. On such occasions Matt would make his way back to his old stamping ground, let himself in and crawl up the bare wooden stairs. He didn't mind that Johnny only had one bedroom and a double bed.

Johnny, knowing that Matt started work at 6a.m., had left a message with the desk sergeant saying that he had been attacked, had spent the night at Bart's and now needed some cash and a change of clothes.

However, a different policeman was sitting by his bed when he next opened his bleary right eye.

"Been meeting your adoring readers again?"

"Constable Watkiss. What an unexpected pleasure."

"Don't sound so disappointed. Matt sent me. I've brought you what you asked for." He nodded to a brown paper carrier-bag with string handles. "Nice place you have. Live alone, do you?"

"For now." Why hadn't Matt come? Was he still angry with him?

"Any idea who did this to you?" The copper's sloe-black eyes bore into him. "Any idea why?"

"I didn't see them coming — literally. I was running down a passage off St Andrew's Hill. I turned a corner and the next thing I knew, a fox was licking my face."

Someone — Watkiss? — had pulled the curtains round the bed. To all intents and purposes they were alone. The policeman leaned forward and poked him in the ribs.

"Ow! Fuck off! What d'you do that for?"

"I don't believe you."

"That's your lookout. Pass me that glass of water." His tongue felt like pumice stone. The policeman did as he was told. "Thank you."

"Need some help?"

"No." Watkiss knocked his elbow. The stale, lukewarm liquid slopped out, soaking the front of his pyjamas. Johnny threw the rest of it in Watkiss's smirking face. The curtains swept back.

"What's going on?" A portly doctor, flanked by the matron and a younger, flaxen-haired nurse, stared at the dripping copper. There was no sign of Millie.

115

"Nothing, Doctor. It's like a Turkish bath in here," said Watkiss.

"Wait till you get outside." The medic stood back to let him pass.

"I have a few more questions for Mr Steadman."

"I trust you're not going to arrest him for assault."

"No point. My sarge wouldn't stand for it." He dabbed his face with a chequered handkerchief.

"Very well. Please wait over there by Sister's desk." The doctor turned his attention to the patient. "Well, John, if your temper's anything to go by, you seem to be rallying swiftly. The concussion will make you feel rather wibbly-wobbly, so take it easy for a couple of days. I'm probably wasting my breath, I know, but only go to work if it's absolutely necessary. Whatever you do, avoid strenuous exercise. Your ribs need time to mend. The swelling round your left eye should soon subside. You've taken quite a kicking. Anything else?"

"Only wounded pride."

"Not going to write about your misadventure then?"

"Depends if it's got anything to do with the stories I'm investigating. There's nothing intrinsically newsworthy about a reporter being roughed up."

"Even when it's by a City of London policeman?"

Johnny looked into the pill-pusher's bloodshot eyes. Was he referring to Watkiss or someone else? He chose to overlook the doctor's question.

"May I leave now?"

"You may. Sister has kindly telephoned your newspaper. They are aware of the situation and have agreed to pay the outstanding five guineas."

"Thank you."

The white coat, closely followed by the bumptious matron, continued on its rounds. As the nurse closed the curtains she gave a grin and whispered: "Millie said she'll see you next Tuesday."

Johnny immediately got out of bed. His legs felt stronger now. The light-headedness had gone. He had just removed the damp pyjama-top when Watkiss appeared through the curtains and picked up the carrier-bag.

"Looking for this?" He made no attempt to avert his gaze.

"Why are you being such a prick?" Johnny held out his hand.

"Not so fast, Steadman. I'll stop playing around when you do. A straight answer gets you one item of clothing. What were you doing in St Andrew's Hill?"

"I was interviewing someone."

"If you want these" — he held up a pair of off-white cotton drawers — "you'll have to do better than that."

If it weren't for his wounds, Johnny would have launched himself at his inquisitor.

"Colleagues of Graham Yapp, the chap who was killed by Frederick Callingham."

"There you are." Watkiss threw the underwear at him. "I'm afraid I couldn't find the frilly ones."

Johnny ignored him and, feigning nonchalance, slowly started to get dressed.

"What time was this?"

"I arrived around six-thirty p.m. and left about twenty-five minutes later."

A shirt came flying over the bed.

"Why are you so interested in Yapp?"

"I'm not convinced his death was an accident."

A pair of trousers followed the shirt.

"And what did you find out?"

"Not much. Yapp seems to have been something of a saint."

"That's suspicious in itself." Watkiss, losing interest in his little game, sat down and tossed the well-used bag to Johnny. It contained a pair of socks and a jacket. He only owned two suits so he would have to find out what had happened to the one he'd been wearing.

"The coroner hasn't released either body yet."

"Check your facts, Steadman. It was announced at nine o'clock this morning. An open verdict and accidental death."

"Not suicide? That's a bit premature, isn't it?"

"There's no evidence one way or the other, so the coroner didn't have a choice. Besides, he doesn't want to hang on to stiffs any longer than is absolutely necessary. People are dropping like flies. The mortuary was flooded yesterday: the fridges can't cope with the heat."

"So I was wasting my time."

"Indeed — and yet someone took the trouble to try and stop you sniffing around."

"It doesn't make sense." Johnny retrieved his shoes from underneath the bedside table. He sat down and wiggled his feet into the scuffed black oxfords. Bending down to tie the laces produced a grimace of pain.

118

"Penterell thinks your secret admirer might be behind the attack. Need some help?"

"I can manage."

"No, you can't. Here, let me." The copper, apparently keen to make up for his churlish behaviour, knelt down and grabbed a foot.

"My secret admirer, as you put it, is trying to attract my attention, not warn me off. Besides, how could he have known where I'd be?"

"He followed you, of course."

Johnny felt stupid: the dope must still be running through his veins. The thought of being shadowed made the hairs on the back of his neck stand up. Then again, if that were the case, the person who followed him would surely have been outside the front of the house, lurking in Wardrobe Place. Even if they were aware of the back entrance they would have no reason to think that he would leave by a different door to the one he had entered. Maybe there were two of them . . .

Watkiss stood up and patted his knee. "All done!" He took out his wallet. "Matt asked me to give you this."

"Thank you." Johnny slipped the crisp new oncer into his pocket.

"He said you can pay him back when you see him tomorrow."

"Absolutely." A wave of relief swept over him. Matt had not cancelled the invitation so he couldn't be that angry — and, if he knew that he was fit enough to travel, he must have enquired about the nature and extent of his injuries.

Watkiss opened the curtains. There was no sign of the old biddy. The adjacent bed had been stripped.

"Keep your eyes open, Steadman. Well, the right one at least. Your attacker might try again — and do a better job next time." He pointed at the table. "Don't forget your watch." It lay next to the mysterious key. He started walking out of the ward.

The dial was cracked — which explained why it hadn't been stolen. Twenty past ten. Stella had been at work for over two hours.

Johnny stood up and nearly fell over. Watkiss had tied his laces together. The policeman, loitering in the doorway, gave a cackle and vanished.

CHAPTER
THIRTEEN

The bells of St Bride's were striking the eleventh hour as Johnny got out of the taxi. The traffic had been nose-to-tail all the way down Ludgate Hill and Fleet Street. The smell of petrol did little to mask the medieval stench of the drains.

"Ain't you got nuffink smaller?"

"Sorry — that's all I have." The driver, muttering under his bad breath, produced a pocket ledger from beneath his seat. He slipped off the rubber band that kept it closed and swapped the pound for a ten-shilling note. He fished the rest of the change out of a dirty calico bag then laboriously counted it out into Johnny's outstretched hand. It was quite a performance.

"That's for your trouble." Johnny returned one of the shillings. "Don't forget the receipt." This prompted another bout of muttering. "What's up? The cat got your budgie? Look around you: the sun is shining and all's right with the world."

The cabbie snorted in derision. Johnny diagnosed an irony deficiency. "I 'ate this fuckin'' 'eat." He let off the handbrake and stuck his bonnet out into an imaginary gap between the two cars that were crawling by. Both drivers immediately put their hands on the horn and kept them there.

Johnny, instead of ignoring the din, laughed out loud and waved at the idiots. Why was he suddenly in such a good mood? A side-effect of the morphia, or plain relief that he had survived to see a new day? His rumbling stomach reminded him that he had not eaten since the previous afternoon.

His eventual arrival in the newsroom, clutching a bacon sandwich from the canteen, created a gratifying stir.

"Blimey!" said Dimeo. "What did you say to Stella?"

"You can't be that bad if you've got an appetite," said PDQ.

"You've got another postcard," said Patsel, mopping his brow.

"Would you like me to contact the police?" asked Timothy Tanfield.

"No, thank you," said Johnny. "I'm quite capable of doing it myself — when I'm good and ready."

The cub reporter meant well but his unbridled ambition often made him overstep the mark. Although he was a foot taller and at least six inches broader, Tanfield reminded Johnny of his younger self. His grey eyes seemed to glow when, for no reason other than to show off, he would call out the number of letters in any particularly long word that cropped up in conversation.

If PDQ, for instance, were talking about the disproportionate response of Franco's thugs to a press release from the International Brigades, Tanfield would cry "sixteen" and earn himself a nod of recognition. At

122

odd moments Johnny would test his remarkable ability by simply shouting out a word — "honorificabilitudinity" — to see how long it took him. A couple of seconds was usually enough, even for the longest word in Shakespeare: "Twenty-two!" He had managed to stump him just once with "floccinaucinihilipilification", the longest word in the *Oxford English Dictionary*, and that was because Tim didn't know how to spell it — or what it meant. Johnny had explained it thus: "If I were performing the action it describes I might say: *I estimate your talent to be absolutely worthless.*"

He sat down — carefully — at his desk. "Did you empty my pigeonhole?"

Tanfield shook his head.

"I did," said Patsel. "I wasn't sure you were coming in."

Dimeo, behind his boss's back, put an index finger on his upper lip and goose-stepped back to his own desk. The hooting stopped as soon as the news editor spun round. As usual he was too late to catch the culprit.

The postcard was a black-and-white image of the Venus de Milo in the Louvre. A single stanza was written on the reverse:

The sinful painter drapes his goddess warm,
Because she still is naked, being drest:
The godlike sculptor will not deform
Beauty, which limbs and flesh enough invest.

Aphrodite was not revered by the Catholic Church: so much for the hypothetical alphabet of saints. The

123

significance of the statue must lie in its missing limbs, but only one arm had turned up — so far.

"You must write up the story today," said Patsel. "We don't want anyone else breaking the news. This pervert will contact another newspaper if we don't give him what he wants. Loads of colour, Steadman, if you please. The Venus de Milo is immediately recognisable. She will make a good illustration."

"Better than the decomposing arm, at any rate."

"We can use that as well. I took the precaution of having it photographed before the police arrived yesterday."

Johnny's lip curled in distaste. "You're the boss."

"Yes, I am. Thank you for reminding me. Describe your escape from death as well."

"But that's got nothing to do with the story!" Johnny looked to PDQ for support.

"You are sure?" Patsel pushed his glasses back on to the crook of his shiny nose. "It is something of a coincidence, no?"

"The attack might just as well be connected with his digging around the suicide in St Paul's," said PDQ.

"I agree," said Johnny. "After all, I'd just come out of the house where the dead churchman lived."

"No matter," said Patsel. "The violence enhances the story of the postcards. It adds menace to the mix. The only people who can contradict you are the offenders themselves."

"The attack places me at the centre of the story," said Johnny. "I thought the whole idea was to give the Looney Tune a spot in the limelight."

124

"Such bashfulness isn't like you, Steadman." Patsel laughed humourlessly. "You have had the stuffing knocked out of you. Six hundred words by one p.m."

PDQ shrugged his shoulders. There was nothing he — or Johnny — could do.

As soon as he was left alone, Johnny snatched up the receiver and gave the Hello Girl the number for C. Hoare & Co.

"Good morning. Mr Dismorr's office."

"Stella! It's me." Her distinctive huskiness made his heart swell. He had feared that he'd never hear it again. Her voice had changed though. A hint of steel could be detected beneath her usual seductive tone.

"Everything OK?"

"Yes."

"Have a nice time in Brighton?"

"Not bad."

"Why didn't you let me know?"

"There wasn't time. Look, I've got to go. Come round tonight." She didn't even say goodbye. Johnny stared at the receiver. She was usually grateful for any opportunity to chat on the telephone; being a secretary was far less fun than she had expected. Something had happened. What though? He wasn't going to wait till the evening to find out.

He had an hour before Stella's lunch-break began. Ninety minutes before his deadline. He got up stiffly.

"If anyone calls, I'll be in the library, Tim." He needed to find out the significance of the postcards.

Apart from the librarian there was no one in the stuffy chamber that stretched across the rear of the

125

fourth floor. Some journalists only pushed open its frosted glass doors to sleep off a long lunch in one of its secluded, cosy carrels. The section on religion was not a large one. Johnny quickly found a dusty, broken-backed volume with the title *A Catholic Martyrology*. He sneezed as he opened it — immediately wished he hadn't — then sneezed again.

Saints Anastasia and Basilissa shared the same feast day: 15th April. They were Roman matrons who, during Nero's persecution of the Christians, retrieved the victims of torture and gave them reverent burial. When the emperor learned of their ministrations he had them sent to prison where they were scourged with whips, had their skin scraped by hooks and had their bare flesh branded with hot irons. Nevertheless, the two women refused to renounce their faith in Christ and were eventually beheaded with swords.

The very word "torture" paralysed Johnny's mind. Not only was he unable to imagine such agonies — the overwhelming, unremitting pain; the humiliating loss of bodily control — but he also couldn't comprehend how one human being could subject another to such maltreatment. He was aware that it did go on — people were at the mercy of others in prisons the world over — yet could not explain why it happened. The usual motives — revenge, hatred, insanity, political necessity — seemed too petty for such enormous evil. Now it appeared likely that some poor girl was suffering a similar fate today. He fervently hoped that it was nothing to do with him.

The reference section was much larger. *Bartlett's Familiar Quotations* — the title always amused Johnny; if they were familiar why would you need to look them up? — revealed that the inscription on the back of the latest postcard was taken from Ralph Waldo Emerson's *Painting and Sculpture*. Perhaps the sender was a religious maniac, or an art lover, or both: a crackpot Catholic aesthete.

"So there you are, Steadman. Looking the worse for wear as usual, I see."

Victor Stone, the editor of the *Daily News*, may have been short in stature but he still exuded a powerful physical presence. His restless nature often made him forsake his suite on the seventh floor and prowl all over Hereflete House. His staff never knew where he might pop up. He liked to think it kept them on their toes. The librarian made no attempt to tell him to lower his voice.

"I'll survive, sir."

"What did you say this time?"

"Nothing! I didn't get the chance."

"Well, I look forward to reading all about it. I believe Herr Patsel has charged you with producing a picturesque piece. Only a maniac would send someone an amputated limb. Take care, Steadman. You know where to find me if you need help with anything — including Herr Patsel. Don't let him bully you into doing something stupid."

"Thank you, sir. I seem to have done that already."

"Maybe. We'll decide that when you've found out what started all this." He turned on his rather thick heels and, with a cheery "good morning" to the librarian, swept through the swing doors.

Johnny returned to the newsroom. Forty minutes later the article was written.

"Laid it on a bit, haven't you?" PDQ raised his eyebrows. "Your injuries sound positively gruesome."

"If Pencil wants colour, I'll give him colour. The readers should know how much we suffer for our art."

PDQ smiled indulgently. "Where you off to?"

"Just going to get a bite to eat. I won't be long."

"You've just had a sandwich!"

"So? I've got to keep my strength up. In my book, suffering for your art doesn't include starvation."

The lunchtime editions had already hit the street. Boys in flat caps, large satchels round their narrow shoulders, yelled out the headlines: "MINIMUM MARRIAGE TIME CUT FROM FIVE TO THREE YEARS!" "JAPAN ATTACKS CHINA!" The heat made the bandage round his head feel like a tightening iron hoop. He slowed down, aware that his fellow pedestrians were giving him a wide berth. His bruised, unshaven face was enough to cause anyone consternation, but he was unprepared for Stella's immediate reaction when he touched her arm. She screamed.

"I'm all right. It looks worse than it is."

"I didn't recognise you." She turned to the mousy girl in thick glasses. "Go ahead, Myrtle. I'll catch you up. I'll have tongue and cress."

Her colleague looked Johnny up and down with a mixture of pity and disgust before marching off towards the Royal Courts of Justice. At this rate there wouldn't be a patch of grass left in Inner Temple Garden.

"What happened?" Stella's annoyance at being ambushed gave way to genuine concern.

"I was jumped on last night."

"Anyone you know?"

"Of course not. At least, I hope not. What sort of question is that?"

"You must have asked yourself who would do such a thing. What were you up to?"

"What else? Chasing a story." Stella, torn between affection and irritation, hesitated. Johnny continued: "I've missed you."

"It's only been four days!"

"What about our date in St Paul's?"

"I'm sorry. I should have let you know. There really wasn't time though. It was all so last minute."

"You haven't got a tan. I thought you'd be as brown as a berry."

"Don't want to look like a gyppo, do I?" She glanced at her watch. Johnny was pleased to see she was wearing it. "Why are you here? I thought we'd agreed to meet tonight."

"Do I need a reason?" A wave of exhaustion swept over him. Why was she being so difficult? "Is there anything you want to tell me?"

"No."

"Is there anything wrong?"

"No."

"Who was the man you were with?"

"What man?" Her green eyes flashed. "Been checking up on me, have you?"

"I was worried about you. Who was he?"

"No one!"

"Stella, look at me. I might have had my head kicked in, but my brain's still working. What's going on?"

"Nothing! Just let me be." Her eyes filled with tears. Johnny went to embrace her but she pushed him away. His complaining ribs made him groan. "Oh! I'm sorry. I didn't mean to hurt you."

"Your lies hurt more. Something's up. Are you in trouble? Let me help you. Whatever it is, the two of us can sort it out."

She laughed bitterly and wiped away her tears. "It's too late for that."

"What is?" Panic began to stir in his stomach. For some reason she wouldn't say what was on her mind, but that didn't mean he had to keep quiet too. "I love you."

"I know you do. Sometimes, though, love isn't enough." She looked at her watch again. "I must be off. Forget about this evening. Let's meet up later in the week." She turned to go.

"Hey! What about a goodbye kiss?" She looked at his swollen lips, hesitated, then pecked him on the cheek.

She might as well have slapped him across the face. He knew then that it was all over.

CHAPTER
FOURTEEN

He stared after Stella as she weaved her way through the milling lawyers, clerks and secretaries. She was an evil witch who, with no need of a magic wand, had made his future vanish — *poof!* — in the midday sun. Nevertheless, Johnny loved her.

He needed a drink. No, make that several drinks. What had he done wrong? It was not like her to be so evasive. He clenched his fists in frustration. Until he knew what the problem was, he couldn't work out a solution.

Few people realised that a romantic soul lurked behind his cynical façade. He believed that love, if strong enough, could find a way out of any predicament. At the moment, though, he was groping in the dark.

The hot flagstones beneath his feet felt like trapdoors that might open at any moment. Knowing that the Tipperary would be full of colleagues slaking their thirsts for beer and gossip, he trudged on a little further to the King and Keys, where he was more likely to be left alone.

The pub was packed with jacketless hacks, most of whom worked for the *Daily Telegraph*. Even so, this didn't stop them dropping their fag-ends in other men's beer — or punching anyone for the slightest perceived offence.

Johnny pushed his way through to the back where an open door afforded a splendid view of a poky yard piled high with empty barrels and sun-bleached crates. The yellow flowers of London rocket stood out against the soot-blackened wall.

He ordered a double Scotch. Before he could pay the apple-cheeked landlord a familiar voice made his heart sink.

"Allow me." For once his trademark scent of sandalwood provided welcome respite from the odour of a hundred sticky armpits.

"Hello, Henry." He picked up his glass and emptied it.

"Interesting choice of headgear. It suits you. Makes you look like a wounded powder monkey."

"Don't patronise me. I'm not in the mood."

Simkins smiled benevolently. "Another? You look as if you need it."

"That's very kind of you. It won't loosen my tongue, though."

"Spoilsport." He ruffled the carrot-coloured hair not covered by bandages. Johnny bridled: only Matt was allowed to do that. "Don't you want to tell me what happened?"

"There's nothing to tell. I was attacked and left for dead. You can read all about it after five o'clock." He had to be careful. Simkins still had time to get something in the *Chronicle*.

"Any arrests?"

"No."

"So you don't know who your attackers were?"

"It's flattering that you think there was more than one. Did you pay a couple of thugs to silence the only man to interview Callingham's grieving widow?"

"If I had, you wouldn't be standing here now. Besides, as you well know, it was a wild goose chase. Sometimes things are exactly what they seem."

"Namely?"

"A ghastly accident."

"Perhaps."

Simkins raised a well-groomed eyebrow. "Are you suggesting there have been developments?"

"Wait and see."

"The coroner's released both bodies."

"I'm aware of that."

"So?"

Johnny wasn't going to give his rival a head start by suggesting a connection between the two dead men and the attack, or the attack and the postcards — even if the latter only existed in the mind of Gustav Patsel.

"So, I've got other things on my mind."

"Such as?"

"Private matters."

"Ah, that explains it." Simkins tossed his chestnut mane. "Girl trouble." He sounded disappointed. "You should try the boys instead. They're much less complicated. Oh, but of course, you already have."

Johnny refused to rise to the bait. He lit another cigarette. He waved at the landlord.

"My turn. What are you drinking?"

"Amontillado."

"Sherry? In this weather!"

"Archie keeps a bottle in his fridge for me. The Spanish drink it chilled. You should try it."

"No, thanks. What are you doing here, Henry?"

"Seeing a friend."

"Anyone I know?"

"I very much doubt it. Perhaps you'll meet him on Friday. I trust you're still coming."

"I suppose so." He had never felt less sociable. On such occasions he was more confident with Stella on his arm. Crowds were more fun when you were part of a couple.

"I guarantee you'll never have seen anything like it."

"Will I know any of the guests?"

"Most assuredly." Simkins smiled into his drink. "There's at least one person looking forward to making your reacquaintance."

He didn't feel like eating and he didn't feel like going back to the office, so he had another Scotch and brooded. He wasn't going to let Stella finish with him without a fight. At the very least she owed him an explanation. He was more than squiffy by the time he staggered outside into Fleet Street, where the lunchtime crush had finally subsided. A lorry loaded with giant rolls of newsprint was holding up the traffic as it manoeuvred into a position that would allow it to reverse into Bouverie Street. The driver must have been a rookie: most deliverymen approached the presses from Tudor Street where they could line up outside the

134

glassworks. Impatient passengers on an open-topped double-decker shouted out instructions and immediately received a volley of abuse in reply. A white-gloved copper marched towards the jam.

Johnny ambled towards Ludgate Circus where he managed to hail a cab. The breeze from the open window cooled his hot skin. Already the alcohol was oozing from his pores. Sometimes he yearned to be away from the racket and rowdiness of the capital — but not for long. He didn't feel safe surrounded by green fields. Smoke was in his blood.

The doors of The Cock were bolted. Johnny kept banging on them till they opened.

"Bloody hell!" Bennion stood there with his arms folded across his broad chest. "What happened to you?"

"Attacked last night. Don't know who by. Don't know why. Can I have a drink?"

"Haven't you had enough?"

"Nowhere near. Still standing, aren't I?"

"Come in." Johnny followed him to the bar. Bennion fetched him a Scotch.

"Thank you."

"She's told you then?"

"Told me what? She won't tell me a damn thing. I've already asked her what's going on twice today: once on the telephone and once in person. She couldn't get away from me fast enough. I don't understand what I've done."

"Nothing, dearie." Dolly appeared from behind her husband, who, only too glad to defer to his missus, went upstairs for his afternoon nap. Years of listening to hard-luck stories had failed to equip him with the skills required to deal with affairs of the heart. It was all he could do to offer meaningless platitudes. Women were better at that sort of thing.

"It's not your fault," continued Dolly. "She'll tell you when she's good and ready. She's got herself into a right old pickle and hasn't decided what to do yet. As soon as she has, I'm sure she'll tell you."

"I was going to ask her to marry me." The lump in his throat made it impossible to say any more.

"Come here." She put her fat arms around him and pressed him to her breast. Johnny gritted his teeth. For once the pain felt good. "You have been in the wars, haven't you? She couldn't have chosen a worse moment."

Johnny knew he was drunk. His whole body, including his heart, ached. He stifled his sobs. Dolly kept holding him and, in her turn, felt herself filling up at the thought of losing yet another prospective son-in-law. She really liked this one. There was something different about him. She had given up lecturing Stella: her beautiful daughter was a law unto herself. Besides, she only listened to her father — and he was not a man of many words. Each of them, in their own way, had spoiled her. Johnny would not be the last suitor to face the distressing consequences.

"I'm all right now." He wiped his eyes with the back of his hand shame-facedly. "May I use the telephone?"

"Of course. You know where it is. How about a cup of tea?"

"Thank you." He followed Dolly round the end of the bar. She bustled into the kitchen; he went down the hall.

"I was wondering where you'd got to," said PDQ. "Patsel, the sadistic bugger, loved your piece."

"I've been interviewing a couple of people." Technically, it wasn't a lie. "I'm not feeling too good. Last night has finally caught up with me. Okay if I take the rest of the afternoon off?"

"I suppose so. If anyone asks I'll say you're following a lead. Call me if you don't think you'll make it in tomorrow."

"No danger. I just need a good night's sleep. Thanks, Pete."

Johnny replaced the receiver. His sense of relief was all too brief. He picked up the notepad that lay beside the Bakelite telephone. Someone — it wasn't Stella's handwriting — had jotted down the number of the *Daily News*. He tore off the page and put it in his pocket.

He had converted one of the pits into a makeshift mortuary. Half a dozen lanterns cast a flickering light over the human abattoir. He was completely unaffected by the eye-watering stench. Mustard gas had destroyed his sense of smell — and so much else — in France.

The mutilated body of his latest victim, the siren of Skinner Street as he liked to think of her, lay on a blood-stained operating table. His timing had been perfect, exploding with a groan as she had finally given up the ghost. Extreme unction, indeed.

As he sliced round the right breast, cutting through gland-tissue, fibrous tissue and fatty tissue, he reflected that his time studying medicine at St Thomas's — until he had been asked to leave after a "misunderstanding" with a nurse — had not been entirely wasted. The ligament of Cooper had always amused him, not that he could identify it now. Sir Astley Cooper's only claim to fame had literally made him a bit of a tit.

If everything went according to plan, he was going to be remembered for rather more.

Johnny alighted from the tram at Islington Green where mothers with prams, tramps with grog-blossoms and unemployed men with nothing to do were taking advantage of the shade provided by the giant plane trees. He bought some bread, cheese and tomatoes in St Peter's Street then walked round the corner to his flat in Cruden Street. A bottle of milk was still on the doorstep.

Having dumped his purchases on the kitchen table, he opened the sash window, then put the kettle on. As soon as he opened the milk he could tell it was off: it had curdled in the sun. He couldn't be bothered to go and get some more so he took a cup of black tea up to his bedroom.

Although the room appeared as tidy as usual, he could tell that someone had been through his belongings. Watkiss must have taken the opportunity to have a snoop around. Johnny owned little worth stealing — apart from his mother's jewellery — but, as far as he was concerned, his journal was priceless —

and, instead of where he had left it, on his bedside table, it was lying open on his bed.

It was too much to hope that Watkiss had been unable to decipher his handwriting. He should have devised a code like Samuel Pepys. The young, red-blooded copper must have wanted him to know that he had read it, and if he had read the entries relating to last December, it would explain his animosity towards him that morning. Johnny didn't care what he thought. However, the prospect of him relaying what he had read to Matt made his blood run cold.

When Johnny had started his journal on his twenty-first birthday in 1927 he had promised himself that he would always tell the truth and nothing but the truth. The vow proved far more difficult to maintain than expected. It was easier to be honest with others rather than yourself.

There were times when he was ashamed of his behaviour, embarrassed by his emotions and annoyed at his perceived weaknesses, but he reckoned it was precisely these passages that would provide his children with the most entertainment if not edification. His aim was full-blown biography, a warts-and-all portrait of a common man, not breathless hagiography.

His investigation into corruption at Snow Hill police station had led him to a homosexual brothel where he had discovered an unexpected — and certainly unacknowledged — part of himself. While interviewing an attentive male whore he had found himself, much to his horror, becoming aroused. Furthermore, a photograph of Matt, naked and unconscious in the arms of another man, had made a deep impression on him. He had tried to erase it from his memory without success. The moment when he had finally faced up to his feelings and written about them had made him both proud and ashamed.

Johnny rarely re-read what he had written in his journal — it invariably stirred up a welter of emotions — but he forced himself to find the incriminating passage:

When Matt showed me the photograph I was immediately struck by how beautiful he looked. It is a strange word to apply to a man but, even in the unflattering glare of the arc-light, his muscular body was an image of perfection. Most people, men especially, look better with their clothes on, but Matt, appearing so strong yet vulnerable, his private parts on show for all the world to see, made my heart leap. Matt would kill me if he ever found out I felt this way — but he never will.

No wonder Watkiss had been so antagonistic towards him. However, would he — could he? — tell his superior officer that he was guilty of invading his closest friend's privacy? Perhaps the knowledge that he would only get himself into trouble had increased his frustration and revulsion.

One of the reasons Johnny had started to write *Friends and Lovers* was to explore these feelings that were deep yet taboo. Where did the boundary between friendship and physical attraction begin to blur? Did they have to be mutually exclusive? He didn't think so: it was impossible to be friends with someone you didn't like the look of. His alibi, should it ever be published, would be that it was only fiction, a sustained exercise in unbridled imagination. If D. H. Lawrence, the son of a Nottinghamshire coal miner, could explore this territory, then so could he.

A novelist had to entertain several points of view at the same time — that was the basis of characterisation — yet lead the reader towards some kind of resolution if not a concrete conclusion. It was the business of novels to analyse and investigate the innermost workings of the mind. The truth could be revealed in different, equally valid, ways.

Writing fiction, like any artistic endeavour which made something out of nothing, was bloody hard work. Non-fiction was much easier: as long as you said true things, stuck to the five Ws — Who? What? Why? Where? When? — you couldn't go far wrong. Sometimes, exhausted by the intolerable wrestle with words, he felt like ditching the novel in favour of starting, for example, a racy account of Jean Harlow's torrid life. He had persevered, though. Had Watkiss tampered with his typescript too?

Johnny, muttering a prayer even though he was a devout atheist, went back downstairs. He wrote at the kitchen table, the endless tapping of the keys often producing answering taps on the floor as the old bat downstairs bashed her ceiling with a broom. However, he hadn't touched the novel for a couple of weeks. The last thing he felt like doing after a long day at work was sitting down in front of a typewriter again. He kept telling himself that he needed to live an eventful life to have something to write about — it had been a good excuse to take Stella dancing or to the movies — and yet the only way he would ever finish the book was by staying at home alone. Well, it seemed he was single once again. He opened the table drawer: it was empty.

The thought of having to go back to page one was unbearable. What was Watkiss going to do with the unfinished novel? Give it to Matt? Hold it to ransom? He was so shattered he couldn't think about the painful repercussions now. His whole life — and body — seemed to be falling apart.

He drank a couple of glasses of water, ignored the food he had bought, and, not even bothering to brush his teeth, undressed and crawled into bed. It was not yet six o'clock but, lying there naked, rejecting the cover of even a single sheet, he drifted into a fitful slumber.

Matt signed the Occurrence Book and slammed its marbled covers shut. It had been a typically fraught day dealing with the lost, deluded and demented — and they were just his own men — so he was looking forward to a quick pint before catching the train home. The garden, for once, could wait.

He was almost to the door of the duty office when the telephone rang. He stared at the blasted thing — was there a simpler instrument of torture? — before sighing and picking up the receiver.

"Sergeant Turner speaking."

"Have you told your journalist chum about the postcard yet?" Commander Inskip had neither the time nor inclination to observe social niceties.

"No, sir. I thought it would be best to do it in person. I'm seeing him tomorrow."

"Very well. Let's just hope whoever sent it keeps to his self-imposed deadline."

"Deadline. That's a good one, sir."

"It wasn't a pleasantry: I'm being serious. Something tells me that the sender isn't mucking about either. I believe Steadman was attacked last night." He paused as if to relish the scene. "Perhaps we should take him into protective custody."

"He wouldn't stand for that, sir." It was true. Johnny would cry foul and start ranting about the freedom of the press. Would removing him from Fleet Street silence him? He could still phone in his copy, but he would be unable to visit crime scenes, interview witnesses or chase up leads. He would soon go mad and start bouncing off the walls of a safe house. Johnny was at his happiest away from the office, in the thick of the action. It stopped him thinking too much.

"Well, it's his lookout. I sometimes wish we were back in the days when a man could be plucked off the street with impunity. Of course, if push comes to shove, we can always get him on a technicality. Any reluctance to accompany a police officer can be interpreted as resisting arrest."

"I appreciate you have his best interests at heart, sir." Matt knew nothing of the sort. The token investigation into the corruption at Snow Hill had cleared the commander, but Johnny, for one, was still convinced that Inskip had been involved. However, the words of a dead man hardly constituted proof. The top brass who hid behind massive desks at Old Jewry, the headquarters of the City of London Police, instinctively stuck together. They enjoyed having scrambled egg on their shoulders — but not egg on their faces. The HQ lay just a few yards from where the Great Synagogue had been burned down in the thirteenth century. A fitting location for a notoriously anti-Semitic force.

"Poppycock! If anything else happens to the blighter we'll be the ones in the firing line. That's what concerns me. I can see the headlines now: POLICE INACTION KILLS REPORTER. We've got to protect our own skins as well — and I'm not talking about sunburn."

"Yes, sir."

"You must impress upon him the need to take precautions — for all our sakes."

"Yes, sir. I'll do my best." What else could he say? Johnny would have most likely pooh-poohed the idea of extra security — until today. Perhaps the beating had knocked some sense into him.

The faceless figure stood at the foot of the bed. Johnny could not move. He lay there naked, holding his breath, straining his ears for the slightest sound, any sign that the stranger was about to pounce. The sweat poured out of him. Why didn't it say anything? What did it want?

144

Johnny yelled but no sound emerged from his parched throat. He tried to roll off the bed but his limbs were lead. Was he dead already?

Finally Johnny wrenched himself back into the land of the living. He stared into the darkness, dreading what the future might hold. One thing was for sure: it wouldn't be pleasant.

CHAPTER
FIFTEEN

Wednesday, 7th July, 7.40a.m.
The cries of a rag-and-bone man, trying to steal a march on his competitors, woke him. Horse-drawn vehicles had been banned from the West End since January but, away from the centre, they continued to impede traffic and leave rich deposits that were quickly shovelled up by gardeners and allotment-holders. Johnny lay there listening to the sparrows chattering in the eaves.

The nightmare was always the same. He had hoped he'd finally managed to lay it to rest — the intruder had stayed away since January — but he'd obviously been fooling himself. The dream's paralysing dread still lingered, heightening his ferocious hangover. He had a head like Birkenhead.

He got up stiffly and padded barefoot into the bathroom. The wiry, white-skinned figure looking back at him from the mirror could have been a stranger. The swelling round his left eye had subsided, but was turning a magnificent shade of purple that matched his bruised ribs. He still couldn't breathe through his nose. He removed the sweat-soaked bandage from round his head. It might appear as though he had been trampled

146

by a herd of stampeding wildebeest but, physically at least, he was on the mend.

Twenty minutes later, having shaved and bathed as best he could, he unlocked the front door. The milkman was not the only person who had called: a parcel, wrapped in brown paper and tied up with string, sat on the doormat. Johnny stood the milk-bottle in a jug of cold water in the kitchen then, determined not to be late, set off for work with the parcel under his arm.

Three number 38s came along at the same time so he managed to get his favourite seat, the rearmost one on the upper deck. He had never liked the sensation of someone looking over his shoulder. An envelope, addressed by hand to J. Steadman Esq., had been slipped under the string. The flamboyant script and black ink were familiar. He ought to wait until he was in the office where he could take more care not to smudge any fingerprints but he was burning with curiosity. Besides, something told him that he was not dealing with an idiot — and if he were there would be plenty more prints inside the parcel.

The postcard showed the Martyrdom of Saint Agatha by Sebastiano del Piombo in the Pitti Palace in Florence. A big-boned woman, clad only in a white sheet wrapped round her waist, was being tortured by two men, each of whom was twisting one of her nipples with a pair of giant pliers. Three other men, including two soldiers, looked on with varying degrees of interest. The dark-haired saint did not appear to be in pain. A large knife, its sharp edge gleaming brightly, lay in the bottom right-hand corner of the painting.

Johnny turned over the card. As expected, beauty reared its ugly head.

Everything has beauty, but not everyone sees it.

It was just a paraphrase of the proverb, "beauty is in the eye of the beholder". However, the lunatic must have been beholding him. He knew where he lived. Johnny, in spite of the warmth, shivered. He was being silly: the maniac had only shown a physical interest in women — thus far. Why then did he feel threatened by these unwanted "gifts"? Perhaps they would stop now that he had given him the publicity he apparently craved. The thought of being spied on was almost as unpleasant as the prospect of being forced from his home. Surely it wouldn't come to that?

He looked round at his fellow passengers. Some were staring out of the window, watching the never-ending movie that constituted life in London, others had their noses stuck in newspapers, including the *Daily News*. Johnny's lurid little story would add spice to another hot and dreary day. If they only had a clue what was sitting on his knee . . .

The thought of what it might be turned his already churning stomach. He took a deep breath. One thing was for certain: he was not going to find out until he was alone.

The lift-boy raised an eyebrow when Johnny failed to get out on the first floor.

"What? I'm going to the library."

"Got something for Amy?"

The librarian's new assistant had attracted a lot of male attention since she had started in June. Her swept-up blonde curls and infectious giggle — totally unsuitable in her job — had prompted more than one reporter to set foot in the library for the first time.

"I'll have something for you if you don't button it."

He pushed open the frosted-glass doors and walked softly down the middle of the room. The highly polished parquet floor was dangerously slippy. The ancient librarian peered at him over the top of his new bifocals and nodded a silent greeting. There was no sign of the toothsome Amy.

He retrieved the *Catholic Martyrology* from the shelf and sat down at the table in the distant cubicle. However, instead of opening the book, he slid the string off the parcel and, using a clean handkerchief, removed the paper to reveal a sturdy blue box. Holding his breath, he lifted the lid, parted the tissue paper and saw what he had feared all along: a single female breast.

It rested on a bed of stained cotton wool, the once pert nipple sunk into the nut-brown areola. The bloodless, soggy mass of flesh resembled a large, unappetising dollop of junket. There was a faint whiff of disinfectant.

It was too much for his crapulous constitution. He started to sweat profusely. His vision blurred. Was he going to faint?

He stuck his head between his knees and breathed deeply. Please God, no. He grabbed the waste-paper basket and heaved. Fortunately, as usual, he had skipped breakfast. He retched again. Bile trickled into his mouth. He spat it out.

The librarian, alerted by the strange noises coming from Johnny's carrel, and observing there was nobody else in the room, decided to break with protocol.

"Everything all right, Mr Steadman?"

"Yes, thank you." He'd hardly got the words out before his stomach convulsed again. "Hayfever. I'm trying not sneeze."

The nausea passed. Johnny, admonishing himself for entreating a non-existent deity in his moment of weakness, replaced the now slightly soiled wagger-pagger-bagger and sat up. Averting his eyes, he put the lid back on the box. It must have been delivered before his story had been published. If they hadn't held fire for twenty-four hours the owner of the breast might still be alive. Theoretically, of course, she might not yet be dead: women did survive mastectomies — sometimes. However, he doubted this one had been carried out under sterile conditions in a hospital.

He turned to the holy encyclopaedia. St Agatha was the patron saint of bellfounders, bakers, jewellers and nurses.

Her feast day was 5th February — no significance there, then. A wealthy noblewoman, she spurned the advances of Quintianus, a low-born Roman prefect, who persecuted her for being a Christian. She was given to the brothel-keeper Aphrodisia and her nine daughters who, despite their best endeavours, could not persuade her to make sacrifices to pagan idols. Her

150

breasts were sliced off before she was finally executed by being rolled naked upon a bed of live coals.

Johnny closed the book in disgust. Why were Catholics so obsessed with torture? Yes, Christ suffered on the cross, but he did so in order that his followers would not. It was downright sick to harp on and on about humiliation, agony and death. Life was not meant to be one long guilt-laden journey.

Tanfield looked up from a pile of news agency reports that had come in overnight. It was his job to sort the bulletins and distribute them to the relevant correspondent who would decide whether they were worthy of further investigation.

"What's that?" The boy's eyes fixed on the blue box.

"Good morning, Mr Steadman. How are you feeling today?"

"Sorry, Johnny. Good morning. You look better without the headdress. Almost human — if you ignore the shiner."

"Thanks awfully. I've received another present from the amateur doctor."

"What part this time?"

"Something you haven't seen since you were suckled by your mother."

"Ha, ha, ha, thud. That's the sound of me laughing my head off. Can I see?"

"No, you can't. A cup of tea might change my mind." Tanfield was on his feet immediately, shooting off to the canteen. "Two sugars!"

"Making a clean breast of it, is he?" Dimeo gave an exaggerated wink. His crisp white shirt emphasised his innate Mediterranean tan. "Come on, don't be a spoilsport. Give us a peep."

"Don't miss much, do you?" He must have the ears of a bat.

Johnny, using his handkerchief once again, reluctantly removed the lid.

"Ugh! It's enough to put you off your greens."

"I very much doubt it. You don't recognise it then?"

"Not in that flabby state. My presence usually makes them perk up."

"And is your presence here absolutely essential?" Patsel, having materialised silently, nodded and bared his false teeth in an attempt at a smile. Johnny almost expected him to click his heels together. Dimeo returned to the sports desk.

"Was there a postcard also?"

Johnny showed him the painting of St Agatha. "Don't touch it. There might be fingerprints." The horrid image seemed to please the German. Johnny turned it over.

"*Everything has beauty, but not everyone sees it.*"

"Confucious," said PDQ. "Is there a prize?"

"Mr Steadman has already got his hands on it. Such a story is indeed pure gold," said Patsel. "I don't know what he did to earn it — nothing, in my estimation — but it will be interesting to learn what today's report produces in its wake. This pervert is like a cat presenting its owner with tributes of dead birds. A thousand words this time. Make sure you repeat all the

152

gory details of the story so far and find out what the police are doing to catch the killer."

"We don't know that he has killed anyone yet."

"You joke, Steadman. How else is he getting these body parts? Where is he cutting up these women?"

"It might be just one woman."

"In this heat? The same body would be putrid." Patsel stooped over the box and sniffed. PDQ rolled his eyes. "This is the smell of eupad or eusol, not formaldehyde. It has not been preserved."

"Edinburgh University Pathology Department," said Tanfield, placing a cuppa on Johnny's desk. "Edinburgh University Solution."

"Quite so, Mr Tanfield," said Patsel in admiration. "It makes a welcome change to have such an educated junior on the staff."

"How the hell did you know that?" Johnny did not miss the dig at his lack of a degree.

"Lexiko. Useful words if you need to get rid of unwanted vowels."

Johnny's smile broadened when he saw Patsel's face fall.

"I believe you have calls to make, Mr Steadman. If, for some obscure reason, you don't wish to exploit this story to the utmost I'm sure Mr Blenkinsopp would be only too delighted to relieve you of the burden." Johnny looked over to where Bert was reading the *Chronicle*. Having clearly heard every word, he waved back cheerily. "Don't let the cops have the titty until it's been photographed," said Patsel. "Peter, a word." They moved off to the centre of the newsroom from where Patsel could observe all his subordinates with ease.

Tanfield was still lurking. Johnny flipped him a penny for the tea then lifted the lid of the box. Its contents made the boy blanch.

"Happy now?"

For once the clever cub was dumbfounded. Johnny took a swig of tea then picked up the telephone receiver. It was Matt's day off so he asked to be put through to DC Penterell.

"I've got something for you."

"What?"

"A female breast."

"Just the one?"

"Yes. It was left on my doorstep this morning."

"I knew it was a waste of time having the GPO monitor your post."

"Don't you need a warrant for that?"

The detective ignored the question. "Was there a postcard with it?"

"Yes. It shows another saint and has another quotation about beauty. And before you ask, I've been careful not to leave any dabs."

"Thanks ever so much." There was that bone-dry tone again. "I'll send someone round to collect it."

"Hang on. Have you got anything for me in return?"

"Such as?"

"Well, I wasn't thinking of a bunch of flowers. Has a body turned up? Has anyone reported a missing woman?"

154

"That's for me to know and you to find out." He hung up.

Johnny shrugged. If that was the way Penterell wanted to play it, that was fine by him. Stonewalling always suggested ignorance, idleness or incompetence. The more public indignation he could create the better.

The morning flew past. By the time he had finished the piece, the breast and postcard had been snapped by a chain-smoking staff photographer and collected by a Scottish detective in plain clothes who asked him a few obvious questions and suggested he might like to stay with friends for a few days: "Better sure than sorry." Johnny said he would consider it. The promptness of the response implied the police were giving the case priority. Penterell would regret not being more forthcoming.

A sweaty messenger dumped a large parcel on his desk. "You the bloke what's been getting women's bits?"

"In a manner of speaking."

"Well, Reg says not to worry: it's just clothes." He didn't wait for a reply. The messengers prided themselves on their apparently preternatural ability to see through brown paper. Although Reg had quite understandably failed to guess the additional contents of Monday's bouquet, he was right this time. There was a note pinned to the front of his freshly laundered pants: *Call me!*

Johnny grinned. Millie was a sweet girl who would soon be snapped up. However, he was not the man for her: the thought of sex with anyone other than Stella

155

saddened him. On impulse he grabbed the phone and, before he could change his mind, asked for C. Hoare & Co.

"Mr Dismorr's office." Stella sounded subdued, her feigned breeziness the attitude of a professional secretary rather than the natural expression of a happy, beautiful young woman in the best of health.

"How about lunch? Anywhere you like. My treat." The prospect made him realise just how hungry he was.

"I can't, Johnny. I've got to make up for my absence on Monday."

"You were allowed out yesterday."

"That's why the cow made such a fuss." She was no doubt referring to Margaret Budibent.

"I understand. How are you?"

"All right. What about you? How are your bruises?"

"Like a rainbow." He wanted to say so many things: that he missed her, loved her more than any other girl in the world, that he wanted to marry her but, in his heart of hearts, he knew it was too late.

"Was there something else?"

"I've been invited to some kind of secret party on Friday. I've been told it will be a night like no other. Will you come with me?"

"I can't." She sighed. She could postpone the moment no longer. "I'm sorry, Johnny. I'm seeing another man."

CHAPTER
SIXTEEN

Wednesday, 7th July, 2.25p.m.

If he was crossing the Thames on foot he usually stopped to admire the view. The panorama from the middle of any bridge, in reminding him that he lived in the greatest city in the world, never failed to inspire him. Today, though, for the first time in his life, he felt like jumping.

The high tide was on the turn. Wherries, lighters and pleasure-cruisers, all sailing at different speeds, clogged the capital's main artery. A police launch, hooter sounding, weaved among the waterborne traffic. Pedestrians, enjoying the stiffer breeze on London Bridge, lingered to follow its progress. Perhaps someone else had already taken the plunge.

He could see the end of Dark House Lane on the left between Billingsgate Market and the Custom House. If he were still alive on Friday he could drown his sorrows at the party there. He turned his back on the Tower of London and looked upstream towards Southwark Bridge. He could smell the malt from the brewery by Cannon Street station.

The sinking feeling of the past few days had vanished as soon as Stella had delivered her thunderbolt. He had known something was amiss but had never suspected that she was being unfaithful. He had reached rock bottom now. There was a metallic taste in his mouth. Every action required an immense amount of effort. Was there any point in going on?

He would be thirty-one next month. Most men were married at that age. What was wrong with him? Why had she ditched him? How could he have been so blind?

He was full of incoherent rage and yet, strangely enough, he didn't feel angry with her. He loved her as much as ever. Perhaps he was still in shock. He had to snap out of it, shake off this malaise. There was no point in feeling sorry for himself, torturing himself with what might have been. He was a survivor. His speciality was kicking against the pricks. He was determined to find out the identity of the other man. But what would he do then? He stared at his feet and, in spite of his misery, gave a rueful smile. He would cross that bridge when he came to it.

Johnny disliked loose ends. The anticipated announcement had appeared in *The Times* that morning. He would attend Frederick Callingham's funeral on Friday — a far more positive step than thinking about his own. Then there was the question of who was sending him female body parts and why. And who had stolen his novel? No, there was too much to do: topping himself would have to wait.

He had told PDQ that he was going to meet a police informant in Kent and would not be back until the next day. It was true: Matt was a copper and he told him things. The deputy news editor, intuiting that Johnny had received bad news, decided not to quibble. His favourite reporter was having a hard week.

As the 2.50p.m. rattled over the points outside London Bridge station, the slums of Bermondsey beneath him, smoke from chimneys — each blazoned with a vertical advertisement: IDRIS, PYRENE, GUINNESS — commingling with the steam, Johnny realised that, although he was playing truant, he did not feel the slightest bit guilty. After all, he had ended up working on Saturday, even though it had supposedly been his day off. He had seen the deaths of two men that afternoon and had just been contemplating his own.

It was unlikely that Matt would want to discuss Frederick Callingham on this, his day off. Matt despised suicides. It wasn't that he lacked compassion. He saved his pity for those who deserved it, not those who, in his words, took the easy way out. Johnny attributed such toughness to the fact that the sergeant often had to pick up the pieces — literally.

Izane Road was a good twenty-minute walk from the station. Johnny had to stop and ask for directions twice and soon realised he might as well have taken the train to Bexleyheath as Bexley. It had been difficult to tell on the map. He could now appreciate why Lizzie had settled on this particular new development. It was not that far from the old town centre. However, its clean air and green fields made it feel a million miles from London.

The rutted road surface, still unmetalled, had been baked hard by the sun. He couldn't remember the last time a cloud had blemished the azure sky. A pair of workmen, feet dangling from scaffolding, were smoking instead of plastering. They watched in silence as Johnny plodded past. He hadn't felt like eating after talking to Stella and was therefore wilting almost as much as the cornflowers he had bought for Lizzie.

Matt had already planted the front garden of the gabled semi. Young rose bushes filled a border that had been dug along the wall which separated the plot from the newly laid pavement. A couple of pink hydrangeas dominated another border below the bay window. Between the borders, the large square pegged out with string was destined to be a lawn. Alyssum and lobelia lined the path, their alternating white and blue flowers like bunting left over from George VI's coronation.

Johnny, aware of the twin trickles running down his sides, paused in the shade of the red-tiled porch. The lack of noise was unnerving. He turned to assess the view. The identical mock-Tudor house across the road was still unoccupied. Would he choose to live here, even if he could afford to do so? Hardly. He would go bananas. Perhaps it was just as well he seemed destined never to be a family man.

He rapped on the door. After a minute he did so again and peered through the stained glass. He detected no sign of movement. No one came.

Johnny walked down the side of the house towards the garage, which was also gable-ended. The kitchen door, which smelled of fresh paint, was wide open, but the room was empty. He continued round the corner of the house.

Matt was at the bottom of the garden with his shirtless back to him. Johnny opened his mouth then closed it again. His friend was oblivious to everything except the spade, the soil and the sun. Sweat poured off him.

"A policeman's lot is not a happy one."

Johnny started guiltily.

"My God! You're enormous!" He put his arms around Lizzie and kissed her.

"Leave my wife alone and get your arse over here." Matt, his blond hair stuck to his forehead, rested his foot on the spade. His flat stomach rippled as he caught his breath.

"I'm an invalid. Got to rest my cracked ribs. Doctor's orders."

"What the hell are you doing here then?"

"To see you, of course. What else?"

"Charming. And it's good to see you too," said Lizzie irritably. "I wouldn't have got up if I'd known."

"You know I'm only kidding." He gave her the flowers.

"Thank you. Come in. You look like you need a drink."

Johnny, as though seeking his permission, glanced in Matt's direction. His friend waved a hand dismissively and resumed his digging.

Lizzie filled the kettle and set it on the stove. She placed both of her hands in the small of her back, pushed her shoulders back and, with a groan, stretched her spine.

"I can't wait for the little stranger to arrive."

"Two weeks will soon pass." Johnny hung his jacket on the back of the chair.

"That's easy enough for you to say. There's nothing like being in the family way to teach you about male chauvinism. Men either treat you like an invalid or assume giving birth requires no more effort than it does for a hen to lay an egg."

"False analogy," said Johnny. "You did the laying months ago. The egg's about to hatch."

"What would you know about it?" The unexpected sharpness of her tone made Johnny flush. Her jibe was more accurate than she realised.

It wasn't so long ago that he'd have sworn on his life that he was in love with Lizzie. Now, looking back at his infatuation, he could see that he had actually been in love with what lay between her and Matt. He'd been besotted by the whole idea of romantic love — and then he'd found it with Stella. Or at least thought he had. Perhaps it was merely the last of his illusions to be shattered. God did not exist. Good was not stronger than evil. All men were not equal. The truth was not more powerful than lies. Love did not conquer all . . .

"I'm sorry," said Lizzie. "Don't pay any attention to me. I've been surprised how much I dislike being pregnant. It peeves me to have my frailties underlined."

"You're one of the strongest people I know," said Johnny.

"That kettle boiled yet?" Matt burst into the kitchen. Heat seemed to radiate off him. He went over to the

162

sink, filled a mug with water, emptied it in one go, and got a refill. Johnny watched his bobbing Adam's apple.

"Get out of here," said Lizzie. "You stink."

"I thought you liked it when I was hot and sweaty."

"And look what happened! Go on, I'll bring it out to you."

She went to the window and watched her husband return to what would become his vegetable patch with a mixture of amusement and annoyance.

"So, don't sit there like a sphinx — tell me all the gory details."

"About what? My assault, or my so-called secret admirer?"

"I've read about those already — and I can see the evidence for myself. I do keep tabs on you, you know. After all, I don't have much else to do these days and Matt, with a bit of gentle prodding, keeps me informed." She sat down with a sigh. "You're an open book, Johnny. Always have been to me. You wear your heart on your sleeve — which is why it gets broken. What's happened now? Did Stella say no?"

"I didn't even get the chance to ask her. When I invited her out to lunch today she told me she was seeing another man."

"And you believe her?"

"Why on earth would she lie about something like that? She knows how much I love her."

"Precisely. It is possible to love someone too much."

"Balderdash. I refuse to accept that for a second. You either love someone totally or not at all. Besides, Stella spent the weekend in Brighton with a man."

"Oh." The news came as no surprise to her, but what could she say? On the two occasions that she had met Stella — at the pictures and at a boxing match — she had struck her as a woman with an eye for the main chance who would only stick with Johnny for as long as it suited her. However, she had kept her counsel and hoped, for his sake, to be proved wrong. Unfortunately it seemed that Johnny had picked the wrong woman — yet again.

"Still think she was telling fairy stories? Don't move. I'll make the tea." He got up and poured boiling water into the teapot.

"You didn't warm it first."

"We're in the middle of a bleeding heatwave."

"And don't I know it. Some nights I've hardly been able to sleep — especially with that lump next to me." She nodded in Matt's direction. "Did Stella tell you about Brighton?"

"No, her mother did. But when I asked Stella about it she didn't contradict me — or Dolly. Her parents were going out of their minds over the weekend. It was completely out of character for Stella to go off like that. She told them she was staying with a female friend on Friday night but later telephoned to say she had decided to extend her stay."

"It doesn't exactly sound like a dirty weekend, does it?" Lizzie rested her hands on her bump. "Where's the man come into it?"

"He called her parents and her office on Monday morning."

"I presume you don't know who he was?"

"I wish I did. I'd soon get some answers out of him." He caught her pensive expression. "So you accept that someone else is involved now?"

"Yes — but my feminine instinct tells me that it's not how it looks. Or rather, not how Stella wants it to look."

"You mean she wants shot of me so badly that she's set up a fall guy? This isn't the movies."

"Don't take this the wrong way . . ."

"Why does anyone ever say that? As soon as the words are said, offence is guaranteed."

"Shut your cakehole and listen." She heaved herself on to her feet and lined up two cups and saucers along with the mug that Matt had already used. She fetched a bottle of milk from the new Frigidaire. Johnny was strangely comforted by the fact that she still remembered how he took his tea. She had given herself enough time to rephrase what she had to say.

"When I said that you can love someone too much, I meant that sometimes the loved one comes to resent their lover's feelings. They can be a burden" — she took a deep breath — "especially if they are not returned to the same degree."

"All relationships are unequal. There's always a kisser and the kissed."

"Bingo!" She clapped her hands. "That's all I meant."

"The first time we ever went out she talked about 'holy padlock'. I honestly thought that she wanted me to propose. Over the past six months we've become closer and closer."

"That's not a long courtship, Johnny. Matt and I went out for three years."

"I know. I was there."

"How could I forget?" She smiled and took his left hand in both of hers.

"I've always been the kisser not the kissed. I guess that's the role of a man."

"Not necessarily. I'm the kisser in this marriage."

"I don't think Matt would agree."

"Maybe not — but remember: I chose him. And he did give me the choice."

"You mean whether or not to accept his proposal?"

"That came later. He told me that if I wanted you instead of him he wouldn't stand in your way."

"He's never told me!"

"Well, think about it. He wouldn't, would he? He's always had your best interests at heart. The way you stood by him after he told you we were getting engaged just proved to us both that you're a good man. Even if Stella has decided that you're not the right man for her, believe me, someone else will soon see what a catch you are."

"I'll be thirty-one next month." Where had his life gone?

"The best is yet to come. Why don't you take Matt his tea? I'll find a vase for the cornflowers before they give up the ghost completely."

He took a cab to Copenhagen Street. The driver's shock at his potential fare's appearance — and initial impulse to put his foot down and leave him standing on the street — had evaporated at the sight of the ten-shilling note. It never ceased to amaze him what so

166

little money could achieve. On the other hand, the thought of what his life would have been like had his parents not been well-heeled terrified him. He was the most fortunate unfortunate alive.

He sat back on the cool leather seat and hid behind his newspaper. Steadman had finally started to take him seriously. The slightly mocking tone of the article, as if challenging him to reveal himself, was irritating though. All in good time. The game was going to be played by his rules or not at all. And he would most certainly win.

He had chosen the Copenhagen because it catered for those who did not wish to be dazzled by the bright lights of Upper Street and the Holloway Road. The former shop was a local cinema for local people. Prices were lower, and the audiences poorer, which would make his offer seem all the more generous. He checked the hypodermic in his pocket: better sure than sorry.

The main feature was a local product too. Its title — *Dr Syn* — had tickled his fancy. However, as George Arliss pretended — unconvincingly — to be a presumed-dead pirate pretending to be the vicar of Dymchurch, his interest in the tale of eighteenth-century smugglers on the coast of Kent gradually dwindled until it couldn't even be aroused by the haughty looks of Margaret Lockwood. His concentration wasn't helped by the fact that each time someone went outside to the lavatory daylight flooded the screen.

He switched his attention to the late afternoon audience. The advantage of sitting in the back row on the left meant that he could survey the whole house and if any lovers, coming up for air, cast their eyes in his direction they only saw his good side. There! She looked a suitable patient. He waited for another burst of sunlight. Yes, she would more than do.

The thought of speeding her through the darkness, away from the long arm of the law, to treat her however he wanted made the blood surge through his veins. She would soon become his own buried treasure.

"Thanks. I thought you'd forgotten all about me." Matt set down his spade and reached for the mug of tea.

"Hardly. Sorry about Monday. I thought I was doing the right thing."

"It's not the first time you've gone against me and, more than likely, won't be the last." He mopped his forehead with a crumpled handkerchief. "How're you feeling?"

"As if I've gone a full fifteen rounds with you." Johnny held up his hand. "Don't say it. I know I wouldn't last one round."

"There's different ways to win a fight. Fancy footwork can be just as important as brute strength. Lord knows, you run rings round me sometimes — or rather, you try to."

Johnny wasn't sure about his feet but he did believe his wits were quicker than Matt's — most of the time anyway.

"Thanks for helping me out yesterday."

"If you'd really been on your deathbed I'd have come myself. Watkiss do as he was told?"

168

"Yes, I think so." Would Matt have asked the PC to search for his novel? "Did he say anything when he got back to the station?"

"Nothing of note. He just said you'd been discharged and gave me back your door-key. Why?"

"It doesn't matter." Now was not the time to raise the spectre of Christmas Past. At least, he hoped it wasn't. He gazed round the back garden. "I'd every intention of getting stuck in. I feel like I've let you down."

"Don't worry — as you can see, I'm making good progress. Having four brothers does have its compensations."

A large area had already been dug over and staked out in preparation for a lawn, and more roses had been planted by the open French window that led off the dining room.

"I received another parcel today. A female breast."

"How lovely! Perhaps the other one will turn up tomorrow. You get more for a pair." Matt ran his hand through his damp hair and sighed in disgust. "That's enough to turn anyone green. Don't mention it to Lizzie."

"As if I would!"

"Well, I'm just saying — she's got a lot on her plate. You weren't supposed to get another one: they were monitoring your post."

"I know. Thanks for telling me."

"There was no point. I knew it would be a waste of time. If the first one was hand-delivered then the second one would probably be too. That's why they put a man on Hereflete House."

"It wasn't delivered to the *News*. It was left on my doorstep."

"Woodling must have been furious." Matt grinned at the thought. "I trust you waited for the detective this time."

"Indeed. I'd hardly replaced the receiver when Stenhouse turned up. Why is this case being taken so seriously when a body hasn't even turned up yet?"

Matt looked him in the eye. "You're not the only one who's received a postcard."

"Does the handwriting match?"

"I'm afraid so."

"Why the hell didn't you tell me before?"

"I wanted to tell you in person rather than on the telephone."

"Why?"

"It was a picture of St Rufus. The message on the back said: *John Steadman, scribbler on the* Daily News, *will be dead by midnight on Sunday, 1st August.*"

CHAPTER
SEVENTEEN

The message was — in both senses of the word — a sentence of death. Above them swifts continued their aerial manoeuvres. Johnny listened to their screams as they chased their prey. He felt Matt's eyes upon him. It was ironic: he had set off here contemplating suicide, only to be told that his death had already been announced.

"It'll be all right," said Matt. "You've always been a cat with nine lives."

"Used most of them up though, haven't I?" He stared at his feet in embarrassment. "I'm really glad you told me. Rufus means 'red-haired' in Latin. Whoever it is must have seen me in real life: my by-line photograph is, of course, black-and-white. This is going to make a sensational story." He could see Patsel's eyes lighting up at the prospect of such copy — and being rid of his most troublesome reporter.

Matt forced the spade deeper into the earth. "Come on. I need a breather."

He led the way over the dusty soil to a couple of green-and-white striped deckchairs that, according to the legend branded on their frames, had once been the property of Southend Borough Council. Johnny glanced over to the kitchen window, but there was no sign of Lizzie.

"You going to take your shirt off as well?"

"Not today."

"It's not like you to be shy."

"The last thing I need is sunburn. I'm already black and blue."

"Let's see."

Johnny undid the buttons.

"Ouch! Whoever it was meant business. Looks like they knew what they were doing."

"What d'you mean?"

"They wanted to cause you the maximum amount of pain with the minimum amount of risk."

"So they weren't trying to kill me. Just giving me a taste of what was to come?"

The warm air felt good on his bare skin so he left his shirt off. He moved his deckchair into the lengthening shade.

"Perhaps."

"At least I now know why Penterell was so convinced there was a personal angle to the case. So who was the postcard addressed to?"

"Commander Inskip."

"He must have thought Christmas had come early."

"Perhaps — but he couldn't just sit on his hands and wait for Santa Claus. The first parcel proved the threat was a real one. Now you know why I was so angry that you'd waltzed off with the widow."

"Yes. I'm sorry." He doubted that his absence had made any difference, but wisely refrained from saying so. "I suppose it's just as well Stella's gone off with another man. There are too many widows as it is." Johnny was gratified to see that Matt appeared genuinely shocked.

"She turned you down then?"

"I never got the chance to ask her. She's been off with me ever since she came back from Brighton — if she ever went there."

Matt scratched the side of his head. "I thought she was better than that."

"She was always too good for me."

"Bollocks! You're too good for her. What're you going to do now?"

"I'm going to demand a proper explanation. I've only seen her for about a minute this week."

"How're you going to do that?"

"*Cherchez l'homme* — I'm going to find the bugger, even if it means shadowing her. I want to know what he looks like. In fact, I've got to find two other men as well: the man who's going to kill me, and George Fewtrell."

"I won't waste my breath advising you to leave it to the professionals, but just remember — us coppers mount man-hunts all the time."

"What about woman-hunts? Have you any idea who the arm belonged to?"

"Not yet. All the pathologist would say was that it probably came from a woman under the age of thirty. The breast — if it came from the same person — may provide further information. I visited the mortuaries at Moor Lane and Bart's myself and drew a blank both times. Every hospital, every morgue and every undertaker's in the capital has been checked. Nothing's gone missing."

"What about missing persons?"

"We're compiling a list of potential victims."

"How many are on it so far?"

"More than forty women."

"That many?"

"That's just in the past six months."

"The arm and breast can't be that old. They hadn't been embalmed."

"No — but if someone is abducting women they may have started before this week."

"There haven't been any reports of mutilated corpses, have there?"

"None that haven't been accounted for. Of course, most people on the list won't be dead. Women go missing for all sorts of reasons. A husband who's too handy with his fists, an over-protective father, an unwanted admirer, an unwanted pregnancy, angry creditors . . . Most of them turn up alive, if not well. It's easier to change your name than change your life. Without money, you can never be free."

"Which is why there will always be those who jump into the Thames."

Matt shook his head. "Being dead is not the same thing as being free." He looked into Johnny's eyes, daring him to disagree. Johnny bit his lip. "Anyway, who's this George Fewtrell?"

"He's one of the God-botherers who lived with Graham Yapp — the bloke who got crushed in St Paul's. I was chasing him when I was set upon."

"Do you really think a man of the cloth would lead you like a sacrificial lamb to slaughter?"

"There has to be a connection. I don't believe in coincidences."

"A coincidence is merely the moment when preparation meets opportunity." Matt was quoting one of Johnny's pet refrains.

"So you do listen to me sometimes!"

Matt's laughter — a joyful, almost girlish, sound that immediately raised one's spirits — came out of nowhere.

"Let's have a beer." After the first swig he cadged a cigarette off Johnny — making sure, like a guilty schoolboy behind the bike shed, that Miss didn't catch him. "I sometimes think it would be easier to give up booze as well as fags, but there's no way I'm going to do that."

Lizzie made Matt have a bath — and Johnny put his shirt on — before they ate. While Matt was upstairs Johnny asked her:

"D'you think it's unreasonable to expect to be loved for the person you are?"

"Unrealistic, perhaps, but not unreasonable. You should be loved for the things you do as much as for what you are. Why d'you ask?"

"Just before Winnie Verloc stabs her husband in *The Secret Agent*, Conrad says that the pornographer had made the mistake of assuming he was loved for simply being himself. I've always found that a devastating indictment. It might explain why I'm still unmarried."

"In one way Stella could be said to have done you a favour. She's broken your rose-tinted spectacles. You have to be clear-eyed about the person you're going to spend the rest of your life with." She plucked a sprig of mint from a bunch that she'd bought and added it to the pan of Jersey potatoes bubbling on the stove. "I can't wait to pick my own herbs from the garden."

"So you have no regrets?"

"Plenty — but not about Matt. I regret having to give up work. I regret losing my independence. I regret having to ask my parents for help."

The doctor and his wife, both insufferable snobs, were of the opinion that their daughter had married beneath her — but, fortunately for her, that didn't stop them supplementing her husband's wages. Matt's hard-won promotion to sergeant had gone some way towards salving his wounded pride.

"So you're glad you moved?"

"Absolutely. Don't think you've avoided the guided tour. I'll show you round later."

"And the baby?"

She turned from buttering the bread to face him. "Is it that obvious?"

"No. You're not the only one who knows their friends. You will regain your figure. I will be able to put my arms round your waist again one day."

"Those days are over — for both of us." She shook her black bob. "It's not that. D'you really think I'm that empty-headed? I've always wanted to give Matt the children he longs for — he'll be an excellent father — but I don't want to be *just* a new mother. I'm

176

determined to be the same old Lizzie — even if I am carrying a babe-in-arms. And the sooner it chooses to arrive, the better."

Matt, his scrubbed skin golden-pink, came into the kitchen. The incongruous scent of Camay, the *white, pure soap for women*, competed with the aromas of frying eggs and gammon. He put his arms round his wife and kissed her on the neck. Johnny, in spite of himself, felt a stab of jealousy.

After the meal, the men returned to the deckchairs to have another beer. The sun was slowly sinking into a sea of orange and mauve. When he asked if Lizzie needed any help in clearing up, she threw a tea-towel at him.

"I must say you're taking the news remarkably calmly," said Matt, smoking one of Johnny's cigarettes.

"What else can I do? I haven't got the energy to run around screaming blue murder."

"There may come a point when you'll be taken into custody for your own safety."

"They can try. I haven't broken any laws. It would look like the police were trying to muzzle the press."

"Inskip is unlikely to offer you any other form of protection — you know, officers posted outside your home and the *News*. He can't spare the manpower. It's not easy tracing missing people."

"I don't want protecting. It would cramp my style too much — as would mooching round a City copshop or being cooped up in some anonymous location in the suburbs. I intend to find the assassin before he finds me — again."

177

"The second parcel — and a second potential victim — will only increase the pressure on Inskip. Sooner or later he'll be forced to go public — to warn everyone and to ask for assistance."

Johnny decided this was not the moment to mention the article that would hit the streets the next day.

"So come on, Johnny — what have you said about it?"

There were times when Johnny swore that Matt could read his mind.

"Ahem." He cleared his throat.

Matt sighed. "Been stirring up a hornets nest as usual?"

"Penterell was less than helpful on the telephone. I suggested that he was stonewalling — probably because there was nothing of interest to report."

"You're no doubt right. It's early days yet. I'll do my best to keep you in the picture."

"I know you will. And I'll do my best to stay alive."

"That's very good of you." He ruffled Johnny's hair. "Okay if I stay over on Saturday?"

"Of course." It would be reassuring to have Matt under his roof. "Won't Lizzie want you here though?"

"The in-laws are coming for the weekend. You know how much Lizzie's mother likes me. The disappointment drips off her. Our Summer Fair is the perfect excuse. Come along, if you want to. The new Artillery Ground, Bunhill Fields from two p.m. It's all in a good cause."

"Yes — good publicity for the boys in blue. God knows they need it."

"The kids will have a ball. There'll be swings and roundabouts, a coconut shy, ice-cream, dogs, horses, a tug-of-war and one of the new gun-cars."

A recent spate of smash-and-grab raids by armed men had prompted the introduction of special vehicles with holes in the windows that allowed officers to shoot while remaining in relative safety behind the doors.

"Will Watkiss be in the pillory?"

"That could be arranged. Want to throw a sponge at him?"

"The book, more like."

"What did he say to you?"

"Nothing much except . . ."

"Except what?" Forewarned was forearmed.

"Well, someone — it might not have been him — has been reading my journal."

"Any particular date."

"No."

"Well, that's something. Watkiss is a good lad but, if he starts dropping hints that he's been prying into our personal lives, I'll drop him."

Johnny didn't doubt it.

A bat, as if dangled on a string, fluttered through the dusk. Here and there lights came on in the new homes: yellow oblongs in the black. Warbling voices emanated from an unseen wireless. There was life here after all.

One of the rosebushes was already in full bloom. Its musky scent percolated the still night air. Johnny sniffed. The smell was familiar.

"A housewarming present from my father," said Matt. "All he does nowadays is tend his roses. Says he doesn't miss the force at all. They're called Beauty."

CHAPTER
EIGHTEEN

Thursday, 8th July, 7.55a.m.
There was no one in the library. Its stultifying silence cried out to be broken. Johnny, whistling "I Get a Kick out of You", went straight to the Religion section and took down the *Catholic Martyrology*. There was nothing like a death threat to give one a zest for life.

He had caught the 6.50 to Cannon Street with Matt. His first night under the same roof as Lizzie had been a strange one. As he lay in the "spare bedroom" — the box room above the front door had already been turned into a nursery — he couldn't help wondering what the murmuring voices through the wall were talking about. Perhaps Matt was telling her about the postcard sent to Commander Inskip, although they rarely discussed Matt's work. Lizzie — for his sake rather than her own — insisted he leave behind the unending catalogue of desperate, depressing acts. She wanted their home to be a refuge, a place — far removed from the smoke and crime of the city — where they could bring up their newborn child in safety.

Ten saints shared the name Rufus. One had died alongside Zosimus, another beside Carpophorus, but only one had received a greeting from St Paul.

181

However, his death was commemorated on 21st November. As soon as he saw the date 1st August he knew he'd found the right saint. This particular Rufus had been executed with several companions in Tomi, a city now in Romania. They had all been publicly vivisected.

For the first time Johnny felt a spasm of real fear. He pulled out a chair, scraping the parquet, and sat down with a grimace. He was not going to be cut open and his organs removed in public. Passers-by would immediately intervene — wouldn't they?

"Quiet please!" The admonition was followed by a giggle. Amy, her round eyes shining with mischief, popped her head into the cubicle. "You're an early bird. Ain't you got a life outside the office?"

"Not really."

"That explains it. You spend more time in here than anyone else."

He wasn't surprised — journalists generally assumed they knew more than they actually did.

"What about you? Does someone have your slippers warming by the fire when you get in?"

"Not in this weather. I live with my parents and two sisters — which is why I'm out most nights."

"I'm sure your dance-card is always full."

"There's the odd gap." She touched her upswept hair. It must have taken ages to do.

"Are you flirting with me?" He had a black eye. She must be toying with him.

"D'you want me to be?"

"How old are you?"

"Old enough." She must have been at least ten years younger than him, but the way she parted her red lips and gazed into his eyes was as old as time itself. Blood flowed into his groin.

The frosted-glass doors swung open and Amy turned tail to greet the librarian. Johnny, feeling that he'd had a lucky escape, took the dingy stairs down to the newsroom. There was too much to do. He could spend August fooling around with floozies — if he survived.

The red light above the panelled doors went out and the green one lit up. Johnny tapped on the polished oak and-entered the inner sanctum of Victor Stone, editor of the *Daily News*. He was on one of his four telephones. Baize blinds shielded him from the blazing sun.

"I don't give two hoots if he is upset. It's our role to upset him. He should know that: it comes with the territory. Yes, yes, of course. It's in the diary: Boodle's, next week." He slammed down the receiver. "Any idea who gave you that magnificent shiner yet?"

"No, sir."

"I hear they're now threatening to do much worse."

"Yes, sir. Herr Patsel's concern is most touching."

The news editor had insisted on informing his superior of the death threat straightaway.

"Cut it out. He's just doing his job. It's taken a long time to lick you into shape and we don't want to lose you now."

Stone, a devotee of callisthenics, spent a lot of his time keeping in shape too. One of his favourite sayings was "beauty hurts".

"I hope you're right."

"Postcards of saints, women's parts, a falling man — you're a magnet for trouble, Steadman."

"Useful, sir, isn't it? I intend to clear up the unholy mess as soon as I can."

"Obviously. Three weeks isn't long. It goes without saying that we'll do everything we can to help. You can always seek sanctuary in Holland Park if you feel your would-be assassin is getting too close. Honoria would be delighted to see you." His wife had taken a shine to Johnny when he'd stayed at the Stones in December.

"Thank you, sir. I'll only trouble you if it's absolutely necessary.

"It wouldn't be any trouble — at least, not for me."

The noise of traffic drifted through the open windows. It was fainter on the seventh floor. Stone studied his protégé: he had followed and — from afar — guided the former office boy and cub up the rungs of the newspaper's ladder. Awkward customers — those who wouldn't take no for an answer — often made the best reporters.

"A barmy butcher, a falling doctor and a flattened priest. Can you handle both stories?"

"You can count on it. My injuries look worse than they are. Cracked ribs are more of an inconvenience than an impediment."

"Sure you wouldn't like Blenkinsopp to assist you?"

"No thanks. He's busy investigating whether the increasing number of shoplifters really do suffer from kleptomania or are just common thieves. I work better by myself."

184

"Well, let me know if you change your mind. And don't leave the office without being photographed. Your black eye will add weight to the death threat. Try not to solve the mystery too soon."

He was only half-joking. The paper's circulation was bound to climb as the day when Johnny's own circulation was in danger of being cut off for good drew ever nearer.

Johnny spent the rest of the morning writing the article which would, he hoped, appear on the front page of the next day's edition. He made much of the fact that the police were keeping him in the dark even though he had not only been attacked but was also being stalked by a potential assassin. Was this because they had no leads on the missing woman (or women), or because he had recently exposed rampant corruption within their ranks?

"Well done," said PDQ. "This should certainly set the cat among the pigeons."

"I'll have shot myself in the foot if it makes them take me into protective custody."

"Fear not — we won't let them. Just don't give them a further excuse. What's your next move?"

"I need to interview George Fewtrell. I was chasing him when I got jumped. He works at St Vedast-alias-Foster."

"Very well. Call the office every two hours — and don't go anywhere without letting someone know. Have you got a weapon?"

"Only my tongue."

"You can't talk your way out of every situation. Here." He opened a drawer in his desk and took out a leather cosh. Keep this in your pocket."

"It's bloody heavy."

"That's the point. It's filled with lead."

"Where d'you get it from?"

"My father was a military policeman. Now you know why they call them coshers."

It was too hot to hurry. Johnny, jacket over his shoulder, strolled up Ludgate Hill. Ahead loomed St Paul's, its black dome thrown into stark relief against the picture-book sky. Three domes created the illusion of a single structure. Could the three stories he was working on — Callingham's death, the postcards and his unprovoked attack — possibly be all part of the same story? The only concrete link between them was himself. It was enough to make anyone paranoid.

Deep in thought, he failed to see Fewtrell coming down the steps of the church, but the curate saw Johnny and fled into the urinal across the road. It was unoccupied. He watched Steadman enter St Vedast then scurried out, crossing the junction of Cheapside and Newgate Street, and disappeared into St Paul's Churchyard.

The church was empty. The three stained-glass windows behind the altar glowed red and green in the sunlight. Wren had certainly been a genius at creating an atmosphere. Whereas the monumental vastness of St Paul's provoked awe — even in a faithless soul like Johnny — a solemn sermon in stones — the intimate and ornate surroundings of St Vedast filled him with a mixture of mystery and tranquillity. He sat down for a minute, appreciating the shadowy coolness. It would be understandable for a man in his position to pray for deliverance, but he was not a hypocrite. He hadn't prayed seriously since his mother's agonising death and he was not going to start again now.

There was a collection box by the entrance. Johnny took out the key given to him by Father Gillespie and tried it in the lock.

"May I help you?"

Johnny swung round guiltily. The key wouldn't turn.

"I was hoping to speak to George Fewtrell."

"I hardly think he'd fit in there." The scrawny old priest had the eyes of a Galapagos tortoise.

"So where is he?"

"May I ask what business you have with my curate?"

"I'm John Steadman from the *Daily News*. I believe he may have some information relating to the death of Graham Yapp."

"Do you indeed? I consider that to be most unlikely."

"They lived together."

"I'm aware of that." The hollow-cheeked man, hands clasped in front of him, stared at Johnny with undisguised animosity.

"So where is he?"

"He's about to go on retreat. Won't be back for a week."

"Where?"

"I don't have to tell you that."

"No, you don't." Johnny, nettled, held up the key. "Father Gillespie gave me this. When we next meet — which will probably be in about ten minutes — I'll be sure to tell him how helpful you haven't been. God bless."

He stormed out of the church, irritated that he was being given the run-around. Why were churchmen so reluctant to give a straight answer? They were no better than snake-oil salesmen, shameless pedlars of useless cures.

Johnny fared no better at St Paul's: Father Gillespie was unavailable. Furious at being thwarted once more, he cut through Dean's Court, passed the Controller's Office of the London Telephone Service, and turned left into Wardrobe Place.

"Blimey! What happened to you?" Haggie stood back to let him in.

"You lied to me." He was in no mood for small talk. "Why didn't you tell me Fewtrell was here when I came back on Tuesday?"

"He asked me not to. What could I do? I'd be in Carey Street if I lost this job." The housekeeper was embarrassed. "Come down to the kitchen. I've a cake in the oven."

"Let me see their rooms first."

"Mr Yapp's has been cleared out. Someone else is moving in next week."

"And Fewtrell's? I presume he hasn't moved out?"

"No — although he is going away tomorrow."

"Where?"

"Search me."

"So where is he now?"

"At work, as far as I know."

"I've just come from St Vedast's. He wasn't there."

"Doesn't mean he's not working: visiting the sick, feeding the poor, attending a meeting. This lot love their meetings."

Hot air was the Church's stock-in-trade, thought Johnny. But he didn't say it.

"I'm not happy about this," said Haggie, opening the door of the third-floor room. "How would you like it if someone invaded your privacy?"

"It happened only yesterday," said Johnny.

"Oh. Having an eventful week, aren't you?"

"You don't know the half of it."

It was stifling in the small room under the eaves. The distempered walls were bare, apart from a crucifix hanging over the head of the single bed. The wardrobe contained clerical vestments and a cheap suit that looked as if it had been bought from a pay-as-you-wear shop. The chest of drawers appeared far more promising, but he had just opened the top drawer, which proved to be full of letters, when Haggie, suffering a sudden qualm of conscience, bundled him out of the room.

"I couldn't look George in the eye ever again if I let you rummage through his things."

"And you don't?"

"Not ever. And I'll thank you not to question my honesty." Huffing with indignation, the old man pushed him towards the stairs.

189

"I was beaten up and left for dead within seconds of leaving here on Tuesday evening," said Johnny, wiping crumbs of walnut cake from round his mouth. "I was, as you know, chasing Fewtrell. Why is he so anxious to avoid me?"

"Only he can tell you that."

"Has he had any visitors recently?"

"None that I know of — but don't forget, I go home at seven. Anything could happen after that."

"Has he been behaving oddly?"

"No more than usual."

"What's that supposed to mean?"

"He's not like the others. Can't put me finger on it. He's always been a bit cagey. Seeing you, though, certainly put the wind up him."

"Glad to hear it. What about Corser and Wauchope?" They sounded like a pair of low comedians. "They been their usual obnoxious selves?"

"They're all right when you get to know them."

"I've no intention of doing that. I got the impression they didn't much care for Fewtrell."

"It's the same old story: they come from a good background. George is a kid from the back streets."

"You mean their families have money." It irritated Johnny how wealth and virtue were deemed by many to be inseparable. In his experience, they were mutually exclusive. "Why enter the Church if they don't need to work for a living?"

"Ain't you never heard of having a vocation?"

"Don't you mean vacation? It's not as if they ever have to break sweat."

190

They were probably too thick to be lawyers, too lazy to be soldiers and too squeamish to be doctors.

"Your problem is that you think the worst of everyone."

"It comes with the territory. The yellow press gives you a jaundiced view of humanity. Call it my vocation."

"Why should I hold my tongue? Steadman is a dear friend of mine." Henry Simkins smiled to himself. He could imagine how vehemently Johnny would have denied it.

"If you still want the photographs, then you're going to have to do as you're told."

"It's been over six months. My patience is not inexhaustible. The police — especially the Snow Hill lot — would be delighted to hear of your return to these shores. I know for a fact that Sergeant Turner would love to get his mighty paws on you."

"I'm relying on you to ensure that never happens."

"Then give me what I want."

"The price has doubled."

"I've already given you fifty pounds!"

"It's not easy being invisible."

"If you hand them over tomorrow night I'll give you the extra money."

"And if I don't?"

"The boys in blue will receive an anonymous tip-off."

"I could just burn them and disappear."

"You could — but you won't. Given the choice, you'd rather have money than revenge."

"True. However, if everything goes according to plan, I'll have both in a couple of days."

She had long since given up crying. Naked, bruised, every orifice sore, she longed for release. However, there was only one way she was going to get that. He had made it quite plain that she would never leave this dungeon. How had she got here? The last thing she remembered was drinking champagne in his beautiful house. He had been so handsome until, outside the cinema, he had turned his face. The pound note had stifled her scream. She had actually felt sorry for him! A wounded soldier, desperate for company. She'd always had a weakness for the underdog. Her kindness had proved her undoing.

At first, when he unlocked the chain from the wall, she thought he had relented, was having second thoughts, but he left the iron collar round her neck, slipped a blindfold over her head then dragged her by the chain into the cell next door. She struggled as much as she could when he picked her up, but to no avail. He was phenomenally strong. Straps were tightened round her wrists and ankles and across her shoulders, waist and knees. The medieval collar was taken off only to be replaced by a leather band across her brow that made it impossible for her to raise her head. The blindfold was whisked off. Her pupils shrank. She was stretched out on a sloping dissecting table that faced a full-length mirror. She struggled against her restraints but could not move. The stench in the room made her choke.

The scalpel glinted in the candlelight. Her abductor, as naked as she was, yet evidently enjoying every second, pressed the blade against her firm, young flesh.

"Such perfect skin," he whispered, stroking it, then himself. "Have you any last words?" Tears that she didn't know she had left ran down the sides of her swollen face. "Don't panic — you're not going to die just yet. Close your eyes."

Cold steel touched one of her eyelids, gently turning it inside out and clamping it open. He repeated the process on the other eye. It was now impossible for her to blink.

He bent down so she could hear each syllable. "This may hurt a little. Watch carefully. I'm about to remove your vocal cords."

It had been a frustrating day. He needed a drink. The Cock was almost due north from Wardrobe Place. He made a beeline for it.

"She's not here," said Bennion. "I'm sorry." He sounded as though he meant it. "What can I get you?"

"Pint of bitter, please." Johnny was almost panting from the heat and exertion. There had been no reason to hurry and yet he had got here as fast as he could. The thought of seeing Stella was enough to make him ignore his aches and pains. He had always thought the best of her, but it hadn't made any difference: she had still betrayed him. "May I make a quick call?"

"Of course."

Johnny rang PDQ and told him that he wouldn't be back in the office until early tomorrow morning — if he was still alive.

"You have my home number, don't you?"

"I do indeed." Johnny wished he could have a telephone. Even if he could afford one, it would take months to have one installed.

"Don't hesitate to call."

"Thanks, Pete."

The retired poulterer had finally had enough. He staggered out into West Smithfield. Johnny slipped on to his stool.

"You just missed her," said Bennion, placing the foaming beer in front of him.

"It's been one of those days," said Johnny. "The sound and pictures of the movie of my life have somehow got out of sync. I don't suppose she said where she was going?"

"She's not speaking to me at the moment. I made the mistake of trying to talk some sense into her. Dolly might know."

"It doesn't matter. I can't make her love me. I gave it my best shot. I'd just like to know where I went wrong."

"The female mind is a mysterious thing."

"You can say that again. I honestly thought I understood her. All I wanted to do was make her happy."

"Well, if you want to make me happy you can buy me a drink." Millie, looking both younger and prettier out of uniform, stood there beaming.

"What would you like?"

"Cherry brandy, please. I must say you look much better than the last time I saw you."

194

"I could say the same. Thanks for getting my clothes laundered."

"You can make it up to me later." She winked. "Let's sit by the window."

Johnny was reluctant to be seen enjoying himself in front of Stella's father but, when he bought a second round, the man who would never be his father-in-law said: "I don't blame you, mate. She's a lovely girl."

Three hours later, as they left the pub arm-in-arm, Johnny had finally made up his mind what to do. All evening the charming diastema had made him long to kiss her mouth — and the rest of her body. For once, though, he was going to resist the temptation. His ribs would complain and he knew that, despite being blameless, he would feel guilty in the morning. Besides, it wouldn't be fair on Millie: he would be bedding her out of a lust for revenge rather than genuine romance.

"I'm sorry, but I can't invite you back to my place — I've an early start tomorrow. I've got to go to a funeral."

"I wouldn't have gone with you even if you had. What sort of a girl d'you think I am?" Her big, brown eyes gazed at him with merriment. "You can walk me back to the nursing home though — if you like."

"Of course." He didn't let on that he knew exactly where it was.

As they headed towards Little Britain Stella emerged from Cloth Fair. She froze, then stepped back into the shadows, watching the happy couple until they turned the corner. A wry smile crossed her face. It hadn't taken him long to find a replacement. So much for being broken-hearted.

CHAPTER
NINETEEN

Friday, 9th July, 7.20a.m.
He had just reached his desk when the telephone started trilling. Someone had placed an early edition over his typewriter. His freckled face stared out from the front page: NEWS MAN SENT DEATH THREAT BY KILLER. The sub-heading read: *Clueless City cops remain tight-lipped.*

"Answer the damn thing!" Dimeo, his hair still damp from the shower — he cycled to work whatever the weather — launched a paper plane at him. He had even drawn Iron Crosses on its wings. It looped the loop then nose-dived to the floor.

"Your taxi's here, Mr Steadman."

"I didn't order one."

"One moment, please." Johnny put down the strawberry shake that he had bought from the new milk-bar across the road. Feeling a little rough after the over-indulgence of the night before, he was hoping it would settle his stomach. He hadn't had anything to eat since the slice of Haggie's cake.

"The driver's adamant, sir. Insists on speaking to you face to face."

"I'll be right down." He licked the sweat off his upper lip. It could only mean one thing.

The cabbie was standing in the marble foyer, gazing at the Art Deco star-burst ceiling. Secretaries, messengers and managers, dreading another long, hot, arduous day, eddied round him. He was holding a parcel.

"Mr John Steadman?" Johnny nodded. "The gentleman was most insistent, sir. I was to give this to you and no one else." He handed over the parcel. It was surprisingly heavy.

"What did he look like?"

"He was a queer fish. All wrapped up 'e was — even on a day like this."

"Can't you be more specific?" The unshaven man gave a crooked grin. He had tombstone teeth. Johnny placed half a crown in the outstretched palm.

"He was tall, dressed all in black, and had a silly big hat on. He'd a white scarf round his face and all. Made it hard to hear what 'e was on about."

"What did he say?"

"He told me to deliver the parcel to the *News* and to hand it over to no one 'cept yourself."

"I don't usually start work until eight o'clock."

"He said that, but I thought there were no 'arm in trying. I were to wait for as long as it took."

"What if I hadn't turned up till noon?"

"Not a problem. He give us a fiver."

"Five pounds!"

The man held up the note with pride. "He ain't short of lolly, that's for sure."

"Did he talk posh?"

"'Ard to say. He whispered like. Creepy geezer, 'e was."

"Where d'you pick up the parcel?"

"Clerkenwell Green."

"When?"

"'Bout an hour ago. I stopped off to have some breakfast. Been workin' all night."

Johnny shook the parcel gently. Something rattled inside. The driver wasn't the only one who'd been busy.

"The police may want to speak to you. The man who hired you has threatened to kill me."

"Sorry to 'ear it — but I ain't no grass. Me and coppers don't get on." He scarpered out of the revolving doors.

Johnny sighed. The man was an idiot. He gave the parcel to a doorman, then followed the driver outside. He had plenty of time to jot down the registration number of the cab. There was something to be said for heavy traffic after all.

Dimeo was perched on the corner of his desk when he got back. "Yum. This tastes really good."

Johnny snatched what was left of the shake off him and drank it. He suspected he was about to lose his appetite.

"Hmm. You're right. Bit warm though." He sat down, opened the top drawer and took out a pair of scissors.

"Is that what I think it is?" Dimeo leaned forward eagerly.

"Has anyone ever told you what a ghoul you are?"

"Not to my face. Go on — I'm on tenderhooks."

"I think you'll find it's tenterhooks," said Tanfield, hanging his jacket on the back of his chair.

"Who asked you?" Dimeo turned back to Johnny. "Keep your whippersnapper under control."

"Fourteen letters!" Tanfield called over his shoulder, heading for the canteen.

"One of these days I'll give that lad what for."

Johnny smiled. "He reminds me of you. Doesn't know when to shut up."

He cut the string and, following the same procedure with his handkerchief as last time, undid the brown paper. He opened the familiar cream envelope first.

The postcard showed a painting by Murillo. Saints Justa and Rufina held what looked like the model of a church tower between them. A few pots lay at their feet. It was a gloomy picture. The women's robes were a medley of muted greens, purples and browns. Justa's eyes were downcast; Rufina's raised to the heavens. Johnny turned the card over to read the inevitable quotation:

Though we travel the world over to find the beautiful, we must carry it with us or we find it not.

He didn't recognise it and knew better than to inquire if Louis did.

"Get on with it!"

"My sentiments entirely, Mr Dimeo." Patsel nodded to his underlings. "Good morning, gentlemen."

Dimeo, curiosity overcoming propriety, stayed put.

"Glad to see you made it through the night, Steadman."

"Thank you. Any guesses what it might be this time?" He shook the box again.

"Bones," said Patsel. "Bloody, broken bones."

Johnny parted the tissue paper. Pencil was right. Scraps of flesh and sinew still clung to some of them. They looked as if they had been snapped or stamped on rather than sawn. Brute force had been employed, not technique. The foul smell, which stung his eyes, made his stomach lurch. He replaced the lid. Dimeo, inexplicably disappointed, returned to his desk without a word.

"You must inform the police," said Patsel. "Finally they might have something interesting to say. I hope for your sake they do: the seventh floor want to go big on this story again tomorrow. Let Mr Quarles know of any developments."

Johnny was prevented from going straight to the library by another telephone call.

"Congratulations, my dear boy. You've made the headlines once again."

"What d'you want, Simkins?"

At the other end of the line laughter tinkled.

"Nothing. Nothing at all. Just ringing out of the goodness of my heart." Johnny doubted there was much of that. "I pray this doesn't mean I shan't be seeing you this evening. I promise to look after you."

"Now I'm really worried. What the hell, though. I'll be there."

200

"Good man. You won't regret it. Toodle-pip."

Why was Simkins so anxious that he attend the party? He always had an ulterior motive. Perhaps he wanted him out of the way of something else . . .

His reverie was interrupted by yet another call.

"Mr John Steadman?"

"Speaking."

"Stay on the line, please. I have Commander Inskip for you."

Johnny sat down and took a deep breath. This should be interesting.

"What the blazes d'you think you're doing?" The roar would not have disgraced a drill sergeant at Sandhurst.

"I might ask you the same question."

"If you want to get yourself killed, then you're going the right way about it."

"Perhaps." He flipped open his notebook. "How are you going about catching the blighter? My readers would like to know, as would I. And don't say it's none of our business. My well-being is your business. I suggest you go public and make a plea for information about any women who have gone missing in the past week."

"Don't tell me how to do my job, Steadman."

"I'm surprised you've still got it. Anybody with an ounce of self-respect would have resigned last year. Why the Home Secretary didn't sack you is a mystery. What have you got on him?"

"Now listen here, you little fuck." He lowered his voice to a growl. "Write any further criticism of me and my men and I guarantee you'll regret it."

"You really have no idea about how to get a good press, have you? You should be buttering me up, not giving me an ear-bashing. It's never wise to threaten a reporter. Whatever your opinion of me — and I don't give a toss what you think — we're actually on the same side in this case. It's in both our interests to see this man caught. I don't want my body to be the first one that's found."

Johnny had never met the commander, but he had seen photographs of him awarding medals, making charitable donations, standing over a bank robber's corpse. He was at least six foot four and had abnormally large hands — which must have made it easy for him to be on the take. Fierce eyes stared out of a craggy face. The overall impression was of a man in his late fifties determined to withstand the ravages of age. Johnny had no doubt that, if they ever met in a back alley, he would not be the one who walked away.

"I've had men working on this all week."

"Are they your best men, though? DC Penterell struck me as still being wet behind the ears."

He could hear Inskip breathing heavily as he struggled to keep his temper.

"Casting aspersions on the professionalism of my men will not solve these murders — if that's what they are."

"I think that's a pretty safe assumption. I received another parcel this morning."

"How?"

"He hired a cabbie. And before you ask, I did take a note of the registration number. You might be able to get a fuller description out of him. Unfortunately, it appears the killer was in disguise."

The commander snorted. "You do surprise me. I presume you opened the parcel?"

"Bits of broken bones. More pieces of the human jigsaw."

"I'll send someone round to collect them. You know you could be arrested for tampering with evidence."

"And what would that achieve? It was addressed to me. If I were taken into custody, the killer would simply wait until I was released. Without me he can't continue his sick little game."

"Why you?"

"I honestly don't know. I've been racking my brains, but I can't imagine what I've done to make him choose me."

"In my opinion, the postcards are a kind of suicide note. He must know that, sooner or later, he'll be caught and sent to the gallows. The longer the game goes on, the more likely it becomes. Each parcel is a way of saying 'Come and get me!' No sane person would announce their intention to commit a murder and think they could get away with it."

"Well, he's obviously not sane — but insanity doesn't preclude intelligence. He's got away with three murders so far."

"You don't know that, Steadman. And I'll thank you not to repeat that in print."

"Are the arm and breast from the same body?"

"No. Preliminary tests suggest the contrary. I'll ensure the bones are taken directly to the lab. My guess is that the results won't match the previous victims. Once you've killed a person — as it were, crossed the Rubicon — it's easier to kill again and again. The killer becomes desensitised and, paradoxically, finds it more difficult to quench his blood-lust."

"I'll take your word for it." Was he speaking from personal experience? Johnny suspected the commander was capable of anything. "Have the envelopes provided any leads?"

"We weren't able to get any decent prints off them, if that's what you mean."

"So it's fair to say you're still clueless?" Inskip swore under his breath. "Would you like me to give you one?"

"Withholding evidence is a crime."

"I'm not sure you can call it evidence — but it's more than a coincidence."

"What is?"

"The postcards I received through the mail were marked Mount Pleasant."

"So was ours."

"The killer hailed the cabbie in Clerkenwell Green. I suggest you focus your attention there."

"He's hardly likely to have been standing on his own doorstep — not if he's as intelligent as you say."

"It was six o'clock in the morning. There was no reason why he should go out of his way. It simply wasn't worth the effort. Think about it. He could have gone all the way down to Brixton to put us off the scent and yet exactly the same question would have arisen. Is it a bluff or a double-bluff?"

"We'll check to see if anyone local has gone missing recently."

"Watch your back — he's a dangerous man."

Inskip snorted. "You too, sonny." The line went dead.

For once there was someone else in the library apart from the melancholic librarian and Amy, who looked over her shoulder at him coyly. Blenkinsopp had a medical dictionary open in front of him.

"What seems to be the problem?"

"That's good, Steadman. I'm having trouble with my Pencil. It's not letting me do what I want." Out of sight, a giggle quickly became a cough. "He's got me investigating whether gastritis is genuinely caused by hurried eating — the bus drivers are threatening to strike again."

The drivers, who were usually so proud of their punctuality, had forced hundreds of thousands of commuters to walk to work in May when, protesting about snatched lunches and two-minute tea-breaks, they had refused to take their vehicles out of the garages. Their sore stomachs had resulted in a lot of sore feet.

Blenkinsopp slammed the book shut as hard as he could.

"Quiet, gentlemen, *please*." The librarian, accustomed to the boorish behaviour of reporters, shook his head sadly. In response the frustrated hack adopted a stage whisper.

"Sure you don't need a hand finding your killer?"

He got to his feet and, with exaggerated care, silently replaced his chair under the table.

"No thanks."

"Well, it's your lookout. Don't forget to write your obit." He blew a kiss to Amy and tiptoed out.

Saints Justa and Rufina were sisters born in Seville in AD 268 and 270 respectively. The object they were holding in the picture turned out to be the Giralda, the bell-tower of the city's cathedral. The pious Christians made pottery for a living, but when they refused to sell their wares for use in a pagan festival the revellers smashed them to smithereens. The sisters retaliated by shattering a statue of Venus. The broken bones must represent the shards of pottery.

Events then followed a familiar pattern. Diogenianus, prefect of Seville, had the sisters imprisoned, stretched on the rack and pierced with iron hooks, yet they would not renounce their faith. They were forced to walk barefoot to Sierra Morena and locked up again without food and water. Their belief in Christ never wavered. When Justa died her body was thrown down a well while Rufina was thrown to the lions — who declined to eat her. Diogenianus, understandably losing his patience, finally had her strangled and her body burned.

It was a typically nasty story, but what was its significance? Their feast day furnished him with one possible answer: 19th July. Had the date 1st August been intended to lull him into a false sense of security? Perhaps he had just ten more days to live.

There were those who believed you should live each day as though it were your last — but Johnny wasn't one of them. It was true that he spent more time

206

looking back than imagining what lay ahead — the answer to why he was being sent the postcards surely lay in the past — however the only way he would be able to deal with the cruel countdown was to treat each moment as it came, paying attention to the present while trying to ignore the future.

He replaced the big book of horrors on the shelf.

"I'm going to the canteen," said Amy, following him out of the library. "Care to join me?"

"Sorry, love. I've got a funeral to go to."

"No one close, I hope. Take care — you know what they say: Someone always catches their death at a funeral."

Johnny caught a train to Barnes Bridge from Waterloo and walked up Church Road. It was 12.15 when he reached St Mary's. The service, as he'd intended, had already started. A late arrival minimised the chances of him being turned away. The medieval church, which had been extended and ornamented by successive generations, was packed out. The massive, studded double-doors had been left open, but even so the atmosphere was suffocating. Some members of the black-clad congregation were fanning themselves with the order of service. Frederick Callingham's coffin lay in front of the altar. The cloying scent of longi lilies mingled with the smell of furniture polish. Johnny made his way along the back of the church until he had a clear view of the front pew.

The boy sitting beside the sobbing Cynthia Callingham had to be Daniel. He was dry-eyed and made no attempt to comfort his mother. Every so often he turned round to survey those sitting behind him. On the third occasion he caught the eyes of someone a few rows back and smiled. With his high cheekbones, even white teeth and curly brown hair he was a more handsome version of his father. Johnny knew that look. It was how he looked — or how he used to look — at Stella.

Hat in hand, he walked down the aisle to identify the object of Daniel's attention. He couldn't believe his eyes — or his luck.

Before the man could leg it once again, Johnny, apologising profusely, pushed his way along the pew and forced the disgruntled mourners to make room for him. He sat down and gripped the man's knee.

"Hello at last. You and me need to have a little chat." This time he didn't attempt to run away. George Fewtrell ignored him. His tear-filled eyes never left the large golden cross on the altar.

CHAPTER
TWENTY

The service seemed to last for ever. The vicar, using the sing-song voice that is somehow meant to impart greater significance but is just plain irritating, made a meal of the eulogy. He emphasised Frederick Callingham's devotion to his family as well as his dedication to the medical profession. The brain-numbing boredom was only relieved when one of the altar boys fainted.

Johnny studied the blank faces around him but did not recognise any of them. He shifted his buttocks again. It was like being back at the Old Bailey. The hard wooden benches of the press gallery were as unforgiving as the judges. If funerals were for the benefit of the living and not the dead, why did they prove to be such ordeals?

The mourners, two bars behind the labouring organist, murdered the final hymn: "Immortal, Invisible, God Only Wise". The priest intoned the valedictory blessing then processed out of the church in front of the pall-bearers. The congregation, gratefully stretching their legs, rose to their feet and watched the brass-handled box pass by.

The Callingham family clearly had connections. There did not appear to be any vacancies in the ancient graveyard, yet a plot had been found beneath a spreading yew tree for the remains of the good doctor. The possibility that he had killed himself was being overlooked. Suicides didn't get laid to rest in hallowed ground.

Johnny, his hand on Fewtrell's shoulder, hung back. Daniel started to come over to them but his friend shook his head and nodded towards the unmerry widow. The puzzled boy went to stand beside his mother.

"How did you meet? You're much older than he is."

"I've just turned twenty. We're both in the choir at St Paul's. He's a tenor. I'm a bass."

"So he knew Graham Yapp?"

"Of course. Everyone knew him." He pushed Johnny's hand off and turned to face him. He raised his chin in a bid to appear defiant.

"Did he dance at the same end of the ballroom as you?"

The young man flushed. "I don't know what you mean."

"Really? I saw the way Daniel looked at you."

"Prove it."

"I don't need to. The mere suggestion that you seduced a boy would be enough to destroy your career."

"But Daniel seduced me."

Johnny laughed. "Perhaps he did — but you should have known better. Either way, it's against the law."

The blood that had rushed to the curate's face now slowly drained away.

210

"For the love of God, please don't say anything. Please . . ." He ran his hand through his straw-coloured hair. "I'll be forever in your debt." His pale blue eyes met Johnny's. They were flecked with gold. Was he coming on to him? "I'd do anything . . ."

"I'm sure you would, but I'm not a blackmailer." Johnny was not averse to pulling the odd stroke while pursuing a line of enquiry, but he would never stoop to blackmail. However, he was well aware that his denial still raised the terrifying prospect of being held to ransom, of being at the mercy of someone else. "Why did you run away from me on Tuesday?"

"I didn't know you were there."

"Why the haste then?"

"I was late."

"What for?"

"I was meeting someone — not that it's any of your business."

"Who?"

Daniel, holding his mother's hand at the graveside, kept glancing over to them.

"Why pick Daniel? You're not a bad-looking bloke. I doubt you'd have much trouble finding someone else. Why not settle for someone your own age?"

"He picked me! I told you, you know nothing. Besides, look at him: how could I resist?"

"You're a man of God."

"Don't be such a hypocrite. You're not a church-goer, I can tell. Whatever else the bible may say about men lying with men, God is love. I truly don't

211

believe he'll send me to hell for loving boys. After all, it's not as if I'm a rabid papist."

"Sure you don't mean rapist?"

"Fuck off!" The familiar four-letter word was more shocking when uttered by a man in a dog-collar. "You've got nothing on me. Just leave us alone. Haven't you got anything better to do? There's a madman after you. Wouldn't you rather be sniffing round women's parts?"

"I'm delighted to hear you read the *News*, but don't change the subject. Daniel's father found out about you and his son, didn't he?"

"No."

"Pull the other one. What about his mother? She'd go straight to the police if she found out."

"She's lost her husband. Why on earth would you want to cause her more pain?"

"I'm trying to protect her son."

"Then go back to the gutter. You can't even prove what I've just told you. Daniel and I could deny everything."

"D'you like the idea of another man probing his arse-hole? A medical examination would provide sufficient evidence to have you arrested." The clergyman cursed and clenched his fists. "Come on then," said Johnny with a sneer. "Give it your best shot. I bet you punch like a girl." Fewtrell refused to be provoked.

"So what if he's had sex? Who's to say I'm his only lover? Who's to say his father wasn't playing hiding-the-sausage with him for years? You know nothing, Steadman. Take my advice. Go and dig for dirt elsewhere. Leave the Callinghams alone. Let them grieve in peace."

Johnny had no desire to make a scene, but this was probably his only opportunity to speak to Daniel before he left for France. If he stuck by Fewtrell the boy was bound to approach them sooner or later.

The coffin disappeared into the ground. A pair of workmen, leaning on their shovels nearby, waited impatiently for the crowd to disperse.

"Why were you crying? Did you know Daniel's father?"

"No, I never met him. Funerals just get to me."

"Must be quite a drawback in your job."

"Most folk appreciate my sensitivity."

"If you care about Daniel, you'll stop seeing him."

The secret lover sighed. "I did try once — I do have a conscience, you know — but he threatened to kill himself. Then he said he'd go to the police. Even if I wanted to end the friendship — which I don't, not any more — I'm trapped."

Daniel, dragging his mother away from a cluster of hand-wringing well-wishers, headed towards them. He was tall for his age but had yet to fill out as Fewtrell had. Even so there seemed fewer than the five years between them.

"Hello, George. Thank you so much for coming." Mrs Callingham smiled tightly beneath her veil.

"It was the least I could do. I believe you've already met John Steadman."

"Yes, I have — but I'd rather hoped never to set eyes on him again." She opened her handbag and took out a pack of Sobranies.

"You're the reporter who saw my father die," said Daniel, his eyes meeting Johnny's inquisitive gaze.

"Yes, I am. He loved you very much."

"How would you know?" His anger came from nowhere. "Why are you here? Come to gloat? Hunting for more juicy details to put in your filthy rag?"

"Don't be discourteous, Daniel," said his mother. "Mr Steadman returned this to me."

She opened her handbag again. The boy snatched the note from her and tore it into pieces. Finally unable to hold back his tears, he hid his face in Fewtrell's chest. The cleric put his arms round him as he wept.

"Why are you here, Mr Steadman?"

"I wanted to meet Daniel and it seems it's not been a moment too soon. I think he's just begun to realise that he's the key to his father's death. Speaking of which, do you recognise this, Daniel?" He produced the key given to him by Father Gillespie.

The boy turned to look and began to sob again. "No. I've never seen it before." Fewtrell did not break the embrace.

"Father Gillespie gave it to me. It was with the piece of paper you just destroyed." The boy hid his face once more and made no attempt to stop crying. Johnny felt like a heel.

"I'm sorry, Daniel. I didn't mean to upset you."

"I think you've done enough damage for one day, don't you?" Mrs Callingham knelt down gracefully and gathered up the pieces of paper scattered on the grass.

"I agree," said Fewtrell. "Do the Christian thing and let Dr Callingham and his family rest in peace."

As the train trundled back across South London, wide-open windows just feet away offering glimpses into other people's mundane lives, Johnny's spirits sank. The discovery of the relationship between Fewtrell and Callingham's son was cause for celebration, but it also reminded him he was single once again. The affair was sordid, against the law, yet their love for one another appeared to be genuine. However, that didn't excuse Fewtrell's exploitation of the boy. Daniel was patently in the throes of first love, still swept up in the novelty and power of his adolescent passions. To bring the fling to an abrupt end so soon after his father's death could well send him over the edge.

Callingham must have learned of his son's inappropriate — and illicit — relationship with Fewtrell. For all their medical knowledge, doctors often turned out to be the most bigoted of men. They saw homosexuality as a disease, something that could be cured by cold baths and the rough company of right-thinking men. As a committed Christian, Callingham was no doubt appalled to discover Daniel was an invert. However, in such circumstances, many fathers would kill — or at least threaten to kill — their son rather than themselves.

Was Callingham, like Jean Harlow's husband, overcome with "abject humiliation"? Did he blame himself for some "frightful wrong"?

It was after six by the time he had completed his account of the latest delivery to arrive at the newspaper. The bones had been taken away for forensic

215

examination. Patsel chortled with glee at Johnny's send-up of the telephone call from the commander. PDQ warned him he was playing a dangerous game, but he didn't go so far as to blue-pencil such good copy. Johnny told them that he had drawn a blank at Callingham's funeral. He would not expose George Fewtrell unless it was absolutely necessary.

The party at the Cave of the Golden Calf wouldn't start till 10p.m. so he had a couple of hours to kill. There was no point in going home. Johnny decided he would have a shower and then get something to eat. Since he had not been invited to the funeral feast, he was starving.

The shower-room — only ever used by men — was on the fifth floor next to a couple of bedrooms where anyone who had worked into the small hours or just returned from a foreign trip could grab a few hours of sleep. They were usually kept locked to discourage office liaisons.

One of the two showers was already occupied. Although the opaque window was tilted open, steam billowed round the tiled room. There was a holdall on the slatted wooden bench. Johnny examined the label. There was no name but its owner had written: *If found please return to the Sports Desk*, Daily News, *Fleet Street*. Journalists were often careful about revealing their home address. However, Johnny recognised the handwriting. He had seen it before — on the jotter beside the telephone at The Cock. He took the piece of paper out of his notebook. There was no doubt about it.

Johnny undressed, stepped into the shower, pulled the curtain to and turned on the hissing water. The other man, alerted that he was no longer alone, began to sing "A Great Big Bunch of You" in a pleasant baritone.

Johnny whipped back the curtain that separated them.

"Hello, Louis. You're in a good mood. Got a date?"

"Of course. Friday night is dancing night. Want to scrub my back?" He turned to reveal more of his enviable physique.

"Who's the lucky girl?"

"No one you know."

"Liar. I'll give you one more go."

Louis continued soaping his armpits. "What are you talking about?"

"I'm talking about Stella." Regardless of the soothing hot water, he began to shake with anger.

"Oh." Louis turned to face Johnny, wiping the water out of his eyes. "She's told you then."

"No — but you just have."

"I'm sorry, Johnny. What can I say?" He looked him up and down. "Perhaps she was fed up with spaghetti and fancied some salami."

Johnny hit him in the mouth as hard as he could, cutting his knuckles on the Italian's teeth. Dimeo, caught by surprise, slipped and cracked his head on the porcelain base of the shower. Johnny, near to tears, finished showering and, breathing deeply, tried to calm down. Dimeo did not move. Johnny turned the temperature control above the sleeping beauty to as

217

cold as possible. With a bit of luck he might die from hypothermia.

Fancy-dress parties were the only social occasions where he felt remotely at ease. He had been looking forward to this evening all week: even if no one else did, he was going to have a ball. The gold paint hid most of his scarring and the eye-mask preserved his anonymity. He just hoped that not too much paint would rub off on his clothes. They had assured him there would be somewhere to, as it were, touch himself up. He chuckled at his little joke.

Wednesday's child was no longer full of woe. In fact, she wasn't full of anything. When he'd finished, her carcass had been virtually empty.

One more girl, and his odyssey would be over. The endgame was beginning.

Johnny, with two brandies inside him to settle his nerves, felt another surge of anger as he passed the Monument. If he had known back in January how Stella was going to betray him he would have shoved her down the 311 steps. The fact that she had done so with a colleague — whom he had secretly admired in spite of his cockiness — just made it worse.

The golden dolphin on the weather-vane atop Billingsgate glowed in the sinking sun. The vast cellars of the fish market stretched below Dark House Lane. He could feel the ancient ice through the thin soles of his shoes.

A pair of flambeaux marked the entrance to the party venue. One of two vaguely embarrassed men, draped in togas, checked his invitation. Unlike those around him, Johnny did not have to pay a hefty entrance fee. A painted dwarf led him down a set of stairs lined in a leopard-skin print and on into the vast basement of the derelict mansion. Its ceiling was one enormous golden mirror. A waitress, also covered in gold paint, a golden figleaf preserving what little remained of her modesty, held out a tray of cocktails. Johnny took a glass and wandered over to the middle of the room where a statue of a golden calf with a ridiculously large penis was spotlit. A jazz band struck up an immediate frenzy.

"Johnny, my dear boy. So glad you could make it."

"Hello, Henry. Thank you for the invitation — I think."

"What happened to your hand?"

"I gave someone a knuckle sandwich."

"Aha! Anyone I know?"

"I don't want to talk about it."

"Shame. Enjoying the cocktail?"

"It's not bad. What's in it?"

"Champagne, honey and calf's blood."

He resisted the urge to spit it out. "Are you serious?"

"Absolutely. It was invented by Frida Strindberg, wife of the miserablist playwright, whom we are honouring this evening. The Cave of the Golden Calf was her creation. Ezra Pound called it a convenient concentration of pleasures which the dull call vices'. It opened in 1912 beneath a hat factory in Heddon Street, just off Regent Street."

"Hence hedonism, I suppose."

"Hardly. It was the centre of the artistic universe. Eric Gill, one of her many lovers, designed the calf. It represents everything opposed by that old killjoy Moses. Jacob Epstein and Wyndham Lewis contributed designs." He indicated the Vorticist paintings that decorated the walls. "Katherine Mansfield, Ford Madox Ford, Osbert Sitwell, Margot Asquith — anyone who was anyone visited the club. Fancy a game of bridge?"

"I don't know how to play."

"Oh, I think you might want to learn tonight."

Simkins, neatly sidestepping a naked negro dancing with a man in women's clothing, led the way to an anteroom. Instead of a quartet sitting round a table, a dozen people were taking it in turns to play with a human deck: golden boys in G-strings, each of whom represented a playing card. Johnny had never felt so out of place. It was probably just as well he hadn't brought — couldn't bring — Stella.

"A thing of beauty is not a boy for ever," sighed Simkins. "Have you received another postcard yet?" He kept his eyes on the seven of diamonds.

"Yes. It arrived this morning — with some shattered bones. You can read all about it tomorrow."

"Sure they're not Billingsgate pheasants?"

"I don't know what you mean."

"Red herrings, you numbskull. Billingsgate doesn't sell game. Perhaps it's all a game. No bodies have been found. Perhaps your world exclusive will vanish into thin air like the Cheshire Cat — except that everyone but you will be grinning."

"I hope you're not suggesting that I'm sending them to myself. That's more your style."

"I'll take that as a compliment. Fancy a glass of Dom Pérignon instead?"

"I'd rather have a bottle, please. Who's paying for all this?"

"Never you mind. You might meet him later — if you play your cards right."

Johnny smiled. "Is Strindberg here?"

"No. The poor thing is stuck in Austria. I doubt she'll ever leave the country again. Still, she'll always be remembered for the Cult of the Clitoris."

"I can't see that being her epitaph. What's the occasion tonight, though?"

"There isn't one. Isn't the pursuit of pleasure a worthwhile end in itself?"

"I'm not sure. If I had this much money I'd be setting up soup kitchens, not organising orgies."

"Why do large hearts and small minds so often go together?" Simkins tossed his mane. "You need to let your hair down, Johnny. Come on."

The heat and noise in the basement were increasing by the minute. More people joined the dancing as the band began to play the "Black Bottom Stomp". A guardsman dandled a dwarf on his lap. Three women, in masks and not much else, kissed each other lasciviously.

"*Why this is hell, nor am I out of it,*" murmured Johnny. On second thoughts Marlowe would have been in his element here.

"Aren't you a trifle warm?" Simkins handed him a saucer of champagne. He produced what looked like a miniature silver salt cellar from his pocket, put it to his nose and sniffed. "Want some?"

Johnny knew exactly what it was. He'd never tried it before. Now seemed as good a time as any. *Carpe diem*. Simkins passed him the bibelot.

"I had it made at Tiffany's. Press the button at the side, turn it upside down, then press the button again." Johnny did as he was told then inspected the perforated nozzle. "Don't worry, it's clean," Simkins assured him. Johnny inserted it into his right nostril and sniffed. "Other side! That's it."

Johnny, heat surging through his veins, waited for the world to change.

"Feel free to disrobe," said Simkins.

A masked man in a cape, his well-defined body painted gold, nodded to them as he passed.

"Someone you know?"

"Never seen him before in my life," said Simkins. "Come on — if you strip, I'll strip."

"It's not my kind of thing. Besides, I'm covered in bruises."

"How d'you know unless you try it?"

"I've never been morris dancing, but I know I'd hate it."

"Suit yourself. I'll see you later."

As Simkins swished off into the milling revellers, Johnny went in search of the cloakroom where he deposited his jacket and tie. The ticket was decorated with an image of the golden calf.

By nature an outsider, he worked his way round the edge of the room, trying to work out the identities of the gyrating guests. No doubt they included the odd film starlet and politician. He discovered an opium den in another anteroom. Half-naked smokers lolled on couches, absent-mindedly stroking the bodies of their neighbours. Fragrant smoke drifted above them.

A wave of euphoria swept over him. Full of newfound confidence, Johnny began chatting to anyone who smiled at him. His glass was topped up without him ever needing to ask. A beautiful Chinese woman, her skin like the purest silk, glued her lips to his then wordlessly moved on. However, when one of the playing cards, a slender, snake-hipped youth, tried to do the same, Johnny turned his head away. The boy just laughed and kissed the man standing next to him.

"Having a good time?" A portly gentleman in an expensive suit, a purple silk handkerchief peeping out of his breast pocket, held out his hand. Johnny shook it.

"John Steadman. Have we met before?"

"I don't think I've had the pleasure."

"Ah! There you are, Johnny!" Simkins, now minus his shirt, his torso gleaming with perspiration, chestnut curls plastered to his forehead, put his arm round the shoulders of the short, well-dressed man, who grimaced.

"Let me introduce you to our munificent host — Mr Walter Apthorp."

"Thank you for inviting me," said Johnny. "Why did you, though?"

"It was Henry's idea," said Apthorp.

"I wanted to broaden your horizons," said Simkins. "Now don't deny it: you're enjoying yourself, aren't you?"

"I'm surprised to say that I am — very much so. I've heard about such events, but never expected to attend one. Why go to so much trouble for the entertainment of other people?"

"It's my vocation," said Apthorp. "If others are happy, then I am happy. The real world is so ghastly and grim that we all need to escape from it sometimes."

"Are you sure we haven't met before?" said Johnny.

Simkins sniggered. "Walter lives in Paris. I hardly think you move in the same circles, Johnny."

"Thank you so much for reminding me." Johnny shook his head to clear it. His brain that had been so sharp now felt fuzzy. Someone was doing an impression but he couldn't work out who was being impersonated. To make matters worse, he was the only one not in on the joke.

"Well, now we have met I feel sure our paths will one day cross again." Apthorp took Johnny's hand in both of his. A large ruby glowed on his ring-finger.

"Enjoy the rest of the evening." He said something to Simkins, who followed him towards the opium den.

Johnny's exaltation evaporated as quickly as it had materialised. The naked and semi-naked bodies that had seemed so attractive now repelled him. What was wrong with him? He would much rather be at home in bed with Stella. Alas, there was no chance of that happening again. Somehow he had blown his best chance of happiness. He stood there, a still point amid

224

the reckless abandonment. He could actually feel his spirits sinking. It was time to leave.

He collected his jacket and tie and, before climbing the steps back to the real world, checked that the cosh was still in his pocket.

"A gentleman asked me to give you this, sir." One of the hairy-shouldered doormen handed him an envelope.

"Thank you."

He ripped it open. Inside was a postcard of St Dorothy painted by Francisco de Zurbarán. A dark-haired woman in a flowing pink dress held a basket of fruit and flowers.

"What did he look like?"

The hulk, who was most likely a porter moonlighting from the neighbouring market, just shrugged. "He was wearing a mask, sir."

Johnny turned the card over. The quotation read:

Beauty is nothing but the beginning of terror.

PART THREE

Sans Walk

CHAPTER
TWENTY-ONE

Saturday, 10th July, 4a.m.

The bells of St Dunstan's, echoed by those of St Mary-at-Hill, struck four. Johnny couldn't believe how late it was. Time had telescoped. He slipped the postcard into the inside pocket of his jacket. It reeked of cigarette smoke. The cool night air soothed his throbbing head.

Dawn glimmered in the east. There was no public transport at this time of night. Lower Thames Street was deserted. However, the market would be opening soon. He would have to walk. Fleet Street was much closer than Cruden Street and he was due to work this Saturday anyway.

As he crossed the road and headed for Monument Street he noticed two men emerge from a passage by the coal exchange. They were both at least a foot taller than him. It was the fact that they were not talking to each other that aroused his suspicion. The hairs on the back of his neck began to prickle.

Instead of continuing along Monument Street he darted into Lovat Lane and, as soon as he was out of sight, sprinted uphill till he reached the mouth of an alley. He stepped into the darkness, and breathing deeply, his ribs complaining, peeped round the corner. Without any hesitation the men turned into the lane. Johnny, careful not to make any noise, hurried down the alley which came out in Botolph Lane.

The men entered the alley and, still without a word, broke into a trot.

Johnny ran straight across the road and into George Lane. If he could make it to the Monument there were so many alternative routes he would have a chance of losing his pursuers. He could hear change clinking in their pockets.

He was about to turn into Pudding Lane when the ground seemed to ripple and shimmer in the half-light. A river of rats, homeward bound after a night's scavenging, cascaded down the hill. They, too, were virtually silent — their myriad claws a mere whisper on the cobbles — as the new day threatened to break. They knew by instinct when it was time to return to the docks.

Thousands of jet-black eyes and a million quivering whiskers registered his presence but ignored him. Like the commuters who flowed in and out of the City each working day — the human rat race — they had somewhere to get to and would brook no diversion. The men came running down the lane but when they saw that their prey had stopped they slowed to a gentle stroll.

Johnny knew that he stood no chance against the pair of giants. He had never liked rats, hated their hairless pink tails and the fact that, since they had no bladder, they never stopped pissing. However, he wasn't just going to stand and wait to be beaten to a pulp. He estimated that it was about one hundred yards to Eastcheap and at least two hundred yards back to Monument Street, so it would have to be uphill all the way.

Motivated by fear rather than courage, he shuffled into the verminous flow as gently as he could. The rats simply swept round — and over — his feet. He increased his pace a little and, inevitably, stepped on one of the rodents. It squeaked in anger and bit him on the ankle. Another one, just for the hell of it, followed suit.

Johnny was about to retreat when he saw one of the men reach into his jacket. He didn't wait to see if it was a gun. He leapt as far as he could, rats hanging off his trousers, and prayed he would not slip when he landed. Tiny spines cracked and flea-bitten bodies burst as he hit the stones. He skidded in the blood but, windmilling his arms, somehow managed to stay upright.

And still the rats — as if obeying the call of a latter-day Pied Piper — came rushing towards him. Johnny, spurred on by sheer panic, hurled himself through the tide, praying the rats would not turn on him en masse. They were not altruistic animals — the fact that their fellow travellers were getting squashed attracted little more than a sideways glance although, the closer he got to Eastcheap, the more frequent the squeaks and the teeth that never stopped growing sank deeper into his flesh.

It was only in the last few yards that he dared to kick out indiscriminately. Furry missiles went writhing through the air and then, at last, he was out of the stampede. He used the cosh to knock away a couple of persistent blighters that were attracted by the blood now flowing freely from his legs. His shoes were splattered with all kinds of evil effluvia.

He crossed the empty road and, shaking with adrenalin, looked back. The rats continued to pour round the corner and down towards the Thames.

His pursuers, still standing on the edge of the exodus, applauded ironically. He flicked them the V-sign and started jogging towards the relative safety of the maze of streets that surrounded the Bank of England.

Henry Simkins coiled and uncoiled in the back of his cab as it rattled along the Victoria Embankment. He had, as usual, taken too much cocaine. Oblivious to the gaudy diorama of the dawn, he stared at the large Manila envelope that he had waited so long to get his manicured hands on. The driver eyed him warily in the rear-view mirror.

He had promised himself that he would not open it until he was once more safely ensconced in his plush Mayfair apartment. However, like the divine Oscar, he could resist everything except temptation. He'd have just one teensy-weensy peek.

What he saw made him chortle with glee. He'd been promised a bonus, but the extra shot was better than he could have ever anticipated. Its potential for mischief was infinite. It really was a wonderful world. He gave the watchful driver an exaggerated wink.

Johnny signed out a key to one of the bedrooms and, assuring the night manager that he needed sleep, not a doctor, took the lift to the fifth floor. The showers were empty. Dimeo must have survived to love another day. Johnny let the hot needle jets perform acupuncture on his aching shoulders. His calves were covered in bites. The soap made them sting. He found some iodine in the medicine cabinet and dabbed the purple potion on them. His wounds stung even more. He would have to get a tetanus injection from the staff nurse in the morning. His body had taken a lot of punishment in the past few days and he was pretty sure it wasn't over yet.

He cleaned his shoes as best he could in the gents, gagging as the fragments of blood and offal came away, then left them on the windowsill to dry. It was almost five when he finally got between the sheets.

Seconds later — or so it seemed — PDQ was placing a cup of tea by his bed.

"So tell me all about it."

Johnny yawned and rubbed his eyes. "What time is it?"

"After nine. I thought you could do with an extra hour."

"Thanks. I need another four at least. Hand me my jacket." He didn't want his boss to see him naked. "I went to a weird party by Billingsgate last night. When I left, one of the doormen gave me this."

PDQ studied the postcard. "Well, there's no double meaning there."

"Two men were waiting for me as well, but I managed to lose them."

"So he's not working alone. You might not be so lucky next time — keep the cosh with you wherever you go. On the plus side, it gives you something to write about for tomorrow's edition. Another exciting episode in the intrepid adventures of Johnny Steadman!"

"My head hurts. I've got a champagne hangover."

"You poor thing." PDQ ruffled his haywire hair roughly. "I want you at your desk in twenty minutes."

He made it in fifteen. Dimeo was not in the sports department. It was possible that he was lying in some hospital but Johnny thought it more likely that it was just his day off. Come to think of it, he had mentioned something about competing in a cycling tournament at Cricklewood. Johnny's hand ached just thinking about hitting the athlete. Would he seek revenge? The Italians loved a vendetta. However, Dimeo — he would never call him Louis again — had got his retaliation in first.

When he had finished his bacon sandwich — which he hoped would settle his queasy stomach — Johnny went up to the library. He had the place to himself: it was only staffed Monday to Friday.

Dorothea of Caesarea — whose parents were both martyred — was put on the rack by the Roman governor Sapiricius when she refused to marry. She believed she already had a husband in Jesus Christ. Imprisoned with two women who had renounced their faith, she not only failed to lose her own but also

234

succeeded in showing the pair of apostates the error of their ways — and was put on the rack again for her pains. She was beheaded on 6th February. As she was being led to her execution a lawyer called Theophilus mocked her by asking her to send him some roses or apples from her husband's garden. As she died, Dorothy saw an angel and bid her send a basket of fruit and flowers to the sarcastic lawyer. He was so impressed that he converted to Christianity and, with wearying inevitability, later suffered martyrdom himself.

St Dorothy was a patron saint of brewers, brides, florists, gardeners, newlyweds and midwives. Was his own failure to propose marriage being mocked? And where was the now familiar accompanying gift? Its absence filled him with foreboding.

The quotation offered little consolation. *Bartlett's* informed him that it was from Rainer Maria Rilke's *Duino Elegies*:

> For beauty is nothing but the beginning of terror,
>   which we are still just able to endure,
> and we are so awed because it serenely disdains to
>   annihilate us.
> Every angel is terrifying.

Did the killer see himself as an angel of death? The change in his tactics — and the proof that he was tailing Johnny — provided plenty to write about. The heat accentuated his hangover. He drank countless cups of tea. The pall of cigarette smoke that always hovered at head-height undulated in the faint breeze that drifted in through the open windows. Johnny suddenly longed to be lying on a beach, exposing an unbruised and unbitten body to the healing rays of the sun. It would be no fun by himself though.

His daydream was interrupted by the telephone.

"So you weren't eaten alive by the rats then?" It was Matt.

"How d'you know about that?"

"They were cops, you bloody fool!" He laughed.

Johnny failed to see the funny side. "How was I supposed to know? They looked a right couple of thugs and they didn't say a word. I'd just received another postcard. I was fucking scared."

"What did it say?"

"*Beauty is nothing but the beginning of terror.*" The threat became more explicit each time he reiterated the phrase. Why had the killer chosen to intimidate him with this particular quotation? He wasn't beautiful like Matt. The words "beauty" and "Johnny" didn't belong in the same sentence.

"Nothing else?"

"No — and no obscene offering either."

"You should have a chat with Penterell."

"I've told you everything he needs to know. How long have I been shadowed?"

"The first shift started yesterday afternoon. I don't know what you said to Inskip, but he's been knocking heads together ever since."

"I hate to admit it, but I suppose it makes sense." Johnny was equally loath to admit that he was now grateful for the security blanket — even if it proved to be threadbare. "Tell him to make sure his bloodhounds stay out of my way — they could scare off the killer. The fact I'm being followed by him and the police must remain a secret. I don't want anyone else to die just because Inskip is pretending to be solicitous about my welfare."

"I'll waste no time in passing on your heart-felt gratitude to him." Matt waited for the expected snort of derision. "I'll have a quiet word with Inspector Woodling as well. That's all I can do."

"Thank you. Any developments to report?"

"We traced the cabbie. The truculent tyke wasn't much use, but he helped our artist come up with what he insists is a reasonable likeness. It could be anybody, though. If you hide the lower half of anyone's face their eyes immediately become piercing."

"When will it be released?"

"Inskip hasn't decided yet. My guess is he'll hang fire till Monday. He won't want to cause panic unless he absolutely has to. Investigating all the inevitable false sightings will only increase our workload. In the meantime he's arranged for extra patrols round the Clerkenwell Green area."

"It's not his patch though. It's outside the Square Mile."

"For once, our friends at the Met were only too happy to oblige. A man-hunt makes a pleasant change from policing demonstrations and strikes."

"Inskip probably just telephoned one of his cronies from the lodge."

"He was at your little get-together last night. Enjoy the scenery, did you?"

"Some of it. Horrid hangover though. Inskip must have been wearing a mask. What was a police commander doing in the midst of such decadence?"

"Same as you, most likely."

"I bet he was paid to turn a blind eye."

"I wouldn't say that if you value your skin."

"Thanks for the advice. No one's untouchable though. He'll get his comeuppance one day. I shall do my utmost to ensure it."

"Well, let's ensure you live to tell the tale. How are you bearing up?"

"Apart from Stella betraying me, the cracked ribs, the rat bites and the thick head, I've never been better. Don't think I can face your summer fair though."

"In the circumstances I don't blame you. You're not the most popular pressman in town."

"Give my regards to PC Watkiss."

"It'll make his day, I'm sure."

"Lizzie okay?"

"Bigger and more bad-tempered by the minute — but otherwise fine. I'm so glad to be seeing you tonight. Don't wait up."

"The way I'm feeling? No chance."

That his apparent pursuers had turned out to be coppers didn't alter the fact that he was being stalked by the killer — the delivery of the latest postcard proved it — so Johnny had no need to alter his copy. PDQ and Pencil had already given it their blessing.

238

He gave the image of St Dorothy to the art department then sloped off for a long lunch with Tanfield. Another opportunity to test the hair-of-the-dog theory.

"So how long have you been murophobic?" asked the cub reporter as they crossed Fleet Street.

"What?"

"Afraid of rats — and mice."

"I'm not, really — they have more reason to be afraid of me. However, I am thanatophobic. Afraid of dying — especially in a slow and painful way."

"Thirteen letters," said Tanfield.

The man in the wide-brimmed hat crossed the deep-pile red carpet of the Angel Picture Theatre. Its magnificent chandelier cast his face in deep shadow. The entrance below the tower that provided Islington with one of its most famous landmarks was for circle patrons only. Those wanting to sit in the stalls had to use the entrance in White Lion Street round the corner. Hundreds of movie-goers — corralled by brass handrails — would often stand in line waiting patiently to buy tickets — but not on a sultry evening such as this.

He didn't normally venture out on Saturday nights — not before midnight, anyway — but time was of the essence. One more week and — assuming everything went according to plan — he would be in self-imposed exile. However, there was much to do before then. Just the thought of having Steadman at his mercy made his balls tingle.

The octopoid organist started to play the "Love Waltz" by Karl Horschna from *Madame Sherry*. The audience, so ready to be pleased by simple things, applauded enthusiastically.

In the event the orchestral performance was better than the main feature: *Night Must Fall*. On Thursday Graham Greene, in *Night and Day*, had written: *Emlyn Williams's pretentious little murder play has made a long dim film*. Robert Montgomery as the psychopathic pageboy with his hatbox of trophies was rather good though. The audience watched spellbound as he continued to hide his delight in decapitation beneath a veneer both meek and mild.

The man gazed down at the rows of heads in front of him. Now which one should he separate from its shoulders?

CHAPTER
TWENTY-TWO

Sunday, 11th July, 8.55a.m.

Johnny woke to feel a man's arm across his chest. He turned his head to see Matt, out cold, lying on his naked stomach. His blond hair, usually so neatly combed, was tousled: it made him look younger. Matt had known him longer than any other person alive or dead. The faintest of crow's feet were beginning to develop at the corners of his eyes. Stubble, the colour of corn, covered his cheeks and chin. His broad forehead was damp.

Johnny had never felt safer. Let the postcard killer come and get him now. He vaguely remembered Matt turning in, well after midnight. Exhausted after the events of Friday evening, he had come to bed at ten. He drifted off back to sleep.

They had spent the whole day playing by the Regent's Canal in Islington. Even then Matt was in the habit of looking out for him. They were so involved in their game of submarines they did not see the gypsies coming. The brown-skinned, sulky-eyed boys had already picked up their discarded clothes by the time Matt noticed them. He got out of the water and, without any hesitation, confronted them. Johnny followed his example.

The thieves, who must have been ten or eleven, had a couple of years on them. They made no attempt to flee. Matt was not afraid.

"Give them back."

"Make me." The taller of the two winked at his brother. The blow caught him completely unawares and almost knocked him off his feet. He flung down the pilfered shorts and T-shirts and lunged at Matt. The other one went for Johnny. The head-butt got him right in the stomach and knocked him to the ground. His grinning assailant jumped on him but Johnny caught him on the chin and managed to roll over so that he was now on top. The vicious urchin tried to bite as well as bash him.

Matt, meanwhile, was straddling the older boy and punching him in the face with alternate fists. The boy wrapped his hands around Matt's neck and squeezed as hard as he could. Matt grabbed his wrists and tried to break the iron grip that was throttling him. The boy beneath him let go and, with a thrust of his pelvis, threw Matt off on to the towpath. Before he could stand up and catch his breath, the gypsy booted him in the stomach again and again. Matt tried to dodge the kicks but fell backwards into the canal.

Johnny and his attacker were now rolling around on the towpath. Sharp stones dug into Johnny's bare back. The older boy, in search of further entertainment, grabbed hold of his soggy drawers, ripped them off, tore them in two and tossed them into the canal.

Johnny, now stark naked, got to his feet and, breathing heavily, quivering with shock, covered his embarrassment. The brothers stood there jeering. He was no match for the two of them. He was at their mercy. What were they going to do to him?

A hand grabbed the younger boy round an ankle and yanked hard. He fell to the ground smashing his face on the edge of the canal as he plunged into the water. He wasn't laughing now. Matt, his face already swelling, heaved himself back on to the towpath.

"He can't swim!" said the gypsy in a panic. "And I can't neither." His brother disappeared below the surface.

"Better get help then, hadn't you?" said Matt. He looked at Johnny's skinny, white body then retrieved their clothes.

When he woke again Matt was still in dreamland. He hadn't even moved. Johnny studied his friend's face, paying particular attention to his lips. They were neither thick nor thin and slightly parted.

He almost jumped when Matt opened his eyes. For a second they were unfocused then their blueness deepened. Another snatch of schoolboy Donne, from "The Extasie", came unbidden to Johnny's mind:

Our eye-beames twisted, and did thred
Our eyes, upon one double string

"Morning." Matt removed his arm and turned on to his back. "Christ, I feel like shit."

"You stink of beer."

"You sound just like Lizzie." He yawned. "Well, shift your arse. Get the kettle on."

"In a second. I want to tell you something." Matt turned to face him.

"Don't say it, Johnny."

"You don't know what I'm going to say!"

"I've a pretty good idea. Please don't say it."

"I don't want to die leaving it unsaid."

"You're not going to die and you don't need to say it. I've sort of known for years."

"That's more than I have."

"Really?" He yawned again, still not bothering to put a hand over his mouth. "Go on, I'm gasping."

Johnny got up and went down to the kitchen. He realised that he was shaking. A cup of tea would solve nothing. If there had been any whisky in the house he would have drunk it.

Matt made a point of giving him a hug before he left for work.

"Keep your wits about you. You can always come and stay with me and Lizzie if you want. Think of your break-up with Stella as a lucky escape. At least she betrayed you before the wedding and not after."

"Every silver lining has a cloud. Thanks for the invitation but, as you say — you've got enough on your plate at the moment."

It was another hot, tiresome, blue-skied day. At noon Johnny wandered up to the newsagent's on Essex Road to buy all the papers. As he was about to put his key in the front door he heard someone moving about inside. He dumped the papers on the step and retrieved the cosh. He slid the key into the lock, turned it and rushed into the hall with his arm raised.

Stella screamed and clutched her chest. For a second Johnny thought of clubbing her anyway. "I thought you'd be out."

"Well, you were right."

"I came to return your key — and this." The typescript of *Friends and Lovers* lay on the table.

"Did you enjoy it?"

"Not really. Proved I'd made the right decision though."

"What decision is that?"

"To stop seeing you."

"Why?" She stamped her foot. Johnny waited for the broomstick. There it was: the witch downstairs never failed. Stella stamped her foot again. The rapping stopped.

"Don't play the innocent with me. You're still in love with Lizzie and, God help you, half in love with Matt as well."

Johnny sighed. "It's only a novel, Stella. Nothing's been going on."

"Not in the real world, perhaps. There's always been too much going on in your head though."

"Would you like a cup of tea?"

"If you're making one." She pulled out a bentwood chair and sat down.

"I've missed you."

"You'll get over it. How's that little minx of a nurse? Always with a different man, she is."

"Did your father tell you?"

"No, I saw you walking her back to her place. Very chummy you were too."

"I'd been drowning my sorrows. Millie was just a bit of company. She looked after me when I was in Bart's. Were you jealous?"

"No. Just surprised how quickly you'd overcome your so-called heartbreak. Or rather semi-heartbreak. It seems our romance was always half-hearted. You can't love two or even three people at the same time Johnny. It's got to be all or nothing."

"I told you nothing happened!"

"That's not what Louis said."

"Oh. I was wondering when we were going to get round to that Eyetie."

"We've been seeing each other for some time."

"Why?"

"Why not? You're not the only one who can't make their mind up."

"I wouldn't trust a man who betrays his colleagues."

"All's fair in love and war."

"He's dark though, isn't he? And black-hearted. Has he told you he loves you?"

"Not in so many words. He told me what you wouldn't though."

"Such as?"

"What happened in December."

Johnny, like Matt, had always refused to discuss the events at Snow Hill.

246

"How does he know?"

"You're a newspaperman. You know better than anyone how people talk. The assault must have unleashed something, let out the queer inside you."

"If that's meant to be a joke, it isn't funny."

It was usually men who made light of homosexuality. They hid their fear of the taboo — Was it contagious? Did it make you queer if a man made a pass at you? — behind a barrage of tasteless wisecracks. Women, on the other hand, seemed to take it far more seriously — as if it were a personal insult.

"Louis simply pointed out that he was all man, but if I was happy with a chap who didn't know which way to turn then he'd back off."

"When was this?"

"Some time in May."

"After I'd introduced you to him in the Tipperary?"

"Yes." Johnny sat down, ignoring the boiling kettle. Stella, rolling her eyes, got up and made the tea. "Louis is a good guy. He's stood by me."

"What are you talking about? The heat must have addled your brain. Don't you get it? I love you. If you hadn't fucked off to Brighton we could have been engaged by now. I was going to ask you to marry me."

"I wasn't in Brighton. I was in Notting Hill."

"I don't understand. Why lie about it?"

"I was pregnant."

Just thinking of the smell of the carbolic soap and disinfectant, the Higginson syringe worming its way inside her, made her nauseous. It hadn't worked, either — which is why she had been subsequently forced to

247

resort to more drastic measures: an ice-cold speculum spreading her wide open, another instrument of torture wrenching the tiny life out of her womb; the bleeding that had seemed it would never stop.

"Was?"

"Louis took care of it."

"How?"

"I'm sure it's not the first time he's got a girl in the family way. He paid for the, er, procedure."

"How d'you know he was the father?"

"I didn't. That's why I couldn't take the risk." She started to cry.

"What risk? Surely what you did was far more risky? Not to say illegal."

"How could I marry you when it might have been his child?"

"I wouldn't have cared!" Was that entirely true? Could he have stood by and watched his putative son slowly turn into the spitting image of Dimeo? He was pretty sure he would have come to love the child just the same.

"We could have had another baby. How many times do I have to tell you? I love you, Stella. I'd have done anything for you — including bring up another man's child."

He put his head in his hands. If not being a husband was bad enough, not being a father — and having your first child murdered — was even worse. It was as if wanting something with all your heart — Lizzie, Stella, a son — immediately made it impossible.

248

"I'm sorry," sobbed Stella. "I didn't know what to do."

Johnny put his arms round her gingerly. When she didn't shake him off, he started stroking her hair.

"You should have told me. I would never have betrayed you." Could they get back together? Could he forget what she'd done? No: on both sides the trust had gone. Perhaps she was better off without him. He pecked her on the cheek. "I hope you'll be very happy as Mrs Dimeo, but with his track record I wouldn't bet on it."

"I've gone off the whole idea of marriage." She pulled a tiny handkerchief out of her handbag and blew her nose. "I'd been waiting weeks for you to pluck up the courage to ask, but at the same time a part of me was also dreading the moment. I was the one in trouble. It was my life in jeopardy, my reputation at stake. The fact that you or Louis could just ride off into the sunset made my blood boil."

"But I wouldn't have done — and Louis didn't."

"How could I have known that?"

If she had truly known him like he knew her — or rather thought he'd known her — she would have come to him straightaway.

"Would you have said yes if I had gone down on bended knee?"

"If I could have been sure the baby was yours, then yes — but only to spare my parents the embarrassment."

"Do they know about the abortion?"

She winced at the word. "No."

"Don't worry, I won't tell them." He took her hand and held it in both of his. "Have you ever loved me?"

"You made me laugh. I loved your adoration of me."

"So that's a no then."

"You don't know how to relax. At first I liked your nervous energy, but in the end I found it exhausting. I never wanted to hurt you, Johnny."

He shook his head in disbelief.

"Of course not. Carrying on with another bloke behind my back was bound to fill me with bliss. Your timing could not have been worse. At least promise me you'll come to the funeral if I die before the end of the month. I'm sure my replacement would be only too happy to dance on my grave."

"He doesn't blame you in the slightest. Says he deserved it. Apparently you pack one hell of a punch."

Johnny gave a sardonic smile. "If Matt has taught me anything, it's how to fight."

"You should show that side of yourself more often."

"Why? Violence is never the answer — and neither is ripping a baby out of the womb."

"I don't have to listen to this." She flung the key at him and stormed out, slamming the door behind her.

So was that how it ended? Would he ever see her again? Johnny picked up the typescript and riffled through the pages to check they were all there. Apparently so. He returned it to its place in the drawer. He felt like smashing up the kitchen. His whole life was falling apart. Frustration, fury, disappointment and despair bubbled inside him. He wanted to scream.

However, before he could do so, someone else did. The quiet enjoyment of a dozen Sunday lunches was shattered by a blood-curdling shriek.

CHAPTER
TWENTY-THREE

Johnny rushed out of the front door and met Mrs Turquand from downstairs coming up the area steps. She was still in a floral housecoat and curlers. She screamed again. Faces appeared at windows up and down Cruden Street. Barefoot guttersnipes, anxious not to miss anything, came scampering up the terrace.

"What's happened?" The old woman, eyes wide with terror, opened her toothless mouth to scream again. "Please stop doing that. Tell me what's wrong."

She pointed a shaking finger at her own front door then allowed herself to be comforted by a neighbour who scowled at Johnny as if the commotion were all his fault.

Johnny entered the dark, low-ceilinged flat. "The Folks Who Live on the Hill" crackled out of the wireless. Mrs Turquand lived alone. There was an open box on the dining table. He pulled out its contents: a large basket filled with roses, apples and the head of a young woman.

He instinctively knew it was real — and yet he couldn't have said why or how. The lidless eyes had begun to turn milky. The bleached hair smelled as though it had been freshly shampooed and rouge had been applied to the now mottled cheeks. To heighten the grotesque effect? If so it worked. The artificially pink lips were so swollen that they had split like overcooked sausages. A semi-clear viscous liquid seeped from the nose.

Johnny, sweating heavily, went back outside. His mounting anger gave him the strength to carry on.

"What were you playing at? It wasn't delivered to you, was it? Why stick your beak in my business?" He knew the answer to the last question: the lonely widow had nothing better to do. She burst into tears.

"Don't you speak to her like that! Who d'you think you are? Can't you see she's upset?" A young mother, one of a number who had come to gawp, folded her arms across her chest. A pair of filthy brats held on to her apron.

"I was doing you a favour, that's all," sniffed Mrs Turquand. "You were otherwise engaged." Her knowing look revealed that she had been eavesdropping on his heated conversation with Stella. The sash windows, of course, had been fully open. "The taxi-driver said he was going to be late for his dinner so I said I'd make sure you received the basket. Beautiful it was, smelled heavenly. Then . . ." — she paused, aware that she was incriminating herself — "I saw that thing in the middle."

"What, dear? What did you see?" asked the straggle-haired mother eagerly.

"A human head. That's what!"

A cry went up from the crowd that was growing by the minute.

"Give us a butcher's, mister. Go on, don't be a killjoy. Pleeeease!" The kids jumped up and down excitedly.

Johnny was almost relieved to see a policeman's helmet parting the ghoulish throng.

It took a while, but eventually a black Wolseley pulled up outside. The gang of kids, determined not to miss any of the action, still held on to the area railings.

"Popular as ever, I see." Uninvited, DC Penterell sat down and crossed his gangly legs. The basket, which Johnny had quickly removed from the flat below, sat in the middle of the kitchen table. He'd had to swat away the hands of those determined to see what lurked inside the box. "I don't suppose you recognise her?"

"No." The thought that he might be in some way responsible for her death was almost as sickening as the sight of her mutilated face.

"Any postcard?"

"No."

"See the man who delivered it?"

"No — and I presume my so-called bodyguards are having a day off. Strange how this maniac doesn't observe the Sabbath."

Johnny realised he had been an arrogant fool — if the killer had wanted him dead he wouldn't still be breathing. He should have accompanied Matt to Bexley. Then again, perhaps it was Matt's presence last night that had saved him.

The cabbie, an idle devil, must have ignored the strict instructions to give the box to him and no one else. Johnny didn't envy the man trying to get a

254

description of the driver from the hysterical woman downstairs. It was very unlikely that she'd had the wit to take down the number of the cab. Its driver, fantasising about roast beef and all the trimmings, would have been at the Angel when she learned what was in the box.

"It's not like you to be lost for words."

"I'm having a day from hell."

"Well, look on the bright side. It's got to be better than hers." He nodded at the head. Its cloudy eyes gazed sightlessly at the *Daily News* calendar that hung on the back of the door. "Crossing off the days, I see. Only twenty more to go."

"He'll make his move before then. My guess is nineteenth July."

"Why?"

"It's the feast day of Saint Rufina — the red-head."

"I wonder what he's got in mind for you." Johnny felt like thumping the callous detective — who saw the anger flare in his eyes. "Go on. Take a swing. There's nothing I'd like more than to arrest you. 'Course, you'd be a lot safer banged up."

"I'm not so sure about that — especially at Snow Hill."

"Don't you worry, I'd look after you." The detective's chuckle did not inspire confidence. "I need you to come down to the station anyway. Inspector Woodling, who's none too pleased at having his day of rest ruined, should be there by now. He wants a word in your shell-like. I'll get Constable Watkiss to bring us some lunch — if you haven't lost your appetite."

"I need to go to the office."

"Fear not, we won't take up too much of your precious time — if you co-operate. We've got plenty to do as well. This is the breakthrough we've been waiting for: someone is bound to recognise the poor cow."

"Well, if you stir your stumps we can run an artist's impression of her with my article tomorrow."

"Woodling might have something to say about that."

"Why? You're going to have to go public now. Thanks to the mob outside, the news will be all over North London by tonight."

In the event Inspector Woodling had rather a lot to say. He wasn't at all what Johnny had expected: seven feet of stern-faced rectitude. He was short for a copper in the City of London Police, around six feet, and, although he had been in the capital for over ten years, had lost none of his Welsh accent or charm. Johnny didn't even mind being called "boyo".

"We're the same age, you and me," said Woodling, after Watkiss, with a scowl, had brought in a plate of ham sandwiches and a pot of tea. He ignored Johnny's request for some mustard: "English, if you have it . . ."

Woodling nodded at the constable's retreating back. "Don't mind him — he's got a sore head. Blames the sun, of course, not the barrel of ale he drank yesterday."

"He reads other people's diaries."

"So I hear. That was a nasty business — before my time, I'm glad to say. Transferred from the Met in January."

"May I ask why?"

256

"You may, but I shan't — well, can't — tell you."

"Are you married?"

"Indeed. To Monique, a lovely lass from Brittany. You?"

"Not yet."

"It's not easy, finding the right girl."

"So it seems."

And then the pleasantries were over. It was like flicking a switch.

"Why does this man want to kill you?"

"I don't know. If I did, I'd have found him by now."

"Leave that to us. That's an order, not a request. Four women have died because of you. You don't want any more deaths on your conscience."

"I didn't kill them. You might as well blame yourself for not giving them the protection they deserved."

"They died to get your attention."

"That can't be the only reason. Revenge? Jealousy? Perverted sexual gratification? The killer could have any — or all — of these motives." Johnny sipped his tea but left the sandwiches untouched. He doubted that Watkiss had been stupid enough to tamper with them, but even so the very idea of eating still turned his stomach. "Did the bones come from a different body to that of the breast and the arm?"

"Correct. And it's probably safe to assume the head came from another. Hence four."

"Perhaps the killer just enjoys slaughtering women. I've given him as much publicity as I can. However, if you were to let me run a picture of the latest victim in tomorrow's edition it might speed up the process of identification."

"An artist is already working on an impression of how she might have looked."

"St Dorothy, the martyr on Friday's postcard, was beheaded. Today a head turns up. The killer's certainly got a sick sense of humour."

"Can you think of any reason why he chose the quotation from Rilke?" *Beauty is nothing but the beginning of terror*: Johnny couldn't get the words out of his mind. Was there a connection to the fact that he lived at the Angel?

"I think he's just trying to put me under greater pressure. He's playing a game and wants to remind me that, one way or another, I'll be the next person to lose my head."

"This business would certainly send some folk to the booby hatch."

"I visited Colney Hatch Mental Hospital once," said Johnny. "I was researching what had happened to those who were still suffering from shell shock and other forms of psychological trauma. I was proudly escorted down the longest corridor in Britain. What does it say about our country that it's in a lunatic asylum? I was told it takes five hours to walk round all the wards but, fortunately, I had neither the time nor inclination to put it to the test. I still have nightmares about some of the things I saw. It's not called Colney Hatch any more. It became the Friern Mental Hospital earlier this year."

"Is any of this relevant?"

258

"I don't know — except whoever's doing this must be mad."

"Send me a copy of the article."

"I'll swap it for your artist's impression of the woman."

"Fair enough," said Woodling.

"Well, don't just sit there. Go and get it."

The thought of Stella being just round the corner at The Cock, possibly in the arms of Dimeo, did nothing to alleviate his ill humour. He crossed Holborn Viaduct then walked the length of Shoe Lane to Fleet Street. He didn't pass a soul. It was, if anything, even hotter. The heatwave was forecast to break by the end of the coming week.

The newsroom was an inner circle of hell. Gustav Patsel, head back on his throne, snored gently. The skeleton staff went about their business and ignored him. The night shift wouldn't turn up till around four. Johnny found an empty paper bag that had contained someone's lunch, inflated it then burst it behind the German. He leapt to his feet in a shower of crumbs.

"*Gott im Himmel!* What are you doing here, Mr Steadman?"

"I've had another human offering: a head in a basket."

"It couldn't have come at a better time. Such a slow news day."

"The cops are going to send over an artist's impression of the dead woman. They think it might be the breakthrough they need."

"Excellent. A thousand words, please. Relate the whole sorry saga from the beginning. We can start the new week with a splash. You'll make the front page again."

The article took him much longer than anticipated. As well as rehearsing his assault and his escape from the pair of undercover cops at dawn on Saturday he listed all the postcards of the saints he had received, along with their feast days: Agatha (5th February), Dorothy (6th February), Rufina and Justa (19th July), Rufus (1st August), Anastasia and Basilissa (25th December). Then there was Aphrodite, the Venus de Milo: the odd one out.

If the dates were not significant — there were too many digits to form a telephone number — then perhaps the initials of the martyrs held a clue? A, D, R, J, R, A, B, V or A. It didn't seem to promise much in the way of an anagram. Perhaps four more postcards — with the names of saints whose initials were C, A, B, and A — would arrive to spell out ABRACADABRA. The J — for Johnny? — might be a red herring. As it was, BRAVADO was the nearest he could come to a word, but the O was lacking. Then O — nothing, zero, love — could represent absence. What if it were a name though . . . J. Bravard? It sounded French but rang no bells. He was fairly certain that he had never interviewed anyone called Bravard. He dug out his old notebooks and checked: nothing. However, he decided not to include any of this wild speculation on the off chance it was nearer the mark than he realised and tipped off the killer.

260

Once Pencil was satisfied with his copy, he looked up Bravard in the telephone directory. There were six with that name but none of them had the initial J. He picked up the receiver.

"It seems rather far-fetched," said Matt. "Why are you telling me?"

"I thought you'd like to suggest the name to Woodling. Do you want to stay in uniform all your life?" Johnny wasn't acting entirely out of altruism — Matt would be of far more use to him in the Detective Squad.

"Thank you. If it leads to anything, you'll be the first to know."

Ten seconds later the telephone rang.

"Have you found the article yet?" Did Woodling have a sixth sense?

"Yes, I have — but I can't see it producing any leads."

"You never can tell. Send it anyway. The picture of the dead woman should be on your desk shortly."

The continuing plight of veterans of the Great War had made a great impression on Johnny. His article had prompted a flurry of letters — full of concern from do-gooders and platitudes from politicians — but had changed precisely nothing. Those with only physical wounds were cared for in hospitals around the capital, including Richmond, whereas those with psychological wounds were sent to Friern Barnet. Many of the patients also had physical wounds: they had lost arms and/or legs as well as their minds. Some were in straitjackets in padded cells; some rocked back and forth in wheelchairs, drool trickling down their chins; and some were stupefied with drugs. However, others had seemed quite sane and proved capable of holding a decent conversation — for a while at least. Johnny concluded that the only reason they were in the original booby hatch fifteen years after the armistice had been signed was because they had no one to care for them or nowhere else to go. The article had appeared under the headline, THE HIDDEN COST OF WAR.

He had forgotten that he'd been strictly forbidden to reveal the identities of those he'd interviewed and had consequently only jotted down their Christian names. He wasn't thinking clearly. He was still reeling from Stella's news.

He didn't feel like returning to his empty house just yet. The words spoken that morning — in love, anger and dismay — would still be hanging in the air. All he had to look forward to was the Torquemada crossword in the *Observer*.

The increasing activity of the office would at least provide some kind of company. Besides, he ought to get Mrs Turquand a box of chocolates by way of an apology and there was nowhere open at this time on a Sunday afternoon. He stayed put and flicked through the day's papers that were strewn round the newsroom.

George Gershwin was on his deathbed in Hollywood. The thirty-eight-year-old musical genius had a brain tumour: another of God's sick jokes. Many of the songs he had written with his brother Ira were listed, including "Summertime", "I Got Rhythm" and "The Man I Love".

Johnny shifted uncomfortably. He did love Matt — but not in *that* way. Not really. And even if he did: what was the point in loving someone you could never have? As usual, Matt had been right: it was better not to say anything, to pretend the moment had never happened, to ignore the whispers of the subconscious mind.

Simkins had been up to his old tricks again. The Minister for Colonial Affairs — or "Colonic Affairs" according to the sniggering caption of the revealing photograph — had been caught in flagrante delicto with a male prostitute. His resignation was expected to be tendered tomorrow. Johnny admired him for not giving in to blackmail. Another blow for the terrible Tories. Simkins Senior must be so proud of his iconoclastic son.

Johnny looked at the photograph again. His heart skipped a beat. He had been in that very same room. He had been in the very same bed — it had been the only way he could interview the very same boy. It was not going to be easy to leave the past behind.

CHAPTER
TWENTY-FOUR

Monday, 12th July, 8.20 a.m.
Tanfield tossed aside the morning edition with a childish pout.

"Seems I missed all the excitement yesterday. You could have called me. I'd have been glad to help."

"I'm sure Mummy and Daddy would have objected to having their dear Timmy torn from their loving embrace on a Sunday."

"Only someone with no family life would say that. I hate Sundays. They seem to last twice as long in Wimbledon."

"You're not the only one who misses work. Time crawls in Islington too."

Johnny had spent the evening writing his journal. Heartbreak and murder made for great copy. He doubted he would ever have so much to write about a single twenty-four-hour period again. Sunday's events had also provided plenty of inspiration for the plot of *Friends and Lovers*.

Like Alice before him, he could escape from reality by passing through the looking-glass. His alter ego could make Stella's surrogate cry with joy — "Oh yes, yes! I will be your wife!" — and nine months later

264

produce a beautiful, bouncing boy. Dimeo's counterpart, meanwhile, could be crushed — slowly, horribly, agonisingly — under the wheels of a packed rush-hour tram. Johnny glanced over to the sports desk. Dimeo, perched like a praying mantis, was typing away and ostentatiously whistling "A Nice Cup of Tea".

Johnny was so busy giving the lothario the evil eye he didn't notice Tanfield studying the notes he had made the day before.

"Of course, *bravard* means 'a cruel man' in French."

"Does it?"

"*Certainement, mon ami.*"

"In that case, I'll excuse your impertinent snooping." Johnny picked up the phone. Matt was out making inquiries so he asked to be put through to the Detective Squad instead.

"Inspector Woodling is currently unavailable. May I help you?"

"That depends, DC Penterell. Can you spell?"

"Have you noticed how Steadman rhymes with dead man?"

"The initial letters of the images on the postcards — A, B, V, R, A, R, J and D — can be re-arranged to spell the name J. Bravard."

"We're aware of that." Johnny waited for him to give Matt the credit but wasn't surprised when he didn't. The plain-clothes pack were all glory hounds.

"Are you also aware that *bravard* means a cruel man' in French? Perhaps it's a *nom de guerre*."

"Indeed." The detective sounded excited.

"There are six Bravards in the telephone directory but none of them has the initial J. Hello . . ." The ungrateful cur had hung up.

As soon as he replaced the receiver, the telephone rang.

"I always knew you were a basket case."

"Good morning, Henry. I suppose congratulations are in order. Why does spreading misery fill you with bliss?"

"Since when have you been on the side of the Tories?"

"Never have been, never will be. I don't like to see a good man destroyed in print though."

"Good? The old bugger was breaking the law."

"Something you've never done, of course."

"That would be telling. As a matter of fact, I've got oodles of things to tell you — and something to give you. Let's have a celebratory lunch — on my expenses, naturally. Should we say the usual place at one p.m.?"

"Very well."

The meal would provide Simkins with plenty of opportunities to gloat but, knowing him, he must be after something else as well. What though? Johnny was sick of freaks bearing gifts.

The white-coated waiter — his face a solemn mask which allowed him to pretend he was not eavesdropping on the conversation — placed the Tanqueray gins, a bottle of tonic water and a bowl of nuts on the occasional table between the leather wing-back armchairs and glided back to the bar.

"So what d'you want then?" said Johnny.

Simkins stared at the cloud-painted ceiling and sighed.

"Why should I desire anything other than to spend time with an esteemed friend and colleague?"

"We've never been friends and you know it."

"That's not my fault."

"Do you feel good, having claimed another ministerial scalp?"

"Cloud nine doesn't come close. It took me months of hard work. I deserve it. The man was a hypocrite."

"Only because the law didn't allow him to be his true self."

"It was his politics I loathed, not his bedtime frolics."

"The photograph was taken at Zick's brothel, wasn't it?"

"I did wonder if you'd notice. Bring back pleasant memories, did it?"

"Hardly. How much did you pay the boy?"

"Not a penny. Zick arranged it all. I haven't the foggiest who the boy is. He was a mere — now what's the *mot juste?* — tool. Ha!"

"Why wait till now to produce it?"

"I only received it on Friday."

"Is Zick back in town, or has his shutterbug finally crawled out of the woodwork?"

"Timney? I've no idea where he is — of course, we know where his son Charlie is, don't we? Six feet under. You put him there."

Johnny refused to be goaded. He hadn't torched the bookshop in which the boy had burned to death.

"Didn't you recognise Zick?" Simkins smirked. "I must say, Cecil was delighted to see you again." He grinned at Johnny's confusion. "Walter Apthorp? You were so polite to him. It was priceless. You really are a prize ass!" His braying laughter shattered the venerable hush. "I do love the way you blush."

"Fuck off! I only ever saw him dragged up as Cecilia. Matt will be very interested to learn he's back on his patch. He's never forgiven him for attacking his wife."

"Too late! He'll be back in the City of Light by now."

"Then he'll arrest you for aiding a fugitive."

"I don't think so, Johnny. Zick gave me something else." He handed over the stiff-backed Manila envelope. Johnny opened it. His heart sank. He had seen the image before: Matt, naked and unconscious, in the arms of an equally naked, unidentifiable man. Before he could tear it up, Simkins snatched it off him. "Just imagine the trouble this could cause if it were to fall into the wrong hands."

"It already has."

"Not necessarily. There is a way to make it vanish."

"I'm all ears."

He couldn't have the so-and-so arrested for the possession of indecent material because the contents of the photograph would rapidly become public. His prime objective had to be to protect Matt. The shame and humiliation that he had worked so hard to forget would destroy him if it became common knowledge. For all that Matt's colleagues might suspect he had been molested there had, until now, been no proof.

268

"Your barmy butcher story has captured the public's imagination. It's done wonders for your circulation, whereas the *Chronicle's* is falling. My exclusive yesterday might have slowed the rot but I need another coup to arrest the decline and regain my reputation as the best newshound in London. I want you to give me the story."

"How can I? It's me he wants to kill."

"True. But I plan to save you from his evil clutches. Give me everything you've got and I'll do my best to see he's caught. Of course, if I fail, you won't be around to regret it. However, I'd prefer you to be there to see me revel in my success."

Johnny drained his glass. He wasn't going to let the bastard steal his story.

"Another?"

"No."

Simkins beckoned the barman anyway.

Johnny got to his feet. "I'll send over all my research this afternoon. I think I know the name the killer is using."

Now it was Simkins who was surprised. "Crikey! You have been a busy boy. You must think the world of Turner to be prepared to sacrifice such a scoop. Then again, he is a very handsome man . . ."

"I expect you to protect my identity. Your source must remain anonymous. I'll be sacked if they find out I've helped you."

"Don't you worry — you're not the only one with connections in the police. Shall we proceed to the dining room?"

Johnny shook his head in disbelief. The urge to wipe the smirk off the bastard's face, to scream abuse at him, was becoming irresistible. He bit his tongue and walked out of the club.

"You owe me. I gave you what you wanted. Can you imagine how hard it was, having to wait outside when I knew exactly what was going on?"

"It was a small price to pay for protection. Who else would have allowed you to keep your job?"

"I did as I was told. Steadman isn't going to let it drop. He's determined to find out what happened. I could go to the police."

"Who are they more likely to believe? Me or you? Do you want to go to prison? You'd never see him again."

"I can't go on like this. It stops now. Leave us alone."

"Or what? If I can't have him, neither can you."

The younger of the two men wiped away a tear, then, catching his tormentor off guard, leapt at his scrawny throat.

If Johnny could have kicked his own backside, he would have done so. He had brought this upon himself by failing to recognise Cecil Zick. The pimp had escaped justice again, while he now found himself trapped — and the worst part was that he couldn't talk to Matt about it.

How could he possibly trust Simkins? He might have several copies of the photograph or, even worse, possess the negative.

Johnny had often felt guilty about his antipathy towards the amoral fop who, until now, had treated him with generosity and a vague, grudging respect. However, by resorting to blackmail, Simkins had confirmed his worst suspicions. How could he get hold of the photograph yet still expose the killer himself? There had to be a way . . .

CHAPTER
TWENTY-FIVE

"Where the hell have you been?" Peter Quarles came bearing down on him. "The head has been identified. You need to go and interview her next of kin and neighbours." He handed him a piece of paper.

"I was meeting an informant."

"And?"

"Cecil Zick, the brothel owner who evaded capture last December, is back in London. He hosted an orgy on Friday evening attended by Commander Inskip. The stink of corruption is growing stronger."

"Never mind about that now. This takes precedence. We need the next instalment for tomorrow's edition. The bonce was delivered to you, so you should follow up the story."

"Who gave you this information?"

"An Inspector Woodling called. He was most anxious to speak with you. You're supposed to let me know of your whereabouts at all times." PDQ's irritation masked what Johnny chose to interpret as relief.

"I'm on my way."

Helena Nudd had lived in Arlington Street behind the Sadler's Wells Theatre on Rosebery Avenue. As Johnny got out of the cab he saw Henry Simkins standing outside the lodging house.

"You really should have stayed for lunch. The veal just melted in one's mouth. Commander Inskip was more than happy to take your place." Johnny handed him an envelope containing his notes identifying J. Bravard as the potential killer. Friern Barnet Mental Hospital had refused to answer his enquiries about Bravard or even confirm or deny someone of that name had ever been a patient. "I suppose Inskip knew Zick was the host on Friday as well."

"That's for me to know and you to find out. How did you know he was there though?"

"You're not the only one with connections in the police."

"*Touché*."

"When do I get the photo?"

"When I've got what I want. I do hope you haven't set me up. By the way, I'm making arrangements that will ensure, should anything happen to me, that the photograph will be sent to every newspaper in the land." He smiled at his own cleverness. "Come on. We might as well do this together. The old bird is already about to fall off her perch."

Simkins led the way into the dark terraced house. It was stifling. A smell of wet clothes and oxtail soup hung in the humid air. The landlady, obese and red-faced in a threadbare armchair, fanned herself with a copy of the *News*. The £2,000,000 national fitness campaign, which was now in its sixth month, had clearly passed her by.

"This is Miss Ody," said Inspector Woodling. "She last saw Helena on Saturday evening when she went up to the Angel Picture Theatre to see *Night Must Fall*. She never came home."

"Why didn't you report her missing?"

"And who might you be?"

"John Steadman from the *Daily News*."

"It's all your bleeding fault!" She flung the paper at him. "Get out of my home!"

Simkins grinned with delight.

"Do you wish to be exposed as the owner of a flophouse?" Johnny wasn't going to be given the bum's rush in front of Simkins and the police. "Is it customary for your young ladies to stay out all night? Or do you let rooms by the half-hour?"

"How dare you!" She was too fat to leap up so looked round for something else to throw at him. Her glasses case came flying towards him. Johnny dodged it easily and tried not to laugh as it landed in a fish tank. The water was so dirty it was impossible to tell if it contained goldfish or piranhas.

"Is that a yes or a no?"

Simkins burst out laughing.

Inspector Woodling had heard enough. "Steadman, a word outside, if you please."

Johnny was only too glad to step out into the relatively fresh air. The roar of traffic from St John Street, less than a hundred yards away, made the street seem an even more unpleasant backwater.

"We're wasting our time here," said Johnny. "Why did you call me?"

274

"I wanted to let you know that J — as in James — Bravard died three years ago."

"So it's an alias, a *nom de crime?*"

"Not necessarily. He had a son, Patrick Joshua Bravard, who inherited the family home in St John's Square. The place is empty. He moved out at the weekend, apparently."

"Have you got a photograph?"

"No. He's not on our books. It seems he has a clean sheet."

"How old is he?"

"Thirty-seven."

"Well, the War Office may have a record of him."

"The thought had occurred to me."

"Friern Barnet refused to tell me if anyone named Bravard had ever been a patient."

"He left in October 1933."

"My article was published in July of that year. If our paths crossed, I must have said or done something to provoke him. What, though?"

"There's no second-guessing the mentally ill. The slightest perceived insult can trigger an over-the-top response."

"What was he being treated for?"

"Major depression. He was seriously wounded in the war."

"He must have recovered pretty well if he can move house and abduct a woman all in one weekend. He didn't have far to send the head though, did he? I live in Islington too."

"I'm aware of that. The question is: where is he now?"

"Perhaps he's done a bunk."

"Aren't you forgetting something?"

"Not at all. Strangely enough, a death threat tends to linger in one's mind."

"I don't wish to unduly alarm you, but his sudden disappearance suggests he's about to make his final move."

"Does Simkins know about this?"

"I haven't told him, but it won't be long before he finds out." The copper did not realise how right he was.

"What can you tell me about the victim? I'm not going to get anything out of Miss Ody now."

"She worked in the linen department of Catesby's in Tottenham Court Road. Her parents live in Manchester. A long-term fiancé went off with another of Ody's tenants a couple of months ago. It hit her hard and she'd only just started going out again."

Johnny's heart went out to her. Talk about bad luck: you pluck up the courage to re-enter the dating game and end up losing your head — literally. He was going to catch the man who killed her — even if it did mean using Simkins as bait.

"He must have known that we'd soon identify the head," continued Woodling. "He must be pretty confident that his bolt-hole is secure."

"Unless he's hiding in plain sight. Where's DC Penterell?"

"You're not suggesting he's got anything to do with the murders?"

"Of course not — he hasn't the gumption. I just wondered what he was up to."

"He's at the cinema, seeing if any of the staff recognise Nudd."

"Are you going to watch the house in St John's Square?"

"What's the point? It's empty."

"Can I see for myself? I'd like to be able to describe where my would-be killer was hiding."

"I suppose so. It's on the way back to Snow Hill. What about Simkins?"

"Let's leave him to his own devices. He's not the one under sentence of death."

Not yet anyway.

He dragged the body down to the crypt. The bloody head bounced sickeningly on each step. Where better to hide a corpse? He would drag it along the ancient tunnel which connected St Vedast-alias-Foster to St Paul's that evening. It was working out even better than expected. The slow-witted cops were bound to be struck by the similarity to Callingham's death and put two and two together and make three as usual. Even the terrier-like Steadman might be convinced. If not, he would have to take further action. It seemed the Good Lord was on his side after all. He forgave genuine penitents all their sins.

Johnny stared out of the open window as the new radio car crawled down Farringdon Road. The City of London Police had only two of them. The booksellers skulked in the shade of the tarpaulins that covered their barrows.

"How did Simkins learn about Helena Nudd?"

"I don't know," said Woodling. "I certainly haven't authorised a press release yet."

"Someone at Snow Hill has a loose tongue."

"And that's news to you?"

Johnny sighed in resignation. As always, who you knew was more important than what you knew.

"Where did the removal firm take Bravard's possessions?"

"They're in storage in Victoria. I've got your friend Sergeant Turner trying to find out exactly where — so we can search them — and the address that the bills are going to be sent to. Commander Inskip has told me I can have as many uniforms as I need. He wants the murderer caught almost as much as you do."

"He had lunch with Simkins today. There's your leak."

St John's Square wasn't a square at all but an irregular oblong off Clerkenwell Road. The door to number six had been kicked in and was now secured with a new hinge and padlocked bracket. All the windows of the smart townhouse were shuttered. Woodling produced a key and opened the lock. It reminded Johnny that Callingham's key — if indeed it had belonged to him — was still in his pocket.

Their footsteps on the dusty floorboards echoed off the empty walls where only the ghosts of paintings remained. Johnny started on the top floor — two small attic bedrooms intended for staff — and worked his way down the other four floors to the basement kitchen. The house was in an excellent state of decoration. Money clearly hadn't been a problem for its owner.

"Is the house going to be let or sold?"

"Let, I believe."

"The bastard thinks he's coming back then," said Johnny. "He actually thinks he's going to get away with it."

He picked up the telephone that was on the floor in the hall. It was still connected. As he replaced the receiver it rang. Both men jumped.

"Good afternoon. The Bravard residence," said Johnny, adopting the tone of a snooty butler.

"So, you found me then. I knew you wouldn't disappoint me." The voice on the other end, although just a whisper, made his blood run cold. He was talking to the man who wanted to kill him.

"I'm afraid I must . . ." Johnny was by no means as good a mimic as Simkins but he did his best to reproduce his upper-class vowels. "Steadman's lost all interest in you, said he had bigger fish to fry, so he's passed your story on to me. I'm his good friend Henry Simkins of the *Chronicle*, I promise I can guarantee you more column inches. Lord knows why you chose the cocky little pleb in the first place."

Johnny imagined he could hear the cogs of the killer's brain whirring as he took in the misinformation. He was pretty sure they had never spoken to each other before, so it was unlikely that his deception would be detected. Before he could say anything else the line went dead. Johnny, frowning with disappointment, hung up.

"You shouldn't have done that," said Woodling.

CHAPTER
TWENTY-SIX

Tuesday, 13th July, 8.40 a.m.

Johnny was ten minutes late for work — the very first time in his career. It had taken him hours to get to sleep and when he did drop off the recurrent nightmare soon returned. This time though the figure at the foot of the bed was Bravard. A large carving knife glinted in the moonlight. "*All changed, changed utterly,*" the maniac whispered. "*A terrible beauty is born.*"

Johnny had woken feeling hungover and unrested. He'd admonished himself for his apocalyptic dread. Yeats was writing about terrorism not torture.

"I thought Bravard had got you," said PDQ. "Seen what he looks like?" He held out a copy of the *Chronicle*. A handsome army officer — the very image of an English gentleman — stared out of the front page: the caption read THE FACE OF A KILLER. Simkins claimed to have unmasked the sender of the gruesome parcels. His article contained exactly the same information as the one Johnny had written on his return to the office the day before — but that was illustrated with a picture of Helena Nudd. "By the way, Stone wants to see you."

Johnny's spirits sank — then immediately rose again. If the editor was going to take him off the story it could work in his favour. If Bravard were to see Blenkinsopp's byline instead of his own it would corroborate what he'd told the lunatic yesterday and fill Simkins with false confidence.

The telephone rang. It was Matt.

"Get yourself over to St Paul's right away. There's been another jumper. It's George Fewtrell."

PDQ assured him that he would tell the editor he was chasing a lead and would visit the seventh floor immediately upon his return. Johnny grabbed his jacket and notebook and hurried out into the sun. Why would Fewtrell have jumped?

The cathedral was closed to visitors. A copper stood by one of the side-doors. "It doesn't take long for flies to find a corpse."

"And it's good to see you again, PC Watkiss."

"Your boyfriend's inside."

"I presume you're referring to Sergeant Turner. Does he know that's what you call him?"

"Doubt it — and you won't tell him, if you know what's good for you."

It was like stepping into another world. The vast stage-set of Portland stone cast a cool, soft light on the cluster of men standing round the curate. There was no doubt that the body had fallen from a great height. Fewtrell had landed on his face — but the back of his head was black with blood.

Father Gillespie was talking to Matt. Johnny waited until they had finished their conversation.

"Don't say it." Matt, as always, appeared more intimidating in uniform.

"What?"

"Two suicides in ten days. It can't be a coincidence."

"Of course it isn't. Are you sure he killed himself?"

"Why?"

"Look at the back of his head, for a start. How come it's caved in if he fell on his face?"

"Perhaps someone turned him over."

Johnny glanced at Gillespie.

"He said he didn't touch him," said Matt.

"I bet he didn't tell you that Fewtrell was screwing Callingham's son, Daniel. He was at the funeral. They both sang from the same song sheet — literally. They were in the choir here."

Matt gave a deep sigh. "Here we go again. Queers are nothing but trouble."

"You might as well blame the Church. Men in frocks in charge of pretty boys . . ."

"Perhaps Fewtrell killed Callingham because the good doctor found out that he'd been fiddling with his son and was threatening to call the police. Fewtrell would have known this place like the back of his hand."

"He told me that Daniel seduced him."

"A likely story. We'll need to talk to the boy as soon as possible."

"The last I heard, he was off to France."

"Very convenient."

"I'll try and speak to his mother today."

"Keep me posted."

"Of course. Who found the body?"

"Father Gillespie. That chap over there."

"Thanks. We've already met. Any news on Bravard?"

"We've traced the removals company that cleared the house in St John's Square. They're under the impression that the owner is moving to Switzerland."

"Switzerland! How? It's not easy getting citizenship there."

"Bravard Senior was a banker."

"Ah, money. The magic key to all doors."

"More to the point: Switzerland doesn't have an extradition treaty with Great Britain. We won't be able to touch him, if he's already there."

"I very much doubt he's left without saying a long goodbye to me. He must want to explain himself, to try and justify his murder spree and why I'm to be his final victim."

"We've alerted the ports and London Airport. Anyone resembling Bravard's photograph will be stopped."

Fewtrell's body was being loaded on to a stretcher.

"Will the investigation into Callingham's death be re-opened now?"

"Your guess is as good as mine," said Matt. "The coroner will only reconsider the open verdict if new evidence turns up."

"Surely a dead body counts as evidence?"

"Let's see what the pathologist says. I'll call if there's any news."

"Thank you. By the way, you might want to ask Watkiss why he refers to me as your boyfriend."

Matt scowled and stormed off towards the exit.

Johnny went over to the deacon.

"A true tragedy. He was a fine tenor."

"Did you know he was Daniel Callingham's lover?"

"Certainly not. What on earth makes you think they were? Fewtrell would have been defrocked. Inappropriate friendships do sometimes crop up, but we endeavour to nip them in the bud. Boys of Daniel's age often go through a period of confusion. Most of them turn out all right."

"Are you sure you didn't notice anything untoward? You know, secret smiles across the nave. Whispers in dark corners . . ."

"To the pure all things are pure. George was an excellent curate. His faith was very important to him."

"Fat lot of good it did him. When did you find his body?"

"Just after eight this morning. He was stone cold. He must have jumped last night."

"How would he have got in here?"

"I don't know. Perhaps he hid somewhere before the sexton locked up. There's no shortage of places. Only half the cathedral is open to the public. It has its own mysteries as well as celebrating the mystery of God."

"Why d'you think he jumped?"

"I've no idea. Are you quite sure about him and Daniel?"

"Fewtrell told me himself. It will all become clear once I — and the police — have spoken to Daniel."

"This news fills me with great sadness. I do hope it isn't going to bring St Paul's into disrepute. However, it may explain why George felt it necessary to end his life. If he was molesting Daniel, the thought of prison, of being separated from the boy, may have unhinged him."

"I can see the headline now," said Johnny. "THE QUIRE OF QUEERS."

"The bishop will do his best to minimise the damage."

"God is truth — but only when it suits you? Would you have gone to the police if Fewtrell had confessed everything? Of course you wouldn't. Mother Church looks after her sons."

"You're a bitter man," said Gillespie. The whites of his eyes were actually yellow. "You must be very unhappy."

"Don't change the subject. I'm interested in the fact that you haven't pointed out the coincidence."

"What — that both Callingham and George jumped from the Whispering Gallery?"

"No. From the condition of the corpse Fewtrell could just as well have jumped from the Stone or Golden Galleries. It can't be a coincidence that both Daniel's father and lover chose to die in the same way — if they did choose suicide and weren't murdered."

"The coroner said there was no evidence of foul play in the case of Frederick Callingham."

"Indeed. It will be interesting to hear what he says about Fewtrell." Johnny pretended to check something in his notebook. "The coincidence I had in mind is the fact that two out of the four residents of Wardrobe Place are now dead."

286

"You have such a suspicious mind. What possible significance could that have?"

"Your training teaches you to think the best of everyone. Mine the worst. Call it the triumph of experience over hope. I think something — something nasty — went on in that house. Perhaps it was where George and Daniel made the beast with two backs. Daniel was a child and he should have been safe there. I must be right — why else would I have been beaten half to death after chasing Fewtrell from the building?"

"I really can't help you there. You should thank the Lord for your survival. If there's anything more I can do, don't hesitate to telephone me. The sooner this ghastly mess is cleared up the better."

"I still haven't found where the key you gave me fits, but I have a feeling that when I do everything will become clear."

Gillespie bowed with a smile. "God speed."

The red light went out and the green one started to glow. Johnny entered the lion's den.

"Steadman. Good to see you. Take a seat."

Johnny, to his surprise, felt butterflies flutter in his empty stomach. The editor's minions weren't usually in the room long enough to sit down. Stone seemed nervous too. A Pifco fan whirred uselessly on his enormous desk.

"Look here, Steadman. Are you an invert?" Johnny leapt to his feet. "No, I am not!" He wasn't going to discuss his sexual orientation with his boss.

"It's all right. I don't mind if you are. There's plenty of them in the Open-Air Tourist Society." Stone's fondness for naturist holidays was a standing joke. "I guess they appreciate the scenery. I've never been bothered with such paltry affairs — except, of course, when they concern matters of state. I heard that you touched Dimeo in the showers."

"I didn't touch him, I punched him! He's been screwing my girlfriend."

"Oh, glad to hear to it — if you know what I mean. This place is full of Chinese whispers. I hope you knocked him out."

"As a matter of fact, sir, I did."

"Excellent. I see, thanks to your sterling efforts, your would-be assassin has been identified. My wife, for some reason, is most concerned about your safety. She has asked me to invite you to stay with us until the man is caught."

"Thank you, sir. However, I need to be where he can find me if I'm to be the one who collars him."

"Simkins seems to have got the bit between his teeth."

"Only because I let him. I'm dangling him as bait."

"I didn't hear that. Such a gambit would be most immoral."

"It's just using a prat to catch a mackerel."

Stone winced. "I must say, I admire your ability to retain your sense of humour in such circumstances — even if it is a poor one. Sure you don't need Blenkinsopp's assistance?"

"I've come this far by myself, sir. I'd like to see it through in the same way."

"Suit yourself. If you change your mind, all you have to do is say the word. Good luck."

As it happened, his luck seemed to be running out. He had just sat down at his desk when the telephone rang. It was one of the Hello Girls.

"You weren't answering so I took a message from a Mrs Callingham. She says her son's gone missing."

CHAPTER
TWENTY-SEVEN

The telephone was answered after two rings. He had expected to hear the affected tones of a housemaid but it was Mrs Callingham who simply said: "Hello?"

"It's John Steadman. I'm sorry to have missed you."

"I've not been straight with you, Mr Steadman, in spite of your kindness, and I now fear I'm paying the consequences."

"You say Daniel's missing. Whereabouts in France was he?"

"He never went there. He refused to leave me by myself. However, I suspect he didn't wish to be separated from George. He's probably with him now."

"I'm sorry to say that he's not, Mrs Callingham, and that's a fact."

"Call me Cynthia. How can you be so certain?"

Johnny hesitated. He should be in Barnes so he could see her face, gauge her reaction, ensure she wasn't lying to him — and ensure that she didn't become hysterical. However, it would be cruel to keep her hanging on.

"I'm sorry to say that George Fewtrell was found dead in St Paul's this morning."

"Did he jump too?" Her voice had hardened. Instead of surrendering to tears she had let iron enter her soul.

"The police think so — but it's too early to tell at this stage. My own opinion, for what it's worth, is that he was murdered." He took a deep breath. "Did you know that he and Daniel were very close?"

"You mean perverts? Not until yesterday. When I confronted Daniel, he admitted that he loved George and refused to accept that they were doing anything wrong. Of course it's all George's fault. He must have led Daniel astray. The thought of him abusing my son turns my stomach. However, Daniel swore that if I informed the authorities I'd never see him again."

"Did your husband know about the relationship?"

"I didn't think so — but I'm not so sure now. Frederick was very concerned about Daniel's adulation of the older boy. He couldn't understand what Daniel saw in him."

"Did he ever talk to George about his friendship with Daniel?"

"Not that I know of."

"George told me that when he tried to end the affair, Daniel threatened to tell the police about him."

"I wish he had. So my son's a blackmailer as well as a pervert."

"He's a mixed-up boy who needs our help. I think someone found out about their friendship, guessed the true nature of it, and turned it against them. I think this person killed Fewtrell and . . ." The doctor's wife gasped.

"Is Daniel also in danger?"

"Quite possibly."

"I can't lose him as well as Frederick. I can't . . ."

"Let me contact the police this very minute. I have a friend who's a sergeant at Snow Hill. I know he will be very keen to speak to you, so stay where you are. I'll call you straight back. Don't worry, we'll find Daniel soon enough."

He replaced the receiver. Before he could call Matt, Tanfield placed a yellow piece of paper in front of him. Perhaps luck had not deserted him after all. It only took five words to save the day:

Daniel Callingham is in reception.

Johnny, breathing a sigh of relief, in too much of a hurry to wait for a lift, hurtled down the stairs to the foyer. There was no sign of the boy.

"Where's the young man who was waiting to see me?"

The doorman shrugged. Johnny ran over to the reception desk. "Well? Where is he? Daniel Callingham. He wanted to see me."

"I'll thank you to keep your voice down, sir. He left a few moments ago with another gentleman.

"What did he look like?"

"Early twenties, fresh-faced." The old soldier paused for effect. "There was one more thing: he was wearing a dog-collar."

Johnny dashed out into Fleet Street. The rush hour was in full flow. All he could see was a mass of milling backs. What should he do? Call the cops now then follow his instinct, or race to Wardrobe Place straightaway? He felt sure that was where Daniel would be taken. The boy's life was at stake. He ran to the telephone exchange at the back of the building. Ignoring the protests of Doreen Roos, he demanded to be put through to Snow Hill. Matt had just gone off duty. He didn't trust anyone else at the station. His wish to see it through by himself had been granted.

The plain bogeys had a different canteen to the officers. It was somewhere they could take the weight off their feet and get any grievances off their chest without the risk of being overheard by their superiors. Only a couple of tables were occupied, but even so the hum of conversation died down when Matt marched straight into it. Herbert Watkiss, a cigarette dangling from his lip, was sitting alone. Matt was amused to see that he was flicking through the *Daily News*, but didn't show it.

"Have you got anything to say to me?"

"Nothing in particular."

Matt bristled. "That's nothing in particular, *sarge*. Why are you giving Steadman such a hard time? He's done you no harm."

"Never said he had. Needs you to stick up for him yet again, does he? Did he come crying to you? Matty, darling, that horrible Herbie's been calling me names."

Matt grabbed his former friend round the throat — alliances forged during training rarely survived when only one party was promoted — and, using just one hand, dragged him to his feet.

"Keep your voice down," growled Matt. He turned to the other table, which had fallen silent. "You lot — clear out."

He waited for the men, muttering in disappointment, to disappear through the doors. The sharp-nosed woman behind the counter didn't need telling to make herself scarce. She and her tea-towel vanished into the kitchen.

"I'm more concerned about what you've been calling me," said Matt. "Why would you think I'm his boyfriend?"

He loosened his grip slightly so that the gasping Watkiss could speak.

"I read his journal when you sent me round to get his clothes." He lowered his eyes in shame at the confession. "Steadman thinks you're beautiful. I assumed he'd told you."

"He hasn't — and he's not queer."

"Well, what is he then? Only women are beautiful."

"Who else have you told?"

"No one. I swear."

"Keep it that way. Johnny's going through a bad time. The girl he wanted to marry has given him the elbow . . ." Watkiss thought better of making a wisecrack. "And this Bravard or whoever he is seems intent on killing him. Cut him some slack. You know what writers are like. I'll deal with it in my own way. And keep your opinions to yourself. They shouldn't interfere with police business." He shook his head in disgust. "Reading other people's diaries? That's low, Herbie. I thought you were better than that."

Two more constables, at the end of their shift, came into the mess. Matt let go of the coughing Watkiss and walked out.

"What?" said Watkiss to the pair of spectators. He wiped his eyes. His throat was on fire. "Never seen a lovers' tiff before?"

Johnny knew it would be quicker to go on foot rather than taking a taxi. In spite of the sultry heat he ran all the way, dodging dawdling pedestrians, and — ignoring horns, hooters and bicycle bells — switching to the gutter when the pavements were blocked. The drains smelled worse than ever. He cut across Ludgate Circus into Pilgrim Street and only slowed down when he reached Carter Lane. His overworked lungs felt as though they were banging against his healing ribs.

He thumped on the door of Number Five. When it opened, he pushed past Haggie and, wiping his face with a handkerchief, stopped by the picture of the Garden of Gethsemane — another scene of betrayal.

"Who d'you think you are, bursting in like this?" The dogsbody was indignant. "And stop dripping sweat on the floor. I polished it today."

"Shut up, if you want to keep your job," panted Johnny.

"The police are on their way. One word from me and you'll also be charged with child abduction. Where is he?" The doorman hesitated. "Where is he?"

His shouting brought Adam Wauchope out of the dining room.

"Mr Steadman! What an unexpected pleasure. We're in here. Haggie, be a good chap and fetch another cup."

Johnny followed the cleric into the dining room. Daniel was sitting at the table, looking scared.

"What's the matter?"

"Why didn't you wait for me?"

"I was worried about George. Adam told me that he was here, so there was no longer any need to bother you. I was going to leave another message, but Adam said there wasn't time."

"I bet he did. I'm sorry, Daniel, I really am, but George is dead."

The boy opened his mouth to speak, but nothing came out. The colour drained from his face.

"He's lying, Daniel." Wauchope moved towards Johnny. "How dare you come in here spreading such evil lies."

"Shut the fuck up. Are you in on it too? Is there anyone in this house who doesn't like boys' bottoms?"

"Ironically enough, Yapp didn't."

"Is that why he was killed?"

"The opposite, I'm afraid. Dr Callingham, having followed Yapp here, made the wrong diagnosis."

"He thought Yapp was abusing Daniel?"

"Indeed. Father Gillespie will explain everything. He'll be here shortly."

"I do need to speak to him, but I'll do it at my convenience, not his."

"I'm awfully sorry, but I must insist that you wait."

As the pot-bellied priest moved towards him, Johnny put his hand in his pocket. The moment Wauchope laid a hand on him the cosh cracked his skull. The pompous priest crumpled to the floor.

"Come on, Daniel. We've got to get out of here."

"Why should I trust you?"

"You're not safe here. Why d'you think everyone's so keen for you not to talk to me? Why come to me at the *News* if you don't think I'm on the level?"

The boy got up from the table. Haggie came into the dining room carrying a cup and saucer. Seeing the unconscious man he knelt down beside him.

"What you gone and done that for? You could have killed him."

"He's still breathing, more's the pity. Besides, he had it coming."

Someone put a key into the lock of the front door.

"Is the basement door open?"

The caretaker, glancing at Daniel, nodded.

"Thank you. I'll make sure you're not implicated."

Johnny grabbed Daniel's arm and pulled him towards the kitchen stairs. "Don't make a sound." Footsteps, followed by raised voices, could be heard as they sneaked out and ran towards the passage that would take them to St Andrew by the Wardrobe and, for the time being at least, a place of safety.

Joshua Bravard — he had never liked his first Christian name — refilled his glass with champagne. He was dressed in a silk bathrobe of a geometric pattern. The doors to the terrace, which had a splendid view of the Thames, were open. The curtains swayed in the welcome breeze. He picked up the telephone.

"Do I have the pleasure of speaking to Mr Henry Simkins?"

"Yes, you do. Make it snappy. I'm off to the theatre."

"Joshua Bravard here. Did you call me this afternoon?"

"No, I didn't."

For once he was so surprised he was momentarily lost for words. "Thought not. Naughty Johnny. Trying to pull a fast one yet again. Would you like to teach him a lesson?"

"There's a lot of things I'd like to do to him."

"It sounds as though you're a man after my own heart. I'm sure we'll get on swimmingly."

"I assume you're not ready to give yourself up?"

"Never. And you'll never get to meet me if you don't understand that. As you know, I kill people who don't do exactly what I want."

"So you're still planning to kill Steadman?"

"Of course. Would you like to watch?"

Simkins had many faults, but sadism wasn't one of them. The thought sickened him. Besides, he couldn't help liking Johnny. Surely the two of them together could defeat this maniac?

"I'd be delighted. Would I be able to write about it?"

"Of course. I'm relying on your powers of lurid description to make me infamous."

"Where are you?"

"Before I tell you, I want your word that you'll come alone and not alert the police. We will meet in a public place so you have no need to be alarmed."

"Very well. However, I shall leave an envelope with the address on my desk and give instructions that it be opened if I haven't telephoned by eleven this evening."

"A wise move, if I may say so. I'm at the Savoy. I'll be in the American Bar. I'll no doubt recognise you from your byline photograph. A handsome fellow like you must be accustomed to fighting off the ladies."

"Very kind of you to say so. What time?"

"Should we say seven thirty? We can have dinner in the Grill Room, if you wish." An image of St Lawrence sprang into his mind. However, Simkins was not going to share his gruesome fate. He had something else in mind for him.

They caught a taxi in Queen Victoria Street. It was only when they were heading West, along the embankment, that Daniel spoke.

"Is it true?" His eyes begged Johnny to deny it.

"I'm sorry, Daniel. He died last night."

"I knew there was a good reason why he didn't turn up this morning." Tears began to run down his face. He made no attempt to wipe them away. "I loved him so much."

"Everything all right, Guvnor?" The cabbie met Johnny's eyes in the rear-view mirror.

"What's it look like? Just drive."

The only safe place he could think of was Stone's mansion in Holland Park. He could hardly take Daniel home with him when Bravard was no doubt sharpening his knives at this very minute.

A maid opened the door. Daniel, overawed by the palatial surroundings, momentarily stopped sobbing. The chequered marble floor reminded him of St Paul's.

"Johnny! What a lovely surprise!" Honoria Stone threw her arms around him. "Victor said you'd declined the invitation. And who do we have here?"

"This is Daniel Callingham. He needs somewhere to spend the night. It isn't safe for him to go home."

"From what I've been hearing, that makes two of you."

"Indeed. Daniel's just had some very bad news. A friend of his died today."

"Oh, I'm so sorry, Daniel." It was his turn to be pressed to her breast. However, he put his arms round his hostess and started to cry again. Honoria stroked his curly hair. "We should call his mother."

"May I speak to her first?"

Honoria nodded her approval. Johnny entered the kiosk under the stairs.

"Mrs Callingham. It's John Steadman. Daniel is safe and well."

"Thank God." God had nothing to do with it, thought Johnny. "Can I speak to him?"

"Of course. For both your sakes, I think it wise if you remain ignorant of where we are until tomorrow. Is there someone who can stay with you this evening?"

"There's my sister — if you think it's absolutely necessary."

"Whoever murdered George is a desperate man. His life depends on Daniel maintaining his silence. He'll do anything to ensure that."

"So you're sure George was killed? Very well."

"My guess is that it will all be over tomorrow and we'll know then the exact reason why your husband died."

"Thank you, Mr Steadman. I underestimated you."

"Here's Daniel."

While Daniel tried to reassure his mother, Honoria studied Johnny like a matron assessing whether a boy was fit enough to start a new term at boarding school.

"You've lost weight, Johnny."

"Loss seems to have become my speciality of late."

"I'm sorry to hear that. You must tell me all about it after dinner. Let me go and make the necessary arrangements for your stay and we'll talk later."

"There's no reason for me to stay."

"Yes there is. The boy needs you. He's in a house full of strangers." As always, she was right. Her unconditional kindness reminded him of his own mother.

Daniel and Johnny waited in the drawing room.

"Everyone's been lying to you," said Daniel.

"It happens all the time," said Johnny. "What have you been lying about?"

"The key you showed me at my father's funeral. It was how George and I used to meet. There's a tunnel that connects St Paul's and St Vedast's. It's not very long. It runs from crypt to crypt. There's a door behind an arras in St Vedast's."

"Why would Father Gillespie give it to me?"

"He was trying to cast suspicion on George."

"Well, he was molesting you."

"He wasn't! We were making love. I seduced him. Gillespie's the molester."

"What?"

"He found out about me and George. He said he'd tell the police if George refused to share me with him. He fucked me every Wednesday afternoon in George's room at Wardrobe Place. It drove George mad."

"I'm not surprised. Did your father know this?"

"He suspected that I was having sex with a man, but I swore it wasn't George. I knew he'd stop me seeing him if I did. He said I was mentally ill. He threatened to send me away to school in France. I said I'd kill myself if he did."

"Can you imagine how much that must have hurt him?"

"He was hurting me! He couldn't accept that George and I loved each other. He said that boys often developed crushes on other boys at my time of life but they soon grew out of them. He even said he'd fallen for a boy at school but, until that moment, hadn't thought of him for years."

"Did you know he was going to kill Father Yapp?"

"Of course not. I was shocked when he said he'd followed me to Wardrobe Place. He planned to force him to resign but was stymied when Yapp denied everything. What else could he do? He was innocent. My father didn't believe him, but he was afraid that if he went ahead and exposed him the newspapers would get hold of the story and ruin all our lives. After all, Greek love is against the law. It's ridiculous — you can't legislate for human nature."

"Why protect Gillespie?"

"I had to protect him to protect George. I didn't want George to lose his job and go to prison. That's why I let Father Gillespie fuck me."

"That's a great sacrifice for a boy of your age to make. You must have really loved George."

"I still do." He started to cry again. "I don't know what I'm going to do without him. I'll never find someone as good as him."

"Now that George is out of harm's way, we can ensure Gillespie hangs for what he's done. He's a rapist and a murderer."

"He didn't rape me — I let him do it."

"It's rape — and sodomy."

"You still don't understand, do you?" The boy wiped his face. "I liked it."

Johnny was shocked. Why were public schoolboys so precociously self-assured? He cast his mind back to when he'd been fifteen: there were times when he was so randy he'd have fucked almost anything. However, apart from pleasuring himself, he'd never given in to his rampant libido.

"You were betraying your boyfriend with a man older than your father."

"I had no choice. By betraying George, I was saving him."

"Daniel, I'm going to tell you something I've never told anyone before . . ." Perhaps his confession would prompt the boy to come clean about how he really felt. "Before I do, you must promise not to repeat it."

"I like secrets. Go on. I won't spill the beans. Cross my heart and hope to die."

"I was raped by a policeman in December. It was the most painful experience of my life. It wasn't about sex. It was about domination." Paul Bern, Jean Harlow's husband, sprang to mind. Being sodomised was far more humiliating than blowing out your brains. "My guess is that Gillespie was acting out of spite. He took pleasure in making George suffer. I think George reached the end of his tether. He realised that your father had killed the wrong man and confronted Gillespie, who had no choice but to silence him."

"I'm very sorry that you were raped — don't take this the wrong way, but there's plenty of men out there who'd like to do the same to you — but Gillespie didn't hurt me. I wish my father had succeeded in killing him, though. If he'd killed the right man, George and I could have lived happily ever after."

Johnny doubted that very much: most homosexuals, forced to pretend they were something they were not, lived loveless lives of misery and despair.

"Why d'you think your father chose such a haphazard way of killing Yapp?"

"It worked, didn't it? Where better to do the deed than the scene of the so-called crime? Well, the seduction at least. My father couldn't accept what I am. He said I'd grow out of it. He seemed to shrivel when I laughed in his face. Perhaps he blamed himself. I rather admire him for, as it were, killing two birds with one stone. He punished the man he thought had polluted his son and ended his own life at the same time."

"Perhaps he was afraid of facing the death penalty." If you were contemplating murder, thought Johnny, any scruples about committing suicide would pale into insignificance.

"Or he couldn't live with the thought that his son was a shirt-lifter." Johnny stared at the boy's tear-stained face. There was defiance in his bloodshot eyes. He hoped it was shock that explained his apparent callousness. "At least this way he spared my mother the stigma of suicide. She still thinks it was just a terrible accident."

"Aren't you going to tell her the truth?"

"Why should I? She won't like it."

"Would you rather she read about it in the *Daily News*?"

"Can't you expose Gillespie without bringing me or my father into it?"

"I don't know, Daniel. Once Gillespie is arrested, God knows what he'll tell the police or say in court. I'll do my best."

"I'd be very grateful." The boy's smile seemed to light up the room. It was like a candle to a moth.

"Why did you come to see me at the *News* this evening?"

"I couldn't think who else to turn to. I knew something must have happened to George. He never let me down. I'll never stop loving him."

"Of course you won't — but George wouldn't want you to spend your life in mourning. Believe me, you'll meet other people — and fall in love with some of them

— but your life will be so much easier if you fall for a woman. Don't you want to have children one day?"

Daniel shook his head. "I don't think so. Men can't have babies, can they? Besides, I'm still a kid, and look at the trouble I've caused. I do know what I am. George showed me how beautiful forbidden love can be. Whatever the bible says, and even though I've lost George, I intend to regain that paradise."

CHAPTER
TWENTY-EIGHT

Wednesday, 14th July, 8.15a.m.

Johnny studied the cherub behind the crossed swords: the symbol of St Paul. Was the child being protected by the weapons, or a prisoner of them? Frederick Callingham must have been temporarily out of his mind — but then, weren't all suicides? Was their self-destruction an admission of defeat, atoning for a frightful wrong, or the ultimate act of self-possession? Perhaps Callingham believed he was protecting his son whether or not he succeeded in flattening his abuser. Perhaps he was afraid of what he would do if Daniel insisted on sticking to the wayward path he had chosen. Fathers and sons: Johnny always felt at a disadvantage when fatherhood was in the frame. *I'm sorry . . .* Perhaps Callingham had been apologising for being a bad father. It was futile trying to second-guess the dead doctor. However, the misguided man deserved his compassion: a physician unable to heal himself.

The cathedral was gradually coming to life. Its calm interior subtly altered as its staff — who appeared like ants from his viewpoint in the Whispering Gallery — scurried hither and thither. The building was a massive machine — a wishing machine — that required constant maintenance. The fact that something so substantial could be built out of something so flimsy and invisible — faith — was a miracle in itself. Wren, a conjuror in stone, had pulled off a magnificent confidence trick. As his son was supposed to have said: *Si monumentum requiris, circumspice.* If you require a monument, look around. God did not exist, so it was nothing more than an extravagant folly, but even so it was a triumphal tribute to the works of man.

What would he leave behind if Bravard had his way? A journal — juicy enough in parts — and an incomplete novel. Memories that would gradually fade in the minds of Matt and Lizzie. A thousand newspaper cuttings that would eventually yellow and crumble.

"Coo-ee!"

The cry echoed round the dome. Father Gillespie, who had just come into view, froze along with the other do-gooders. He beckoned Johnny to come down. Johnny shook his head. The mountain would have to come to Mohammed. He smiled at the inappropriateness of the phrase.

The deacon was out of breath when he emerged on to the gallery.

"I was wondering when you'd turn up."

"Why haven't you run away?"

"Where to?"

"Your sort always have somewhere to hole up."

"My sort?"

"Child abusers. Paedophiles."

"I didn't do anything to Daniel that Fewtrell hadn't already done."

"That's no excuse. The boys loved each other."

"So they said. In my experience, at that age there's very little difference between love and lust."

"How many others have there been?"

"I've lost count."

Johnny felt physically sick.

"Did Yapp know what was going on?"

"He didn't have a clue. Haggie is a whiz at dealing with dirty laundry. When Callingham turned up on the doorstep, Graham denied everything — which just made him seem more guilty."

"Why Daniel?"

"His feelings for George made him more — now what's the word . . . ? — compliant."

"He's only fifteen!"

"That's old enough to bleed."

Anger surged through Johnny's veins. "How can you say such a thing? You're a man of God."

"Lucifer was the most beautiful of the angels."

"Remember that when you're getting the shit kicked out of you in Pentonville."

"What makes you think I'm going to prison? You've only got the word of a deranged boy who has lost both his father and friend."

"And the testimonies of Wauchope, Corser and Haggie." He was sure they would all sing like canaries to save their own necks. "And the blood on the steps of the crypt in St Vedast and in the tunnel leading from it."

That morning Johnny had entered the cathedral via the tunnel to ensure that Daniel was telling the truth. It was an unpleasant place for trysts — dark, damp and festooned with cobwebs. Perhaps the besotted boys, as if to prove that love is blind, hadn't noticed.

"You made, shall we say, a clerical error in not cleaning it up. Were you too proud? You know what comes after pride."

The priest said nothing — a silent acknowledgment of his mistake.

"I told you once I knew where the key fitted I'd have the whole story. Why did you give it to me?"

"To throw you off the scent. I thought it would lead you to Fewtrell."

"Why did you kill him?"

"He attacked me. It was self-defence. I may be old, but I didn't just murmur a few words over mass graves in the war. I fought hand to hand with the Bosch." He smiled at a sudden memory. "Some of them were so young — and beautiful. It's not happenstance that angels have blond hair and blue eyes."

Johnny thought of Matt lying on the pillow beside him. He was no angel.

"How did you know Daniel would be at the offices of the *News* yesterday?"

"I didn't. I sent Wauchope to fetch you. It seems that someone else is out to kill you so I thought I'd do us both a favour."

A terrifying thought struck Johnny. Were two people really after him? There was no such thing as a coincidence. Could it be Gillespie who had sent him the parcels? Had he set up Bravard as a scapegoat, a fall guy? Could the two men have met during the war? Did

310

Gillespie know that Bravard would soon be safe and sound in Switzerland? The voice he heard on the telephone in St John's Square could have been Gillespie's. The first parcel had arrived two days after Callingham fell from the gallery — but the first postcard had already been sent by then. Although he wasn't a left-footer the priest would know all about Catholic saints — but Gillespie wasn't interested in women. Then again, chopping them up was hardly a sign of affection.

"Did you attack me last Tuesday?" He stepped away from Gillespie and grabbed the railings.

"Alas, that was nothing to do with me. I can't imagine there's a shortage of people who'd like to knock your block off." He took a step towards him. "Why are you trembling, Steadman? Death is nothing to be afraid of. As it says over the entrance here: *Resurgam* — I will rise again."

"Thank you, but I've no intention of falling. You should be thinking of your own skin. If there's a hell, you'll be there in seconds." Johnny nodded at the two policemen who had started walking in opposite directions round the gallery.

"Ah. I see you brought the cavalry. Pity: all I did was protect myself from a child molester."

"It takes one to know one. You stood by and watched while Yapp died for your sins."

"I thought you were a non-believer." He took another step forward. Johnny stood his ground. If it came to it, he would shove the devil over the banister.

"What's to stop me taking you with me?" Gillespie's eyes burned with fury, not fear.

"This," said Johnny, producing the cosh. He slapped the life-preserver in the palm of his hand. It made a reassuring sound. He was itching to use it. "Do you know what fishermen call the club they use to kill fish? A priest." He raised his arm. "This is for Daniel and George."

Gillespie, however, refused to give him the satisfaction. He glanced at the two policemen, glared at Johnny and snarled, "Fuck you" then climbed over the railings.

"Wait!" said Johnny. "Did you kill the missing women? Do you know a Joshua Bravard?"

Gillespie whispered something. Johnny, eager to hear, was about to step forward but, before he could do so, found himself held back by Matt's strong arms. Before he too could be grabbed, Gillespie let go of the railings and took the plunge.

CHAPTER
TWENTY-NINE

"Why did you stop me?" Johnny turned to face Matt.

"I'd have had to arrest you for assault — and you'd hardly catch Bravard if you were banged up in a cell. Besides, I could see it in his eyes: he was going to take you with him. I saved your neck — again."

"Thank you." He'd have embraced him if there hadn't been other cops around.

Far below a crowd was already congregating round Gillespie's corpse. The eternal fascination of death.

"Don't be too despondent. You got your man in the end."

"He's escaped justice though — and now he's gone there's no need to expose him as a paedophile. The living must take precedence over the dead. The reputations of Dr Callingham and his son — even though they're a murderer and a pervert — will remain unblemished."

"At least Gillespie can't harm any more choirboys."

"And Wauchope?"

"He wanted you charged with assault until it was pointed out that he could be charged with child abduction. I should think his days in the arms of Mother Church are numbered."

"Sarge . . ." A spotty-faced constable whom Johnny had never seen before came trotting up.

"Yes, Gazzard?"

"Your wife's gone into labour. She's been taken to Bexley Hospital."

"I very much hope not. It's a booby hatch. She's supposed to be going to St Mary's in Sidcup."

The constable blushed. "I knew you lived in Bexley . . ."

"And jumped straight to the wrong conclusion. Go on, since you're here — try and take some witness statements with more accuracy."

"Aren't you going to the hospital?" Johnny was amazed at Matt's calmness.

"When my shift ends at two. I'll only have to kick my heels in a corridor. With a bit of luck, Matt Junior will be waiting for me by the time I get there."

"What about Lizzie? She needs you."

"No, she doesn't. Her mother will be with her. Men aren't allowed in the maternity ward."

"Even cops?"

"We'll see. I don't know why you're more worried than I am. Haven't you got more important matters to attend to?"

They looked at the broken body of Gillespie. His limbs, at unnatural angles, formed a swastika on the marble floor. No one had bothered to adjust his cassock, which had somehow ended up round his waist. His withered legs, riddled with varicose veins, were as thin as sparrow-shanks. It was an undignified pose for a man who had used his respected position to satisfy his unnatural lust. How many childhoods had he ruined? They would never know.

"You're right. The fact that Gillespie killed George Fewtrell will still make a sensational story. If I choose my words carefully, I might be able to get away with implying he was abusing the young man."

"I should think he was an expert in all kinds of abuse. You'll need to make a statement, so you might as well come back to Snow Hill with me now. Inspector Woodling has been trying to get in touch with you. Your dear friend Henry Simkins appears to have gone missing."

In the event, Woodling was not in the station-house so Johnny was soon free to go. Could Gillespie have been responsible for the abduction of Simkins? Had he and Bravard been in cahoots? His brain was buzzing with all manner of crackpot theories.

As he walked down Ludgate Hill he could see a mass of cumulonimbus clouds, giant cauliflowers, towering in the west. It was, if anything, even hotter. The entire capital seemed to be holding its breath, waiting for the heatwave to break.

There was a small parcel on his desk. Before he could open it, Dimeo cautiously approached.

"I just wanted to let you know that Stella's finished with me."

"And why would that be of interest to me?"

"Well . . ." The shame-faced sportsman was disconcerted. "You can try and patch things up now."

"And how, exactly, do you bring a dead baby back to life?"

"Watch what you're saying!" Dimeo looked round the office to see if anyone had heard. "Look, Johnny, I'm truly sorry for what's happened."

"More like sorry I found out. Not used to being given the elbow?"

"I don't mean that. What I did was despicable. Stella loves you."

"No, she doesn't. She never did — not really — but that doesn't let you off the hook. I can just about understand sleeping with a colleague's girl, but what I don't get is why you had to tell her about the assault — it's not as if you don't find seduction easy."

"I thought she had a right to know."

"Why?" Johnny lowered his voice. "I was raped — and there's nothing I can do to change that. I have to live with it every day. That doesn't mean I now find men attractive. You're a handsome devil, Dimeo, but I don't want you to fuck me."

"Jolly glad to hear it. I'm sorry, Johnny, honest."

"Well, I'm not sorry I hit you."

"What's that?" Dimeo nodded at the parcel.

"Strangely enough, it's not addressed to you."

He waited until Dimeo was back at his desk then unwrapped the package. It was from Bravard. There was a postcard of a painting by Jean Vignaud — *Abelard and Héloïse Surprised by Master Fulbert* — the significance of which eluded him. He opened the box slowly: there, on a bed of cotton wool, nestled a pair of what could only be testicles. They looked like lumps of Turkish Delight but smelled slightly fishy. A wave of nausea swept over him. What fresh hell was this? Johnny turned over the postcard:

If you wish to see your so-called friend alive again, do exactly as instructed. A taxi will collect you from the office at 6p.m. Come alone.
JB

Johnny raced upstairs to the library. It was as if he were trapped in a recurrent nightmare. Apparently Simkins — who else could it be? — had succeeded in luring Bravard out of his lair. Johnny almost felt guilty. Simkins may be a blackmailer, but he didn't want his death on his conscience. He consoled himself that, one way or another, Simkins, for the sake of a scoop, had deliberately placed himself in jeopardy. Meanwhile, this was likely to be the last time he would have to decipher one of Bravard's sick pictorial puzzles.

He was relieved to see that Amy's chair was empty. The latest — last? — delivery made the very idea of flirting seem obscene. He ran his fingers along the smooth red leather of the *Encyclopaedia Britannica* before pulling out the first volume.

Peter Abelard, a twelfth-century scholar, had fallen in love with Héloïse, the niece of a canon of Notre Dame in whose house he lodged. When the affair was discovered the canon had Abelard castrated. In spite of his enduring love for Héloïse, the scholar went on to become a monk. Johnny couldn't see Simkins following suit. Poor Henry — it couldn't have happened to a nastier man. On the other hand, the unwilling eunuch could be dead already. If he were, the pornographic photograph could be on its way to the whole of Fleet Street right now.

Johnny reluctantly telephoned Woodling. The Welshman was beside himself with rage.

"You're unbelievable, Steadman. Not only do you tell Bravard that you're Simkins — you tell Simkins everything there is to know about him. Were you deliberately setting up a rival?"

"How d'you know I told Simkins anything?"

"He rang yesterday evening to say that he was on his way to meet Bravard. It was deliberate provocation, a tease. He knew it was far too late to put a tail on him. He's got what he deserves. By the way, he said to remind you about the deal. What deal?"

"I can't talk about it."

"Well, if he dies, it'll be your fault."

"I have his balls in my hand as we speak."

"I beg your pardon?"

"They were delivered in a box this morning."

"Was there a message?"

"No." He couldn't risk telling the truth. Involving the police would only complicate matters.

"How d'you know they're Simkins's balls then? They could be anybody's. If you're lying to me, Steadman, you'll regret it. Wherever you go, you leave death in your wake. I've just heard about Gillespie — not that he deserves to be mourned. I'll send someone to collect the, um, evidence. If you interfere in this case once more I'll have you arrested for obstruction."

"I am the case."

"Not any longer. Keep out of my way. And don't forget to keep us informed about your movements. Simkins's safety takes priority now."

"It's a bit late for that."

Woodling, instead of responding, hung up.

One thing was for sure: Johnny wasn't going to do as either Bravard or Woodling told him. For a start, he wished to remain intact: he had lost quite enough in the past fortnight as it was. However, he wasn't stupid enough to think he could stop Bravard by himself. Perhaps Dimeo would help — he was good at acting surreptitiously and if he lost *his* balls, so much the better.

He took the package over to him.

"Take a look."

Dimeo, surprised, did not hesitate.

"Crikey! Are they what I think they are?"

"Like to help me get the man who did this?"

"I presume he's the same one who's been sending you the other bits."

"Indeed. I need you to secretly follow me in a taxi tonight. I can't inform the police because the ex-owner of these baby-makers will die if I do. You'll need an accomplice. Who do you suggest?"

"What about Tanfield?"

"He's just a boy!"

"He can handle himself though. We've been training together."

"What kind of training?"

"Boxing."

No wonder Dimeo had never actually clipped the cub round the ear. He would have fought back.

"Okay — but I'll have to run it past PDQ."

Quarles agreed — on condition that he came along as well. "There's safety in numbers."

"And three's a crowd."

"We won't be together. We'll travel in different taxis."

"What can I say? I'm touched that so many people are concerned for my safety."

"It's the story that concerns me. If we can get this guy before the boys in blue it will make us look even better."

Tanfield, of course, was thrilled. "Thanks for this opportunity, Johnny. I won't let you down."

"I sincerely hope not." He didn't tell the boy that he had made Dimeo and PDQ promise to protect him at all costs.

He was halfway through writing his account of Fewtrell's murder and Gillespie's suicide when Victor Stone's secretary rang to summon him to the seventh floor.

The red light went out and the green light came on.

"Well done, Steadman. The choirboys of St Paul's can sit easily again."

"If you say so, sir."

"I've had the Bishop of London on the blower."

"Oh yes?"

"He wants me to kill the story."

"There's a surprise. I hope you said he hadn't a prayer."

"He's most concerned that we insist that Gillespie was acting alone."

"But he wasn't. What about Wauchope?"

"He's already been sacked."

"God moves in alacritous ways."

"Indeed. Let me see your finished article before Herr Patsel does."

"Yes, sir. Thank you for your hospitality last night."

"Don't mention it. Honoria was pleased to see you. Daniel's a nice lad."

"Yes, he is. He's had a difficult two weeks."

"He'll get over it. He's young." Johnny was not so sure. "I'm told he was reunited with his grateful mother at Snow Hill this morning."

"It's a damn nuisance that I can't mention him in the article."

"Perhaps — but I don't think either mother or son would be grateful to have Callingham portrayed as a killer who got the wrong man. How's the hunt for Bravard going on?"

"He's sending a cab for me this evening at six o'clock. Mr Quarles, Dimeo and Tanfield are going to follow as unobtrusively as possible. I don't want to get the police involved because a man's life is at stake. I've got his balls in a box downstairs."

"Jesus Christ, Steadman. This gets better and better. Who's the unfortunate hostage?"

"Most likely Henry Simkins, sir."

"Ha! The fellow once had the cheek to turn down my offer of a job. Keep your hair on — it was before your time. He's a damn fine reporter."

"If you say so."

"I do say so — but you'll be top dog if you can rescue him from this farrago. He seems to have been remarkably well informed. Any idea how he found out so much about your story so quickly?

"No, sir. You know how people talk."

"Where would we be without gossip? Well, whatever you do, don't let Bravard get away. I want to know what makes him tick."

"Surely you mean sick, sir?"

"Very funny. Now get out."

Johnny spent most of the afternoon on his article, trying to reveal as much as possible without saying too much. If the man on the Clapham omnibus could be bothered to read between the lines it would be obvious to him that the Church of England was arranging a cover-up. If the organisation put as much effort into helping its flock, rather than itself, the world would be a better place.

Soon after 5p.m. a tremendous thunder-clap shook the building. It felt like the crack of doom and brought home to Johnny that, if things went wrong that evening, these could be his last hours on earth. Having no heirs, he had never made a will, so he scribbled a note, addressed to Matt, leaving all his worldly goods — such as they were — to him and a request that he maintain in good condition his mother's grave in St Pancras & Islington Cemetery. He had no wish to lie mouldering in the ground, so he asked to be cremated and that his ashes be scattered in the Thames. He sealed it in an envelope and labelled it *Strictly Confidential*.

"What is that?" Pencil held a copy of his article in his hand.

"Just a note to a friend — in case I don't come in tomorrow."

"Ach, Steadman. With these three good men on your side, nothing can go wrong."

"Well, that's put the kibosh on it."

"What does that mean?"

Johnny sighed. "Nothing important."

"If you say so. Mr Stone is impressed with your work, Steadman — and so am I. It will be front-page news tomorrow. I do not often say such things, but I would regret most highly were anything to happen to you. I wish you good luck."

"Thank you, sir. You're making me nervous."

The German waddled off.

"*Sir?* You've really got the abdabs, haven't you?" Dimeo and Tanfield, clad in Macintoshes, stared down at him. Their eyes shone with excitement.

"You're hardly the Praetorian Guard."

"We're all you've got, though, so be nice to us." PDQ nodded to the others. "Come on, it's time to get into position. Taxis will be thin on the ground in this weather." As if on cue, the heavens opened and the desultory spitting that had been the first precipitation in almost three weeks was replaced by rain like gleaming stilettos that stabbed everything beneath it. A sweet-sour scent filled the air as weeks of dust were rinsed away. Those closest to the windows scrambled to close them. As Johnny left the building it was like stepping into a cold store. The sudden drop in temperature was remarkable. His gabardine was at home but he didn't mind in the least getting soaked to the skin. It was as if Gillespie's filth were being sluiced off him. He felt refreshed and energised.

The taxi — with a sign saying STEADMAN in the driver's window — was waiting right in front of the entrance. Johnny pushed his way through the forest of black umbrellas and hopped into the back. The storm cast everything in an eerie half-light. Fate appeared to be on his side: any cop trying to trail him would have great difficulty keeping him in sight.

"Evening, Guvnor." The greeting was barely audible. The cabbie, in the *de rigueur* cloth cap, released the handbrake, let out the clutch and nosed his way into the crawling traffic. Rain always slowed it down.

"Where are we going?"

The answer was drowned out by another clap of thunder. Johnny was surprised the driver could see anything through his dark glasses.

"What did you say?"

"You'll find out soon enough."

Johnny, irritated by the whispered reply, sat back. Perhaps he had been paid to keep the destination a secret.

They turned right into Fetter Lane and headed north. At Holborn Circus the driver took the exit to Hatton Garden. Johnny resisted the impulse to look back to see if there were any other taxis behind them. When they turned right again into Clerkenwell Road,

Johnny guessed they were heading for St John's Square. Surely Bravard hadn't returned home?

As they approached the entrance to the square the driver suddenly accelerated and shot down Albemarle Street, a short cut-through from the square to St John Street. He then took the next left into Aylesbury Street — throwing Johnny across the back seat — right into Woodbridge Street and left into Sans Walk. Johnny's heart sank. There was no way any other vehicle could have followed them.

"Here we are." The driver took off his cap and glasses and turned to face his passenger. A flash of lightning — which made Johnny see red — revealed a face of two halves. One was instantly recognisable as the debonair Joshua Bravard; the other, eyeless and corrugated, looked like toasted cheese. No wonder the photograph in the newspapers had failed to produce a response.

"Hello, Johnny." The hoarseness of his voice added to the horror. "We meet at last. Do come in."

The taxi had stopped by a high wall on which a plaque notified passers-by that six people had been killed and fifty injured when a Fenian bomb had exploded on the spot in 1867. The Irishmen had been trying to spring two of their fellows from the Clerkenwell House of Detention, but had succeeded only in destroying the wall and a row of houses opposite. The prison had been demolished at the turn of the century and Hugh Myddleton School now stood on the site. What were they doing here? Bravard clearly

325

wasn't worried about being followed if he intended to leave the cab right here.

"This way." Bravard unlocked a door in the wall and stood aside to let him enter. The windowless room was little more than six feet square but was furnished with a burning oil lamp, ottoman, Turkey rug and a full-length mirror that took up the whole of one wall. "This is the only place where I allow mirrors to be displayed. I don't have to be invisible here. I can be my true self."

"You do surprise me. Did you crack all the others? No wonder you've had such bad luck."

Bravard snickered humourlessly.

"What have you done with the taxi-driver?"

"Nothing. It's mine — so useful for getting around unnoticed. As you can see, I have some difficulty in that department."

Johnny looked round the tiny room. What on earth could it be used for? A head-doctor's consulting room?

Bravard watched him with amusement. "The police were here on Monday. I found the lock smashed in later that evening. The fools didn't search hard enough though." He pressed a switch behind the frame of the mirror. The looking-glass swung back to reveal an iron door. "This is all that remains of the prison. My father used the cellars to store his extensive wine collection, but, as you're about to find out, I sold it and found a far more interesting use for the space. I only drink champagne."

He picked up the lamp and unlocked the door to reveal an iron staircase. As soon as the well-oiled hinges turned Johnny was hit by the vilest of odours. It was a

326

mixture of rotting flowers, blocked drains and open graves. The stench made Johnny retch. His eyes began to water.

"I can't go down there. I can't."

"Don't be such a sissy. I know it's all right for me to say — the gas destroyed my sense of smell — but if you want to save Simkins, you must."

Johnny tentatively stepped towards the door and tried to breathe only through his mouth. A hard shove in the small of his back sent him cartwheeling down the metal steps into the darkness. He landed, dazed and bruised, in a heap on an iron gantry.

"Why don't you take off those wet clothes?"

"No, thanks."

"I won't ask again." Bravard held up a blood-stained scalpel.

Johnny quickly stripped and stood there shivering — out of fear rather than the cold. If the maniac thought being nude would stop him running back into the street, he was mistaken.

They stood on a suspended walkway which ran above six cells. Bravard kicked his discarded clothes — and PDQ's cosh — over the edge and held up the lamp. It was a charnel house. A mirror was screwed to the back wall of each cell. Four of them held mangled corpses in various stages of decay. A fifth contained a naked woman chained to the wall by an iron collar round her neck. Was it a trick of the light, or did she move?

The final compartment on the left had been fitted out as a makeshift operating theatre, Simkins, a leather gag in his mouth, was strapped to the table. His eyes were closed.

"How did you get him here?"

"I invited him up to my suite for a drink. The promise of more champagne was all it took. Of course I slipped a little something extra into his glass. He went out like a light. The staff at the Savoy are extremely helpful — especially when you're known to be a big tipper. Two page-boys helped me load the trunk into the taxi." He slowly looked him up and down. Johnny felt like a bullock at auction. "Let us descend. After you . . ." As Johnny passed him he stabbed him in the right buttock. "Get a move on. I've waited for this moment long enough."

The corridor below the gantry consisted of a succession of brick ovals which made it necessary to step over the foot-high divisions that separated the door to each cell. Prisoners would have only been able to see above their heads — if there had been any light.

They entered the sixth cell. Bravard lit some candles and took off his own clothes.

"Don't worry, I'm not ambisexual like Henry. The blood sprays everywhere." He held the lamp up so Johnny could appreciate his naked body. "Recognise me now?"

"Why would I?"

"Our paths crossed at the Cave of the Golden Calf. I was painted gold and in a black cape."

Johnny remembered Bravard's enigmatic smile. "It was pretty dark. Why were you there?"

"Zick invited me. I've known him for years."

"You can tell a lot about a man from the company he keeps." Johnny knew his only hope was to keep Bravard talking. His three musketeers, if they had somehow managed to follow him, might just recognise the taxi parked upstairs. He was already regretting not involving the police. "Was it you who knocked me out and pissed on me last week?"

"Certainly not." Bravard laughed. "I'd have made sure you were conscious before the baptism. There's no point in humiliating someone if they can't appreciate it." To demonstrate the point, he tilted the table that faced the full-length mirror. He ran his finger over Simkins's outstretched body. The shaved scrotum was crudely stitched together with black yarn.

"It's a terribly simple process. You slice just to the side of the ridge that runs down the middle of the sac known as the raphe, snip the spermatic cords and then tie them off. Of course the writhing makes it a little more tricky. I don't believe in anaesthetic. Pain is what reminds us we're alive."

"That must have hurt a lot too." Johnny nodded at the torturer's disfigured face.

"You'll find out soon enough. Although acid will do to you what fire did to me. What really hurt though was your refusal to look at me."

"When?"

"You don't remember then?" He turned down the corners of his mouth in mock sadness. "We almost met a few years ago. Why d'you think I chose you?"

"I don't know — that's why I'm here."

Bravard pointed to the wall where the following words had been daubed in red paint — or blood: BEAUTY IS NOT SKIN DEEP.

"I was in Colney Hatch." He came closer to whisper in Johnny's ear. His breath smelled of Parma violets. "I'd just been transferred from St Mary's, Sidcup — living proof that not all pioneering plastic surgery is successful — and was having, shall we say, a little difficulty in adjusting to my altered appearance. You came beetling round, full of compassion, a bleeding heart with no bleeding time for ugly beggars like me."

"I was told not to stare. I couldn't speak to everyone."

"You ignored me."

"Not deliberately — even if I had spoken to you, I wouldn't have been allowed to use your name. Is that what this is all about? How an unintended snub made you into a mass murderer? You must be really sick."

"You were flirting with one of the nurses. I couldn't believe your insensitivity, chatting up a woman in front of men — men who had served their country, men who were still paying a terrible price for their bravery, men who would never enjoy the company of a beautiful woman again."

"I was chatting her up to get more information. Flattery sometimes gets you everywhere. You don't know much about journalism, do you?"

"Not as much as I do about the human body. Do you remember what you said to the bitch as you walked down the burns ward?"

"Of course not. It was years ago. I was on your side. Whatever it was, I didn't intend to cause offence."

"Well you most surely did. You said: 'Beauty's only skin deep.'" He laughed ironically. "I'm going to prove just how wrong you were. The miraculous pumping of the heart, the exquisite coral of the brain, the rainbow iridescence of the intestines . . . I shall show you all these things tonight."

Johnny was struck dumb. His mouth was so dry his tongue was shrivelling — and that wasn't the only thing. The thought of being forced to watch the mysteries of his own body — or Henry's — being wrenched into the light made him break out into a cold sweat. It would be no good refusing to look. He remembered the lidless eyes of Helena Nudd.

Bravard lit more candles so that the operating table was circled with a warm yellow glow. Glass jars, each containing a human organ, gleamed in the shadows. "It's amazing what people will tell you, if you know just where to press. Henry hates his father because he loved his late brother far more than him. He likes you because you remind him of a childhood chum who disappeared before he could tell him how he felt about him. Blackmail, though, is a nasty business. I couldn't understand why you suddenly lost interest in me. Simkins described the photograph he used to persuade you. That's why I presented you with his balls. I've cured him for ever of his unhealthy interest in male genitalia."

He slapped Simkins across the face. "Wakey, wakey, sleeping beauty!"

Henry's eyes shot open and, remembering where he was and what had happened, widened with fear. Bravard removed the gag.

"He can't talk. He hasn't had as much as a drop of water in over eighteen hours. His throat will soon be so swollen he'll have difficulty breathing. But you're here now. It's time to change places."

Johnny flashed on the man standing at the foot of his bed in the nightmare. He knew he was as good as dead if he lay down on the table. Bravard began undoing the straps that held Simkins in place. Black terror, pure naked terror, began to stir in Johnny's stomach. It was similar to the claustrophobia that sometimes started to uncoil inside him. This sensation though was far stronger. He had been a total berk to come here alone. A sudden draught made the candles gutter. Bravard, inscribing bloody whorls on Simkins's stomach, seemed oblivious.

"Why the pictures of the saints?" His words were little more than a whisper. "Surely you don't consider yourself a martyr? Talk about delusions of grandeur. They died because they believed in something. What do you believe in?"

"I have catholic tastes and I believe in beauty." Bravard grinned, fully aware of the ghastly effect it had on the spectator. "I know you're stalling — hoping for a rescue that will never come — but I've got all night. You appreciate something far more, Johnny, once it has gone for ever. I also believe in pleasure — and pain."

"Pain is meaningless."

"I intend to change your mind. As you'll find out, the anticipation of it increases the agony."

"I still don't understand why you're doing all this. Why the women? What had they done to you? Why me? Why now?"

"There is no why," whispered Bravard. "Why do I look like this when I was doing my bit for King and Country? Why should you go from strength to strength, bringing down policemen, politicians and prostitutes? Why should you have lots of women and not have to pay for them? Why you and not me? *Why* is an empty word. *Because* carries more weight. Because cruelty is all there is. Because this country is finished. Five years from now it will be changed, changed utterly. Because I'm leaving for Helvetia. Because I wanted to make a grand parting gesture to show the contempt I feel for Britain and the Empire. Because I was bored. Because I was lonely. Because I could. Because . . ."

A metal clank made both of them jump.

"Move an inch and I'll slice one of your eyeballs into confetti."

He darted out of the cell and into the darkness. Johnny realised he couldn't move even if he had wanted to. For the first time in his life — just when it was about to end — he fully understood what being paralysed with fear meant.

The buzzing that had been in the background all along suddenly got louder. It was as if someone had turned up the volume on a badly tuned wireless. Great clouds of flies — bloated bluebottles and glinting

333

green-bottles — disturbed by the unseen Bravard and attracted by the candlelight, swarmed round them.

Simkins's look of disgust and despair brought Johnny to his senses. He undid the rest of the buckles that bound Simkins to the operating table. As soon as his hands were free, Simkins pointed at a tray of surgical instruments. Johnny selected a large scalpel. Simkins palmed it but made no attempt to get off the table.

A scream, the like of which neither man had ever heard, rent the foetid air. So the woman had been alive. Bravard, afraid that she might be making a feeble attempt to escape, was merely tying up a loose end. For one foolish moment Johnny had hoped the police had found the entrance to the torture chamber. Half unhinged by the whole experience, he tried not to cry. He didn't want to die.

Bravard, re-entering the cell, stopped in mock surprise then, in a moment of bizarre hilarity, started to sing. "Oh dear, what can the matter be? Johnny and Henry are locked in the laboratory." He giggled at his rewording of the playground song.

Simkins, summoning up what little strength he had left, stuck the scalpel into Bravard's bare thigh as far as it would go. He gasped and — with just the hint of a grimace; was he high on something? — began to extricate the blade.

"You've no idea how much you'll regret that," hissed Bravard. "I had finished with you, Simkins, but your futile gesture has made a further procedure necessary. Afterwards you won't be able to stick your nose in other people's business again." Turning to re-tie the

334

restraints that had strapped Simkins to the table he realised that all of them had been undone. "What the . . . ?"

It was now or never.

The jar of what Johnny hoped was ethanol smashed at Bravard's feet. The candle seemed to take an age as it flew end over end through the foul air. For a sickening second nothing happened, then the amateur surgeon was engulfed in fire. The make-up on his face melted rapidly and added purple and green to the flames. His mouth gaped in a silent scream.

Johnny helped Simkins to his feet. Unable to stand unaided, he put his arm round Johnny's shoulders. Bravard lurched towards them, a surgical saw in his upraised hand.

The bullet came out of nowhere and blew him into the air. Blood and bone exploded in a brown mist. Shattered specimen jars added their fuel to the fire. Bravard landed on the two naked men who fell together to the ground. The flames from the human torch licked their flesh. They screamed in agony until unconsciousness finally claimed them.

An aroma of roasted meat filled the underground abattoir. DC Penterell couldn't help himself. He wiped his mouth.

"Sorry, sir."

Inspector Woodling had seen many horrors in his career but even he was momentarily silenced. He stared at the scene of carnage, mentally logging every detail. There was no doubt about it: this was one for the memoirs.

CHAPTER
THIRTY

Saturday, 17th July, 2.30p.m.

It bucketed down the next day — St Swithin's Day —
and as usual a special service was held in St Swithin,
London Stone on Cannon Street. Wren's octagonal
dome, from the outside at least, was almost as beautiful
as that of St Paul's. It rained the following day as well
but as the weekend dawned the skies slowly cleared and
the much-needed forty days and nights of rain failed to
materialise. Once again the myth bore little resemblance
to reality. Even so the capital's citizens went about their
business with renewed vigour. They did not miss the
heat: such high temperatures just weren't British.
Johnny's spirits lifted too.

He had been released from St Bartholomew's
Hospital the day before. The burns on his back,
although painful, had proved to be superficial. Cracked
ribs or not, he had still been forced to lie on his
stomach.

The first person he saw when he opened his eyes was
Matt.

"Boy or girl?" His voice was croaky. He let Matt hold
a glass of water to his lips.

336

"A girl. Eight pounds four ounces." He glowed with paternal pride.

"Congratulations."

"You bloody idiot. Did you really think you could handle Bravard by yourself?"

"I had no choice." Revealing that he had been blackmailed would only cause further trouble.

"Woodling saved your life — and Simkins's."

"When did they start tailing me again?"

Matt tried not to grin. "They never stopped. Fortunately for you, we're rather better at it than your Keystone colleagues."

"Inskip must be very pleased with himself. He's very chummy with Simkins. He's still in my sights."

"Sometimes it's better to just let it go. No one can set the world to rights by themselves."

For the second time in a minute Johnny held his tongue.

Peter Quarles was his next visitor. After apologising for his own incompetence and that of Dimeo and Tanfield — "the traffic was murder" — he sat patiently beside the bed while Johnny dictated his account of the previous night's events. The fact that Bravard had operated literally beneath the noses and feet of playing schoolchildren made it all the more horrific. The police had recovered the remains of five women — so far. Had they been loved and missed? Would they be mourned? If there were families and friends they would no doubt think about the manner of their deaths every day for the rest of their lives. Had the women been prostitutes or just poor souls like Helena Nudd, whose only crime

337

had been to want a little company? Had they been motivated by money, pity or desire? If at all possible, he intended to find out.

"Four front pages in a week, Johnny, well done."

"I trust Captain Vic is satisfied."

"He sends his best wishes and said not to worry about the medical bills."

"I wasn't."

Stella was his third visitor.

"You needn't have bothered."

"I only had to come across the road."

Their green eyes met. Johnny saw regret in hers; she saw hurt in his. Perhaps it was delayed shock, perhaps it was the final realisation that whatever had been between them had evaporated. Henceforth they would be strangers. He watched her walk out of the ward dry-eyed.

The Callinghams, having seen the *News* on Friday morning, were his final visitors.

"Did you push old Gillespie then?" Daniel leaned forward eagerly.

"No, I didn't."

"Pity. I hope he didn't die straightaway."

"Daniel!" His mother glared at him. "Thank you for rescuing him, Mr Steadman." She tried to stroke her son's hair but he turned his head away. How much had he told her? Would she ever reconcile herself to his true nature?

"Does it hurt?" The boy was studying his bandaged back.

"Like hell."

338

"Come along, Daniel. We mustn't outstay our welcome."

"We've just arrived, Mama!"

"Thank you once again for your discretion, Mr Steadman. Believe me, it's greatly appreciated."

"Look after your mother, Daniel. You're the man of the house now."

"I suppose I am."

Johnny suspected that the death of the boy's lover had eclipsed that of his disapproving father. It was unrealistic to expect a fifteen-year-old to grieve for two people at the same. He held out his hand. The boy took it straightaway.

"Remember that your father loved you very much."

"It's true, Daniel."

Johnny expected the mother to start crying but, having regained mastery of herself, she retained her composure. In their own way, women were stronger than men.

"Well, he had a funny way of showing it."

Simkins, having fallen on top of Johnny, had come off far worse than him. Bravard, of course, was dead, but the blackmailer would live. Before leaving the ward on the day of his discharge, Johnny stopped by Simkins's bed.

"How are you?"

"I'll survive — thanks to you. There's no sign of septicaemia. It seems Bravard really did want me to live to tell the tale."

"I've already done it."

"So I hear. I owe you, Steadman. I've been an absolute bounder. You might as well know that two of Cecil Zick's former bum-boys attacked you last week. Zick will never forgive you for closing down his brothel. He had you followed as soon as he returned from Paris. As for the lovely picture of your friend — I should feel guilty for using it to my advantage, but I don't. However, I am grateful to you for trying to rescue me. You — and only you — will receive the photograph this afternoon. I presume you'll be at the office."

"Where else would I be?"

"That makes two of us. Work is all that's left to me now."

"You'll have the sympathy of every man in Fleet Street."

"It won't stop them making jokes, though. Who'd have thought my balls would one day be evidence in a murder case?"

"From what I saw, they'll make a very small contribution. Anyway, look on the bright side: George Bernard Shaw said losing one's libido is like being unchained from a runaway horse."

There was a poster advertising *Saratoga*, starring Clark Gable and Jean Harlow, on the platform at London Bridge. Harlow had died before it was in the can but MGM had somehow managed to complete the movie without her. Money always found a way. Perhaps he would take Millie to see it — she had popped in to see him on the ward whenever she could — so it could be his way of saying thank you. Horse racing, though, bored the pants off him — maybe it would bore the pants off her too.

Harlow's chaotic personal life still intrigued him. It might be a good idea to put *Friends and Lovers* in his bottom drawer — for Matt's sake as well as his — and concentrate on the real world of facts instead of seeking refuge in fantasy. Real life was far more interesting than make-believe.

The photograph, as promised, had been delivered to the office by messenger. The large sealed envelope had contained no accompanying note or apology. Johnny had taken the picture home and, having stared at it for longer than he should, burned it in the kitchen sink. As Matt had said: "Just let it go."

He got off the train at Bexleyheath — no one could accuse him of not learning from experience — and strolled south, past fields of buttercups, to Izane Road. Everyone — including both sets of grandparents — was in the back garden. All the roses were now in bloom: none of them were as beautiful as Lizzie.

The proud parents with their newborn babe formed a scene worthy of a picture postcard — one that Johnny would have been glad to receive. Two weeks ago he would have sworn that a wife and child were all he wanted. Now he was not so sure. Could he settle for second best? He had never been good at compromise.

"Lila Mae, this is your Uncle Johnny." Lizzie placed the baby — which looked like every other baby he had ever seen — in his cradled arms. Tiny, pink fingers, with perfect, tiny nails, closed automatically round her father's massive forefinger.

"We'd like you to be a godfather," said Matt, putting a hand on his shoulder. "Are you ready to renounce the devil and all his works?"

Johnny, bracing himself, gazed into Matt's sky-blue eyes.

"I think so," he said.

Guilt by Association

Marcia Clark

A Deputy DA specialising in high-profile cases, Rachel Knight is addicted to her work and fiercely loyal to her friends. But when her colleague Jake is found dead in a seedy Los Angeles hotel room next to the body of a teenage male prostitute, Rachel realises she might not know those around her as well as she thinks.

The police want to write off Jake's death as a straightforward murder/suicide. Rachel doesn't believe it's that simple. Warned off the case but determined to track down her friend's killer, the investigation takes her through the dark and tangled city from its wealthy suburbs to its seamy downtown heart. And a truth so dangerous it could kill her.

ISBN 978-0-7531-8966-5 (hb)
ISBN 978-0-7531-8967-2 (pb)

The Nightmare Thief

Meg Gardiner

Autumn Reiniger wants something special for her 21st birthday. Daddy's bought her the car and the apartment, but now she wants excitement. And what Autumn desires, she gets. Her father signs up Autumn and five friends for an ultimate urban reality game. Edge Adventures alert the SF police that a "crime situation" is underway, so the authorities will ignore any squealing tyres or desperate cries for help.

Then — when working on a case nearby — Jo Beckett encounters a group of men carting six sullen college kids to the woods for a wilderness adventure. Suspicious, she takes a closer look. And winds up with an invite to a birthday party she may never leave . . .

ISBN 978-0-7531-8962-7 (hb)
ISBN 978-0-7531-8963-4 (pb)